JAMES TYNION IV * RIAN SYGH * WALTER BAIAMONTE

THE BACKSTAGERS™

VOLUME THREE: ENCORE

BOOM!
BOX™

BOOM! BOX™

ross richie..ceo & founder
joy huffman...cfo
matt gagnon..................................editor-in-chief
filip sablik................president , publishing & marketing
stephen christy..............................president, development
lance kreiter...........vice president, licensing & merchandising
phil barbaro...........vice president, finance & human resources
arune singh..........................vice president, marketing
bryce carlson......vice president, editorial & creative strategy
scott newman..........................manager, production design
kate henning................................manager, operations
spencer simpson.................................manager, sales
sierra hahn.......................................executive editor
jeanine schaefer..............................executive editor
dafna pleban.....................................senior editor
shannon watters..................................senior editor
eric harburn.......................................senior editor
whitney leopard...editor
cameron chittock...editor
chris rosa..editor
matthew levine...editor
sophie philips-roberts.........................assistant editor
gavin gronenthal................................assistant editor
michael moccio....................................assistant editor
gwen waller.......................................assistant editor
amanda lafranco.............................executive assistant
jillian crab................................design coordinator
michelle ankley..........................design coordinator
kara leopard...............................production designer
marie krupina.............................production designer
grace park........................production design assistant
chelsea roberts................production design assistant
samantha knapp..............production design assistant
elizabeth loughridge......................accounting coordinator
stephanie hocutt................social media coordinator
josé meza......................................event coordinator
holly aitchison...........................digital sales coordinator
megan christopher.........................operations assistant
rodrigo hernandez.............................mailroom assistant
morgan perry ....direct market representative
cat o'grady..marketing assistant
breanna sarpy...............................executive assistant

THE BACKSTAGERS Volume Three, April 2019. Published by BOOM! Box, a division of Boom Entertainment, Inc. The Backstagers is ™ & © 2019 Rian Sygh & James Tynion IV. Originally published in single magazine form as THE BOOM! BOX 2016 MIX TAPE, THE BACKSTAGERS: 2018 VALENTINE'S INTERMISSION No. 1, THE BACKSTAGERS: HALLOWEEN INTERMISSION No. 1, ™ & © 2016, 2018 Rian Sygh & James Tynion IV. All rights reserved. BOOM! Box™ and the BOOM! Box logo are trademarks of Boom Entertainment, Inc., registered in various countries and categories. All characters, events, and institutions depicted herein are fictional. Any similarity between any of the names, characters, persons, events, and/or institutions in this publication to actual names, characters, and persons, whether living or dead, events, and/or institutions is unintended and purely coincidental. BOOM! Box does not read or accept unsolicited submissions of ideas, stories, or artwork.

BOOM! Studios, 5670 Wilshire Boulevard, Suite 400, Los Angeles, CA 90036-5679. Printed in China. First Printing.

ISBN: 978-1-68415-332-9, eISBN: 978-1-64144-185-8

THE BACKSTAGERS

CREATED BY JAMES TYNION IV AND RIAN SYGH

WRITTEN BY
JAMES TYNION IV

ILLUSTRATED BY
RIAN SYGH

COLORED BY
WALTER BAIAMONTE

LETTERED BY
JIM CAMPBELL

"FINDING THE ONE"
WRITTEN BY JAMES TYNION IV AND SAM JOHNS
ILLUSTRATED BY BRITTNEY WILLIAMS
COLORED BY REBECCA NALTY
LETTERED BY JIM CAMPBELL

"LOVE RODENT #9"
WRITTEN BY JAMES TYNION IV AND SAM JOHNS
ILLUSTRATED BY CAITLIN ROSE BOYLE
COLORED BY REBECCA NALTY
LETTERED BY JIM CAMPBELL

"OF MICE AND MUNCHIES"
WRITTEN BY JAMES TYNION IV AND SAM JOHNS
ILLUSTRATED AND LETTERED BY KATY FARINA

"GREASED FRIGHTENING"
WRITTEN BY SAM JOHNS
ILLUSTRATED BY SAVANNA GANUCHEAU
LETTERED BY JIM CAMPBELL

"FRIGHT LIGHTS"
WRITTEN BY SAM JOHNS
ILLUSTRATED BY SHAN MURPHY
LETTERED BY JIM CAMPBELL

"FRIGHT OF THE LIVING TOOL RATS"
WRITTEN BY SAM JOHNS
ILLUSTRATED AND LETTERED BY ABBY HOWARD
COLORED BY WALTER BAIAMONTE

"THE PITS"
WRITTEN BY JAMES TYNION IV
ILLUSTRATED BY RIAN SYGH
LETTERED BY JIM CAMPBELL

COVER BY VERONICA FISH

SERIES DESIGNERS MARIE KRUPINA AND GRACE PARK

ASSISTANT EDITOR SOPHIE PHILIPS-ROBERTS

COLLECTION DESIGNER CHELSEA ROBERTS

EDITOR SHANNON WATTERS

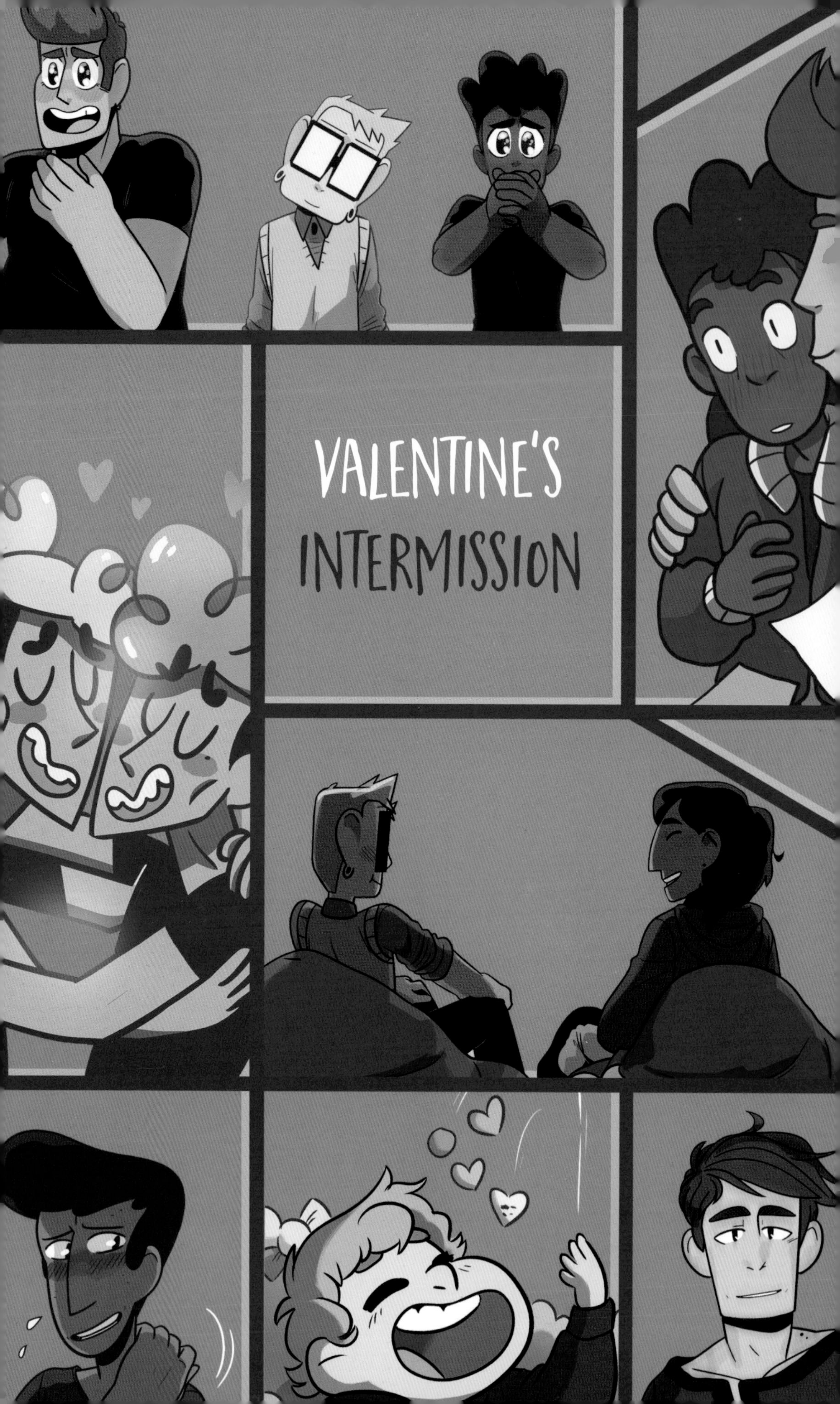
VALENTINE'S
INTERMISSION

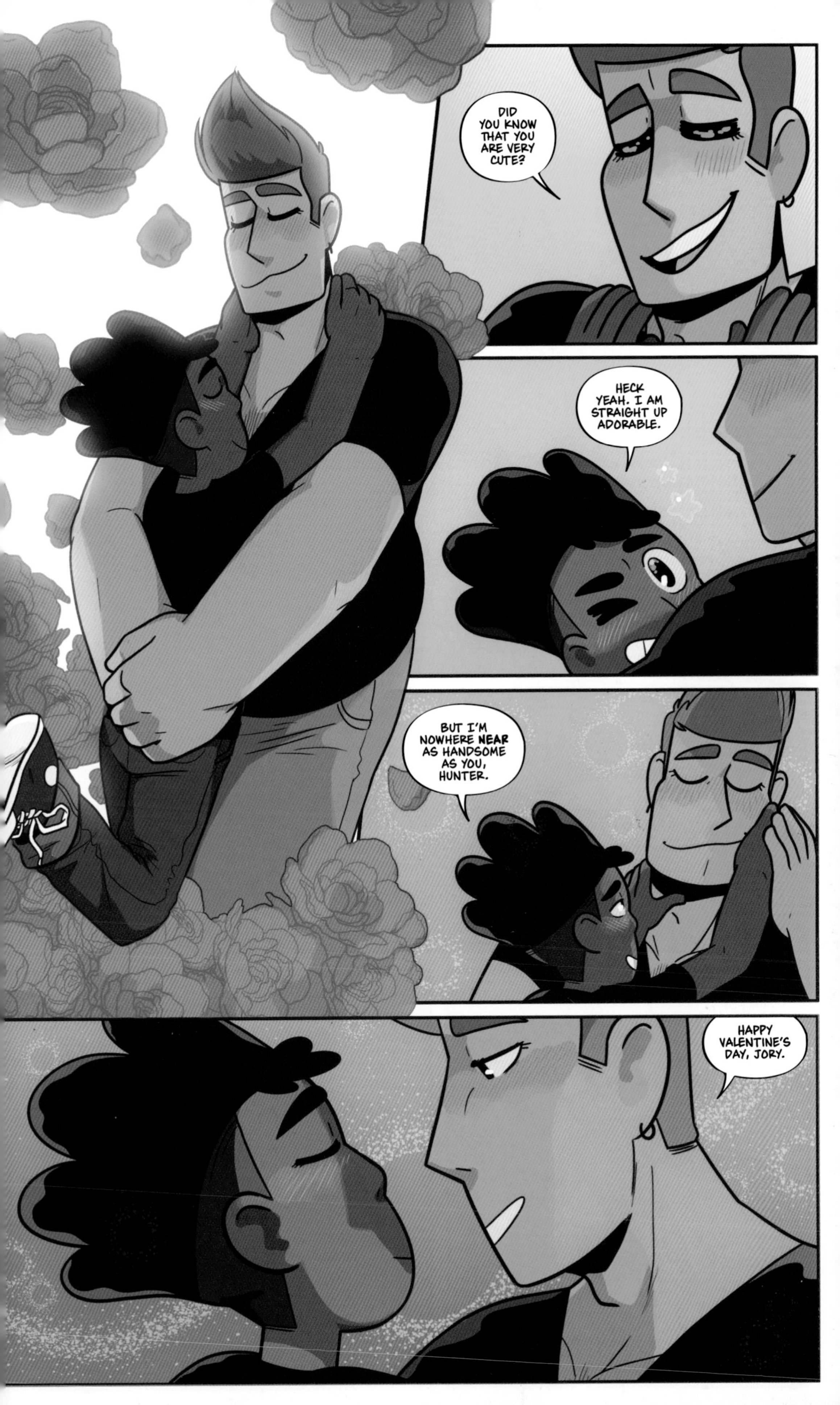
DID YOU KNOW THAT YOU ARE VERY CUTE?
HECK YEAH. I AM STRAIGHT UP ADORABLE.
BUT I'M NOWHERE **NEAR** AS HANDSOME AS YOU, HUNTER.
HAPPY VALENTINE'S DAY, JORY.

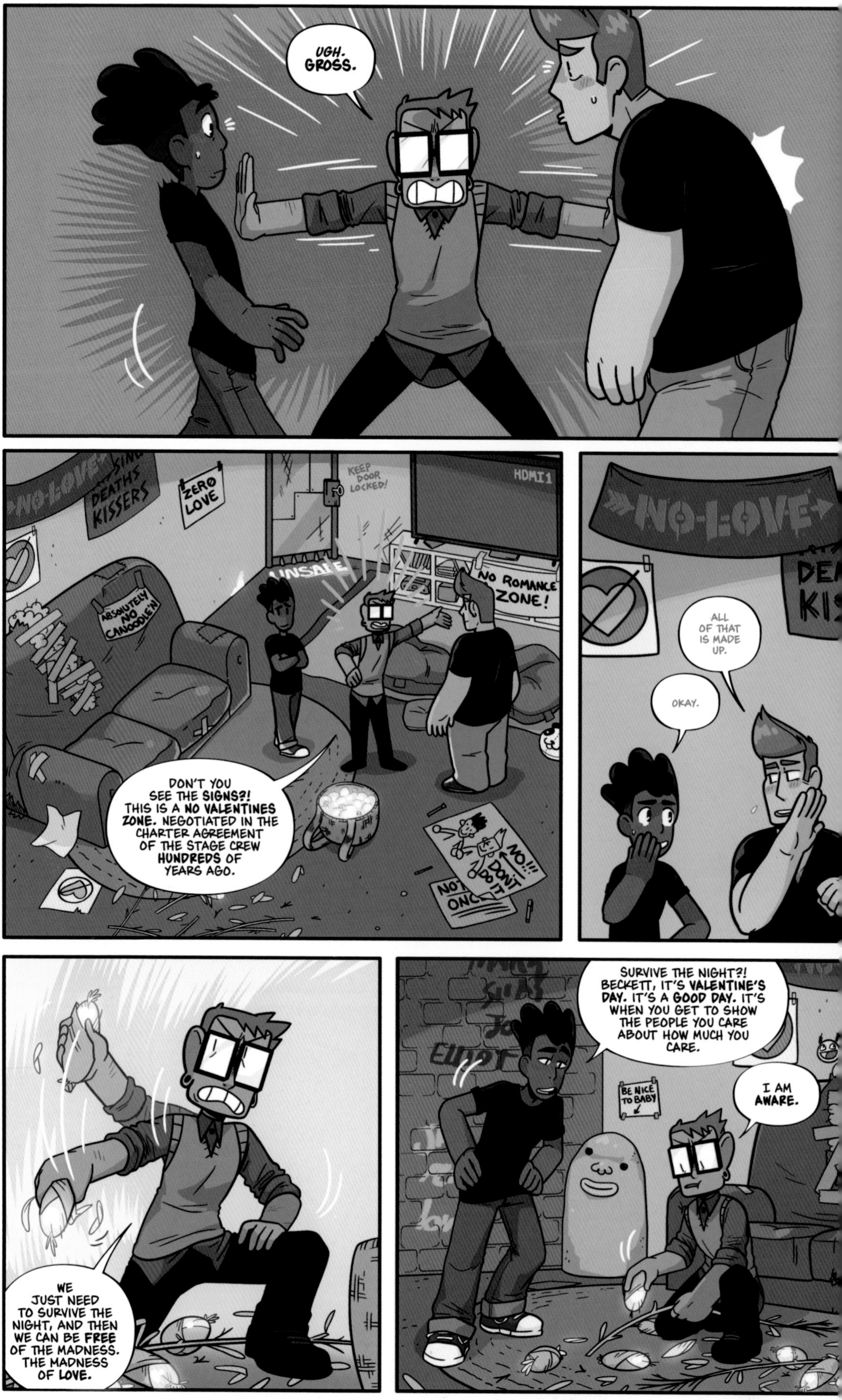
UGH. GROSS.
NO-LOVE
DEATHS KISSERS
ZERO LOVE
KEEP DOOR LOCKED!
HDMI1
UNSAFE
ABSOLUTELY NO CANOODLE'N
NO ROMANCE ZONE!
DON'T YOU SEE THE SIGNS?! THIS IS A NO VALENTINES ZONE. NEGOTIATED IN THE CHARTER AGREEMENT OF THE STAGE CREW HUNDREDS OF YEARS AGO.
NO!!! DON'T DO IT
NO-LOVE
ALL OF THAT IS MADE UP.
OKAY.
WE JUST NEED TO SURVIVE THE NIGHT, AND THEN WE CAN BE FREE OF THE MADNESS. THE MADNESS OF LOVE.
SURVIVE THE NIGHT?! BECKETT, IT'S VALENTINE'S DAY. IT'S A GOOD DAY. IT'S WHEN YOU GET TO SHOW THE PEOPLE YOU CARE ABOUT HOW MUCH YOU CARE.
BE NICE TO BABY
I AM AWARE.

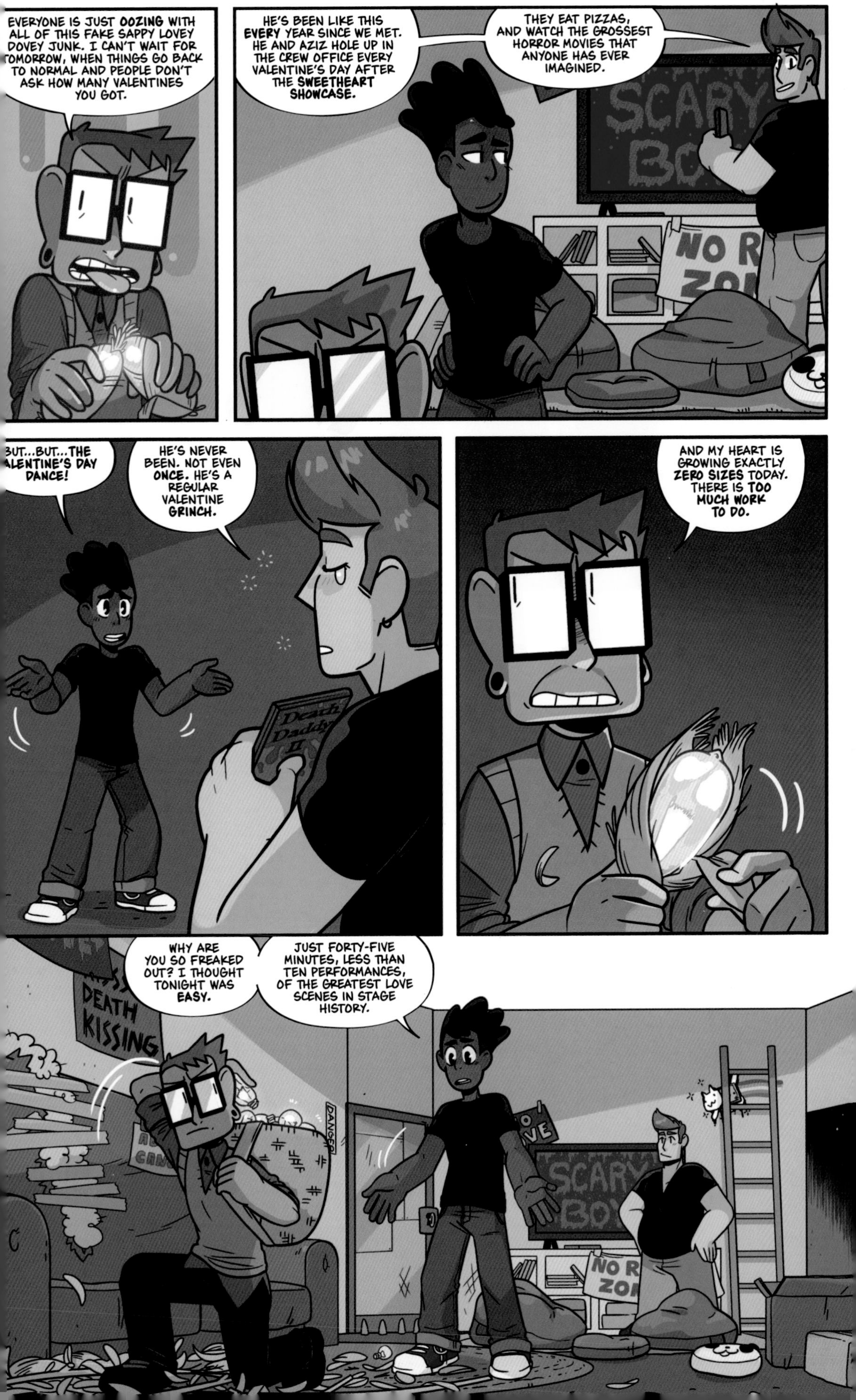
EVERYONE IS JUST **OOZING** WITH ALL OF THIS FAKE SAPPY LOVEY DOVEY JUNK. I CAN'T WAIT FOR TOMORROW, WHEN THINGS GO BACK TO NORMAL AND PEOPLE DON'T ASK HOW MANY VALENTINES YOU GOT.
HE'S BEEN LIKE THIS **EVERY** YEAR SINCE WE MET. HE AND AZIZ HOLE UP IN THE CREW OFFICE EVERY VALENTINE'S DAY AFTER THE **SWEETHEART SHOWCASE.**
THEY EAT PIZZAS, AND WATCH THE GROSSEST HORROR MOVIES THAT ANYONE HAS EVER IMAGINED.
SCARY
BUT...BUT...THE VALENTINE'S DAY DANCE!
HE'S NEVER BEEN. NOT EVEN **ONCE.** HE'S A REGULAR VALENTINE **GRINCH.**
Death Daddy II
AND MY HEART IS GROWING EXACTLY **ZERO SIZES** TODAY. THERE IS **TOO MUCH WORK** TO DO.
WHY ARE YOU SO FREAKED OUT? I THOUGHT TONIGHT WAS **EASY.**
JUST FORTY-FIVE MINUTES, LESS THAN TEN PERFORMANCES, OF THE GREATEST LOVE SCENES IN STAGE HISTORY.
DEATH KISSING
DANGER

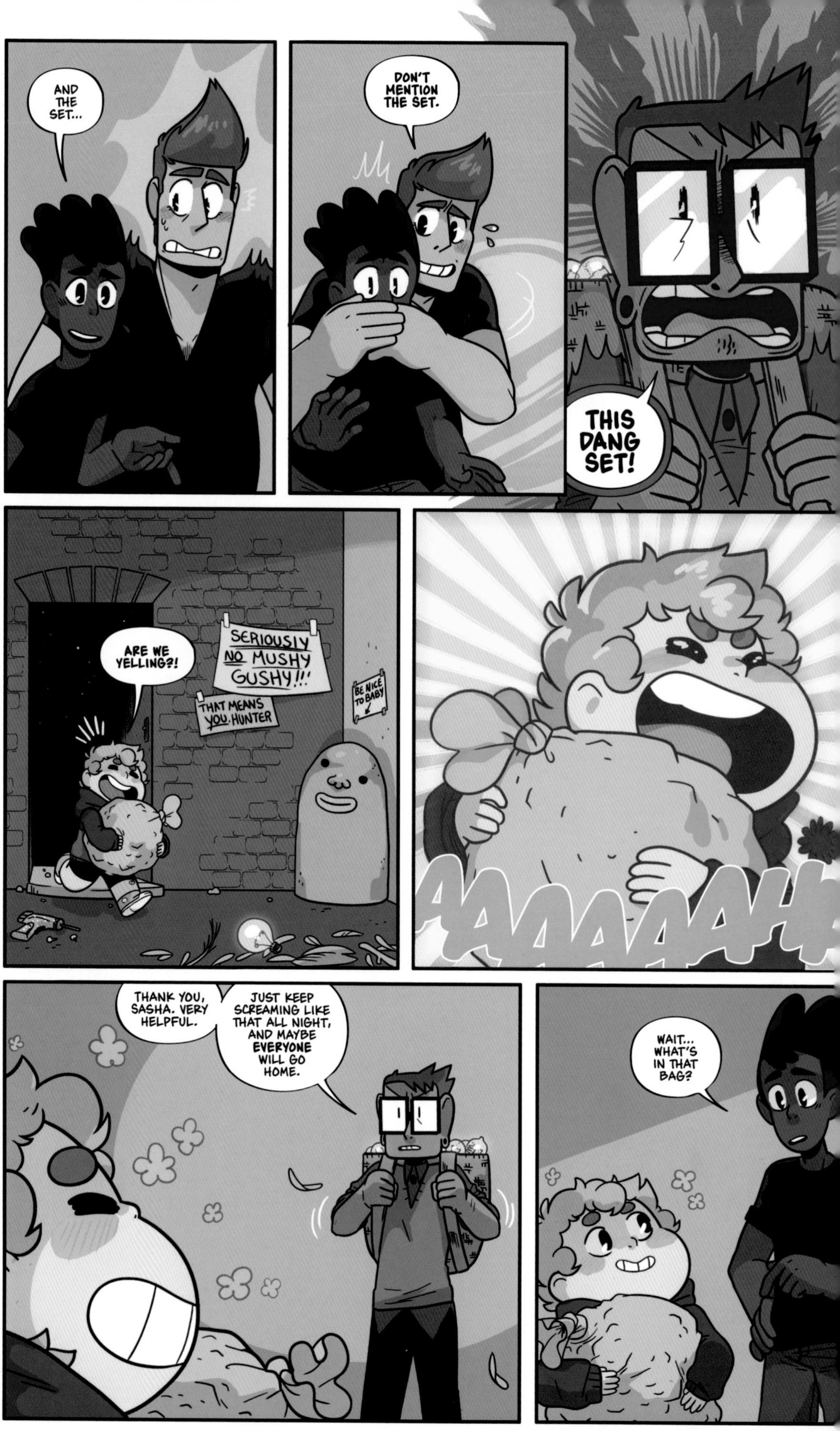
AND THE SET...
DON'T MENTION THE SET.
THIS DANG SET!
ARE WE YELLING?!
SERIOUSLY NO MUSHY GUSHY!!!
THAT MEANS YOU, HUNTER
BE NICE TO BABY
AAAAAAAH
THANK YOU, SASHA. VERY HELPFUL.
JUST KEEP SCREAMING LIKE THAT ALL NIGHT, AND MAYBE EVERYONE WILL GO HOME.
WAIT... WHAT'S IN THAT BAG?

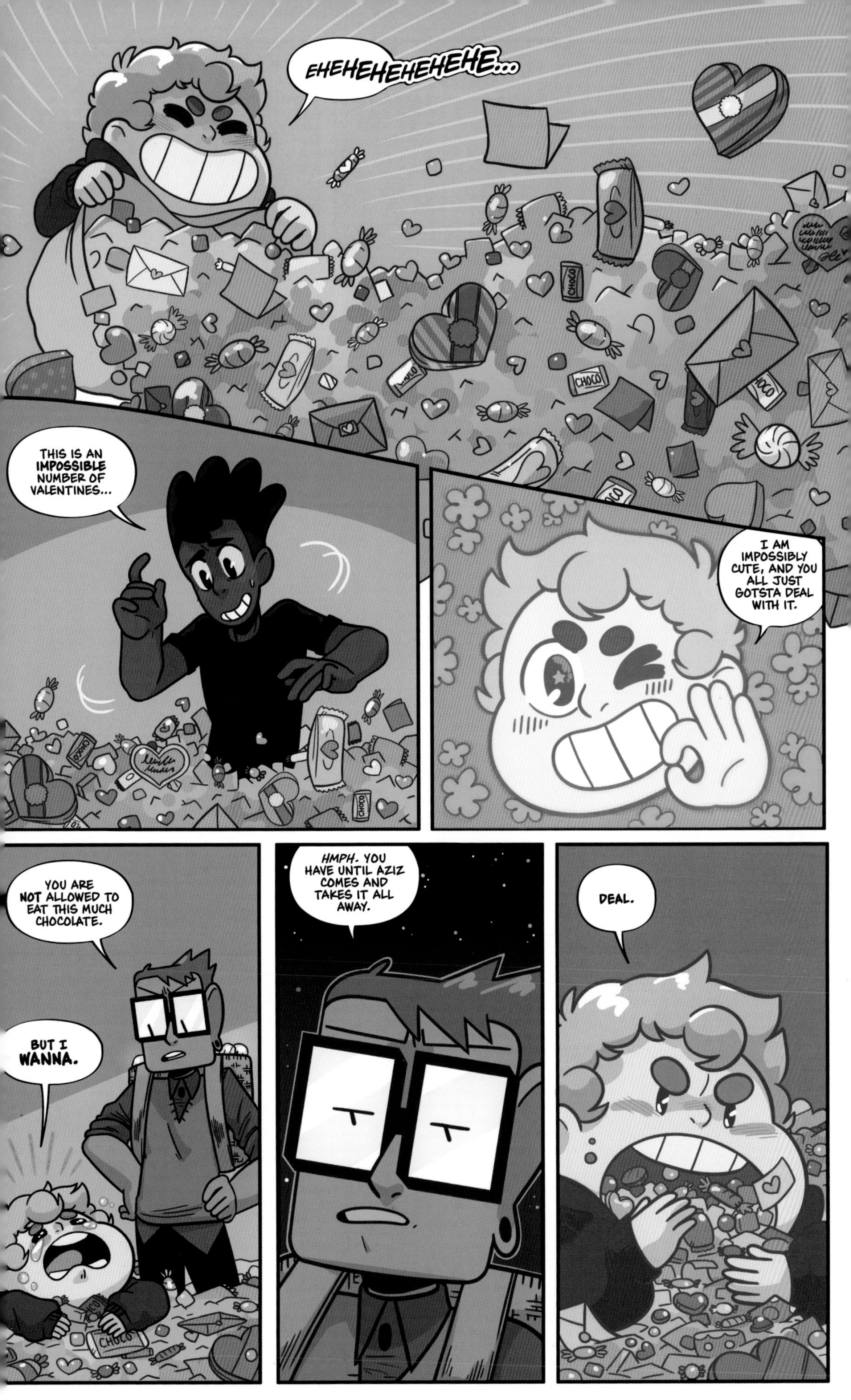
EHEHEHEHEHEHEHE...
THIS IS AN IMPOSSIBLE NUMBER OF VALENTINES...
I AM IMPOSSIBLY CUTE, AND YOU ALL JUST GOTSTA DEAL WITH IT.
YOU ARE NOT ALLOWED TO EAT THIS MUCH CHOCOLATE.
BUT I WANNA.
HMPH. YOU HAVE UNTIL AZIZ COMES AND TAKES IT ALL AWAY.
DEAL.

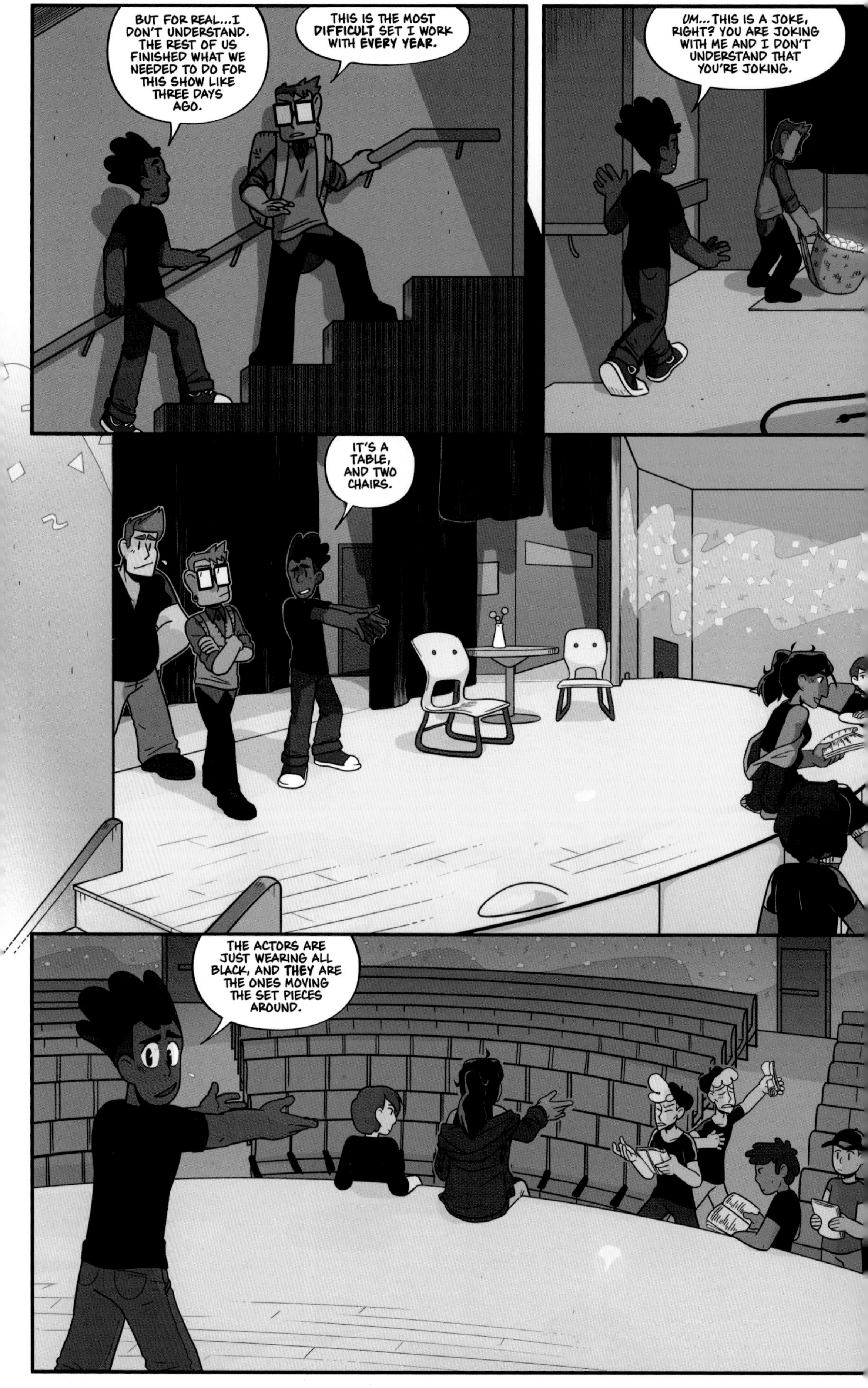

BUT FOR REAL...I DON'T UNDERSTAND. THE REST OF US FINISHED WHAT WE NEEDED TO DO FOR THIS SHOW LIKE THREE DAYS AGO.
THIS IS THE MOST DIFFICULT SET I WORK WITH EVERY YEAR.
UM...THIS IS A JOKE, RIGHT? YOU ARE JOKING WITH ME AND I DON'T UNDERSTAND THAT YOU'RE JOKING.
IT'S A TABLE, AND TWO CHAIRS.
THE ACTORS ARE JUST WEARING ALL BLACK, AND THEY ARE THE ONES MOVING THE SET PIECES AROUND.

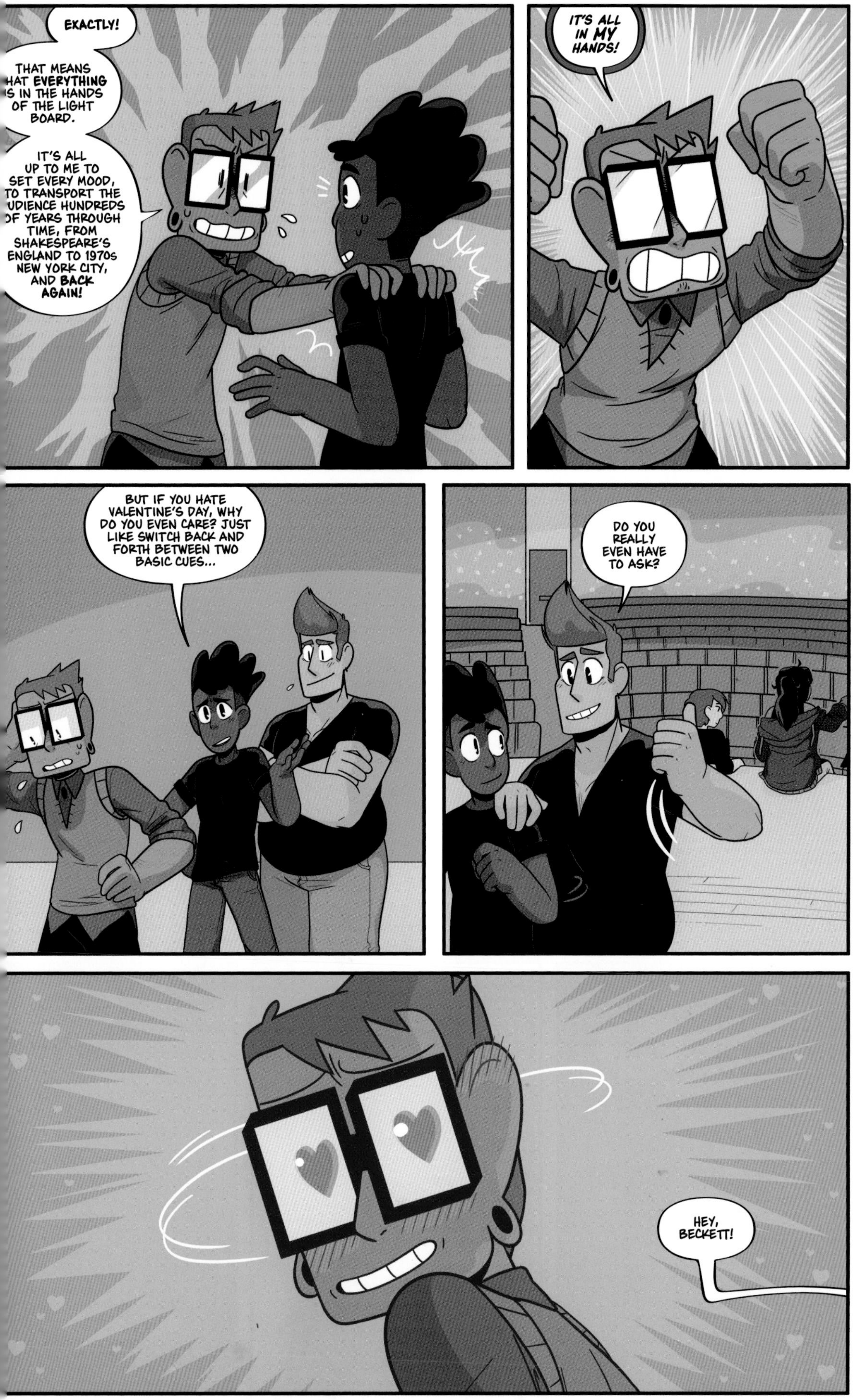
EXACTLY!
THAT MEANS
HAT EVERYTHING
S IN THE HANDS
OF THE LIGHT
BOARD.
IT'S ALL
UP TO ME TO
SET EVERY MOOD,
TO TRANSPORT THE
UDIENCE HUNDREDS
OF YEARS THROUGH
TIME, FROM
SHAKESPEARE'S
ENGLAND TO 1970s
NEW YORK CITY,
AND BACK
AGAIN!
IT'S ALL IN MY HANDS!
BUT IF YOU HATE VALENTINE'S DAY, WHY DO YOU EVEN CARE? JUST LIKE SWITCH BACK AND FORTH BETWEEN TWO BASIC CUES...
DO YOU REALLY EVEN HAVE TO ASK?
HEY, BECKETT!

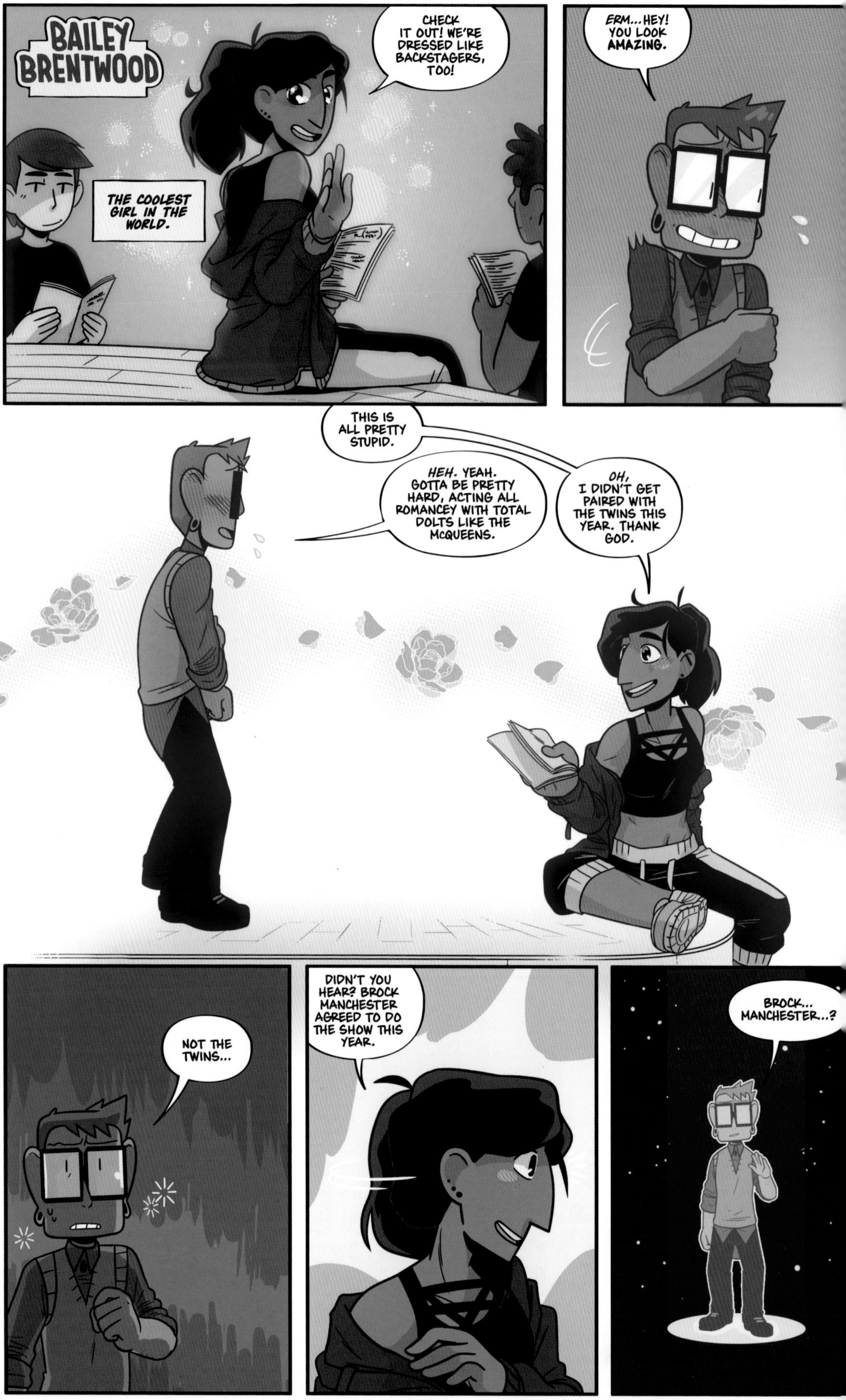
BAILEY BRENTWOOD
CHECK IT OUT! WE'RE DRESSED LIKE BACKSTAGERS, TOO!
THE COOLEST GIRL IN THE WORLD.
ERM...HEY! YOU LOOK AMAZING.
THIS IS ALL PRETTY STUPID.
HEH. YEAH. GOTTA BE PRETTY HARD, ACTING ALL ROMANCEY WITH TOTAL DOLTS LIKE THE McQUEENS.
OH, I DIDN'T GET PAIRED WITH THE TWINS THIS YEAR. THANK GOD.
NOT THE TWINS...
DIDN'T YOU HEAR? BROCK MANCHESTER AGREED TO DO THE SHOW THIS YEAR.
BROCK... MANCHESTER...?

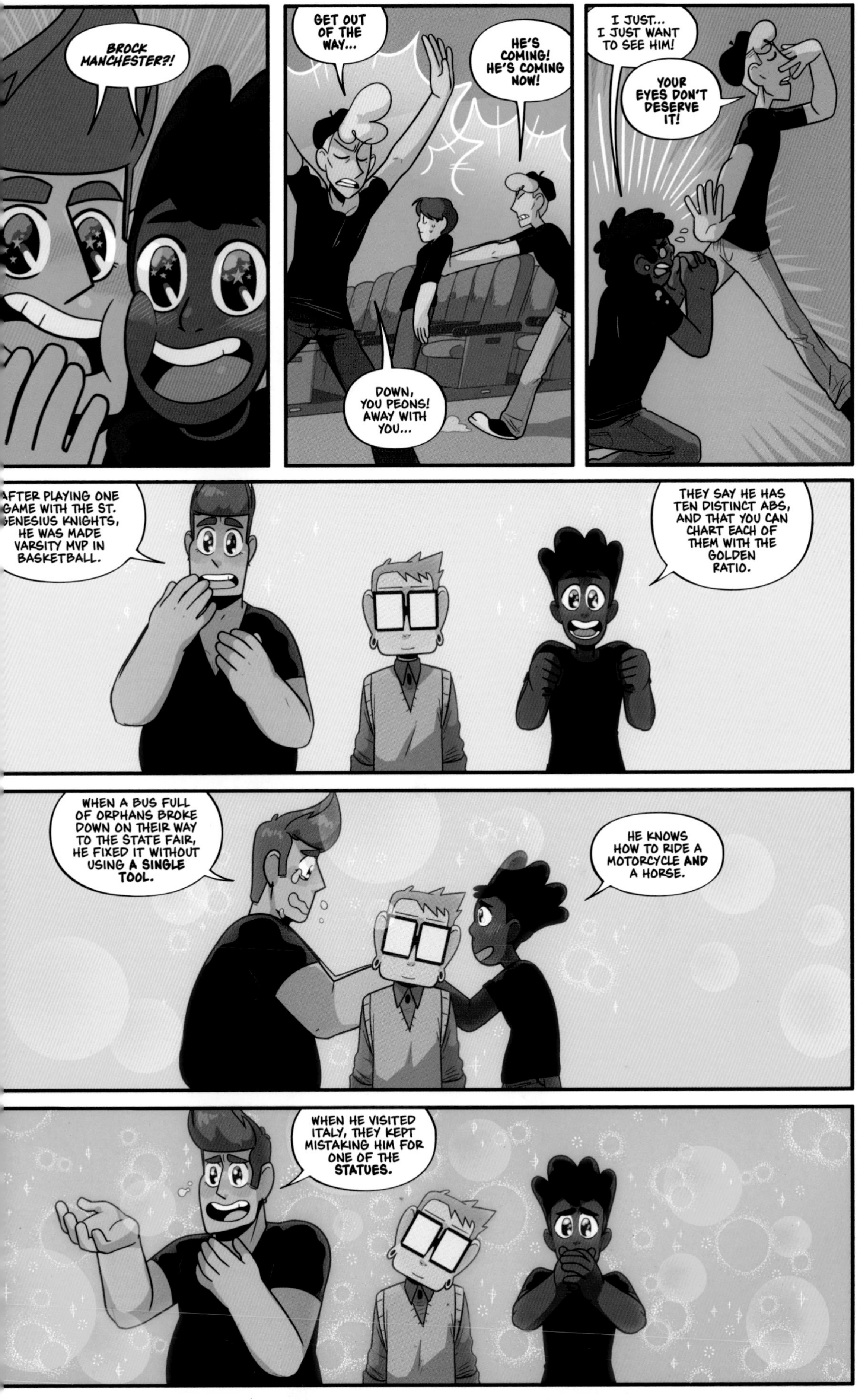
BROCK MANCHESTER?!
GET OUT OF THE WAY...
HE'S COMING! HE'S COMING NOW!
DOWN, YOU PEONS! AWAY WITH YOU...
I JUST... I JUST WANT TO SEE HIM!
YOUR EYES DON'T DESERVE IT!
AFTER PLAYING ONE GAME WITH THE ST. GENESIUS KNIGHTS, HE WAS MADE VARSITY MVP IN BASKETBALL.
THEY SAY HE HAS TEN DISTINCT ABS, AND THAT YOU CAN CHART EACH OF THEM WITH THE GOLDEN RATIO.
WHEN A BUS FULL OF ORPHANS BROKE DOWN ON THEIR WAY TO THE STATE FAIR, HE FIXED IT WITHOUT USING A SINGLE TOOL.
HE KNOWS HOW TO RIDE A MOTORCYCLE AND A HORSE.
WHEN HE VISITED ITALY, THEY KEPT MISTAKING HIM FOR ONE OF THE STATUES.

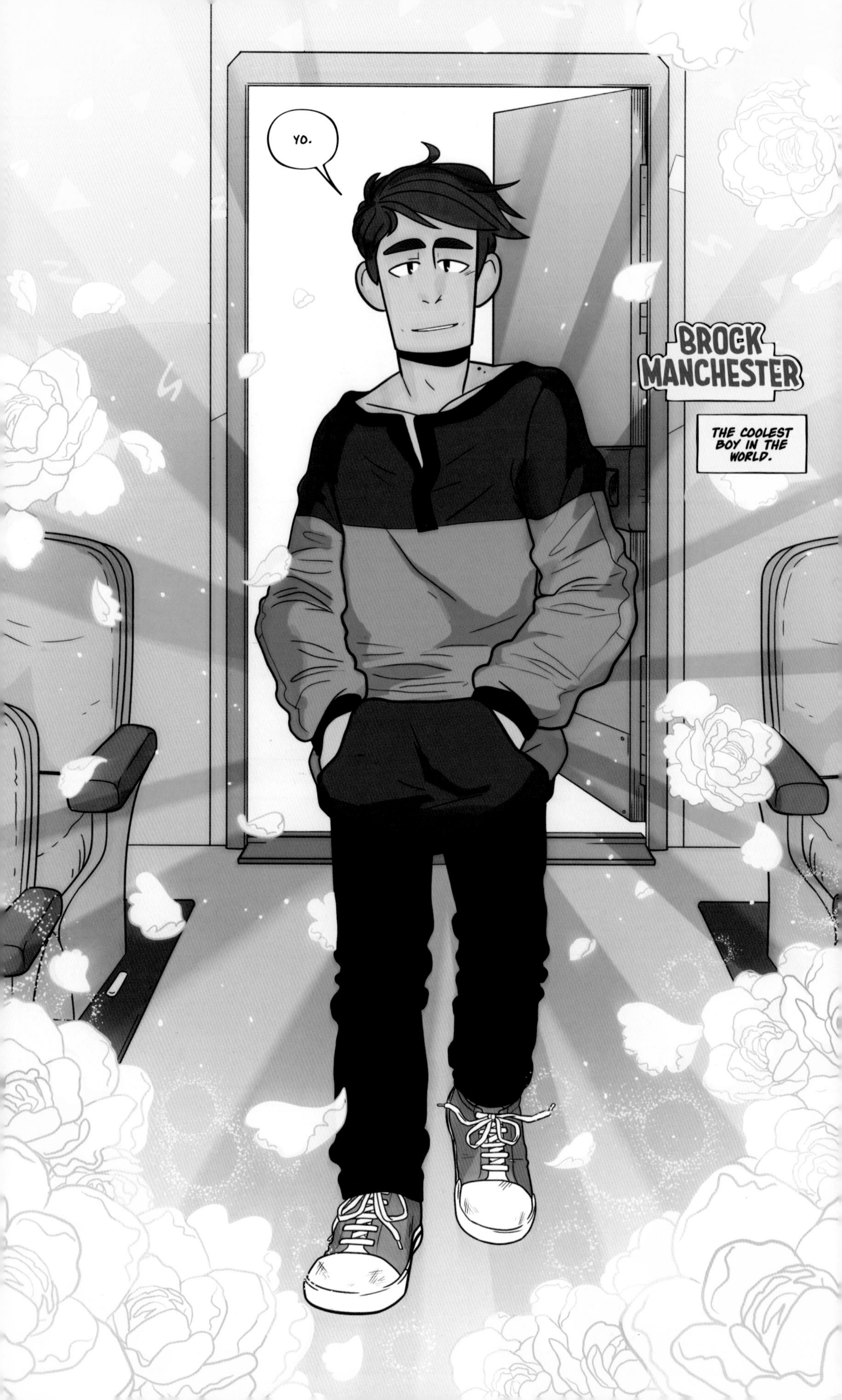
YO.
BROCK MANCHESTER
THE COOLEST BOY IN THE WORLD.

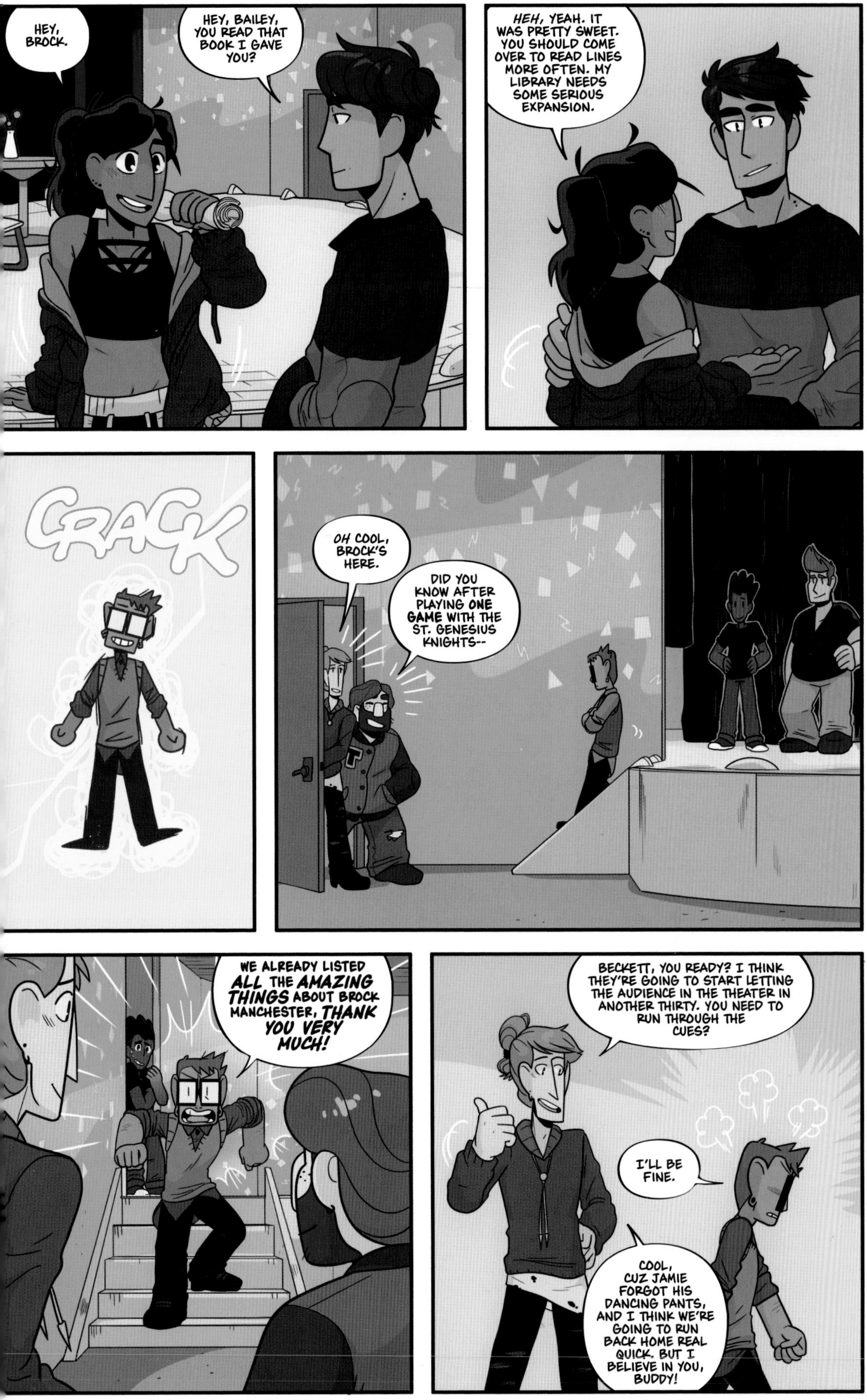

HEY, BROCK.
HEY, BAILEY, YOU READ THAT BOOK I GAVE YOU?
HEH, YEAH. IT WAS PRETTY SWEET. YOU SHOULD COME OVER TO READ LINES MORE OFTEN. MY LIBRARY NEEDS SOME SERIOUS EXPANSION.
CRACK
OH COOL, BROCK'S HERE.
DID YOU KNOW AFTER PLAYING ONE GAME WITH THE ST. GENESIUS KNIGHTS--
WE ALREADY LISTED ALL THE AMAZING THINGS ABOUT BROCK MANCHESTER, THANK YOU VERY MUCH!
BECKETT, YOU READY? I THINK THEY'RE GOING TO START LETTING THE AUDIENCE IN THE THEATER IN ANOTHER THIRTY. YOU NEED TO RUN THROUGH THE CUES?
I'LL BE FINE.
COOL, CUZ JAMIE FORGOT HIS DANCING PANTS, AND I THINK WE'RE GOING TO RUN BACK HOME REAL QUICK. BUT I BELIEVE IN YOU, BUDDY!

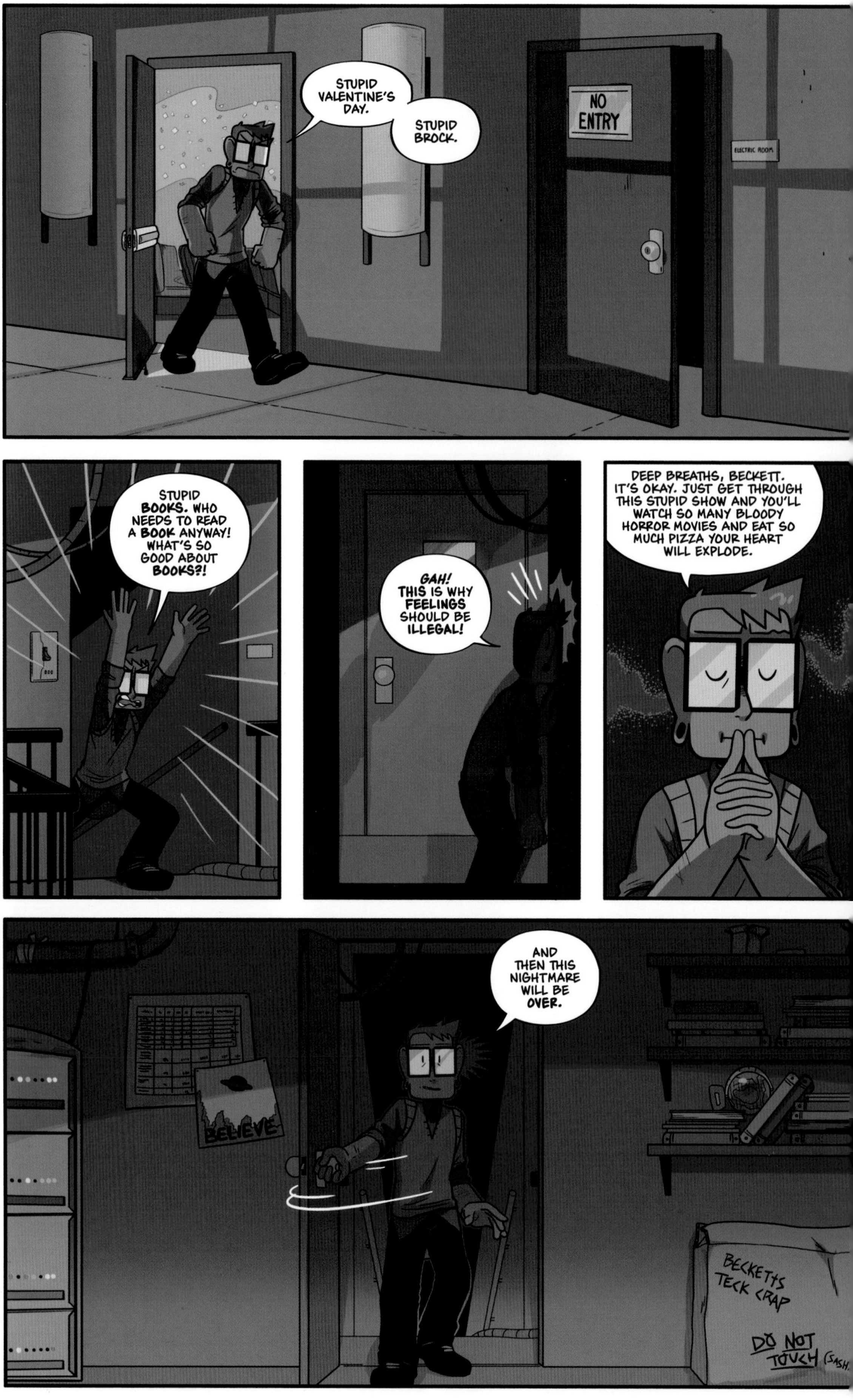
STUPID VALENTINE'S DAY.
STUPID BROCK.
NO ENTRY
ELECTRIC ROOM
STUPID BOOKS. WHO NEEDS TO READ A BOOK ANYWAY! WHAT'S SO GOOD ABOUT BOOKS?!
GAH! THIS IS WHY FEELINGS SHOULD BE ILLEGAL!
DEEP BREATHS, BECKETT. IT'S OKAY. JUST GET THROUGH THIS STUPID SHOW AND YOU'LL WATCH SO MANY BLOODY HORROR MOVIES AND EAT SO MUCH PIZZA YOUR HEART WILL EXPLODE.
AND THEN THIS NIGHTMARE WILL BE OVER.
BELIEVE
BECKETT'S TECK CRAP
DO NOT TOUCH

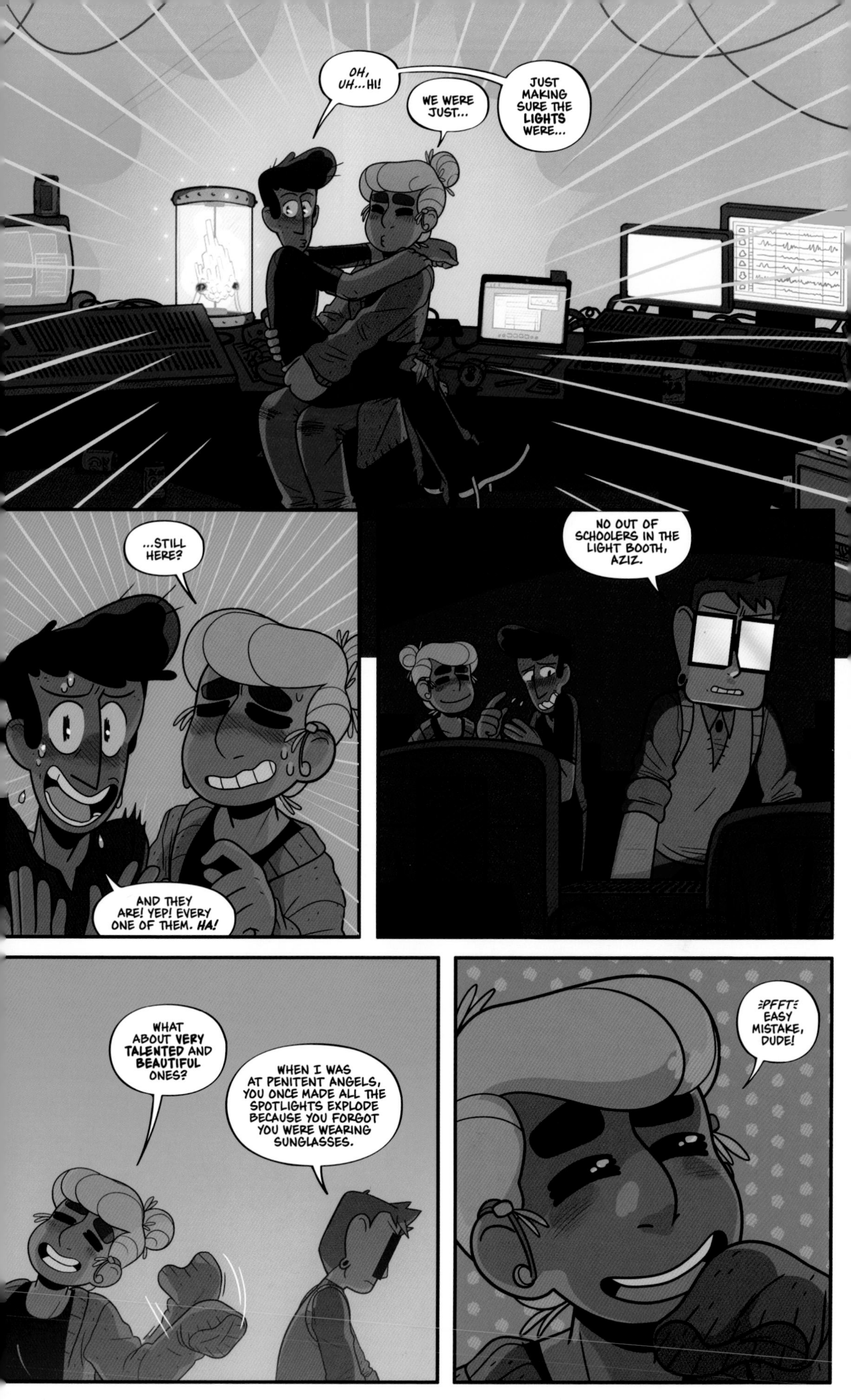
OH, UH...HI!
WE WERE JUST...
JUST MAKING SURE THE LIGHTS WERE...
...STILL HERE?
AND THEY ARE! YEP! EVERY ONE OF THEM. HA!
NO OUT OF SCHOOLERS IN THE LIGHT BOOTH, AZIZ.
WHAT ABOUT VERY TALENTED AND BEAUTIFUL ONES?
WHEN I WAS AT PENITENT ANGELS, YOU ONCE MADE ALL THE SPOTLIGHTS EXPLODE BECAUSE YOU FORGOT YOU WERE WEARING SUNGLASSES.
PFFT EASY MISTAKE, DUDE!

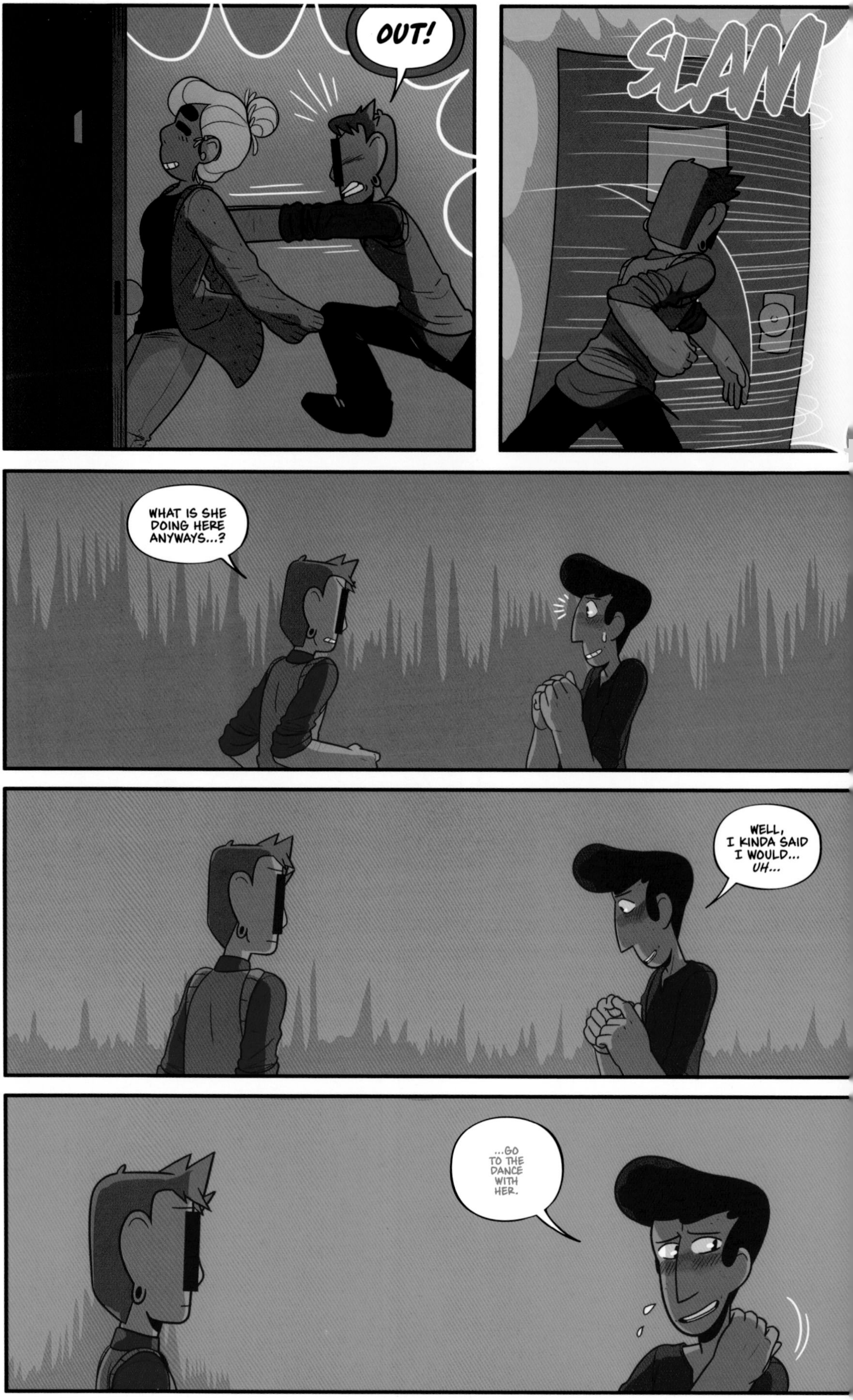
OUT!
SLAM
WHAT IS SHE DOING HERE ANYWAYS...?
WELL, I KINDA SAID I WOULD... UH...
...GO TO THE DANCE WITH HER.

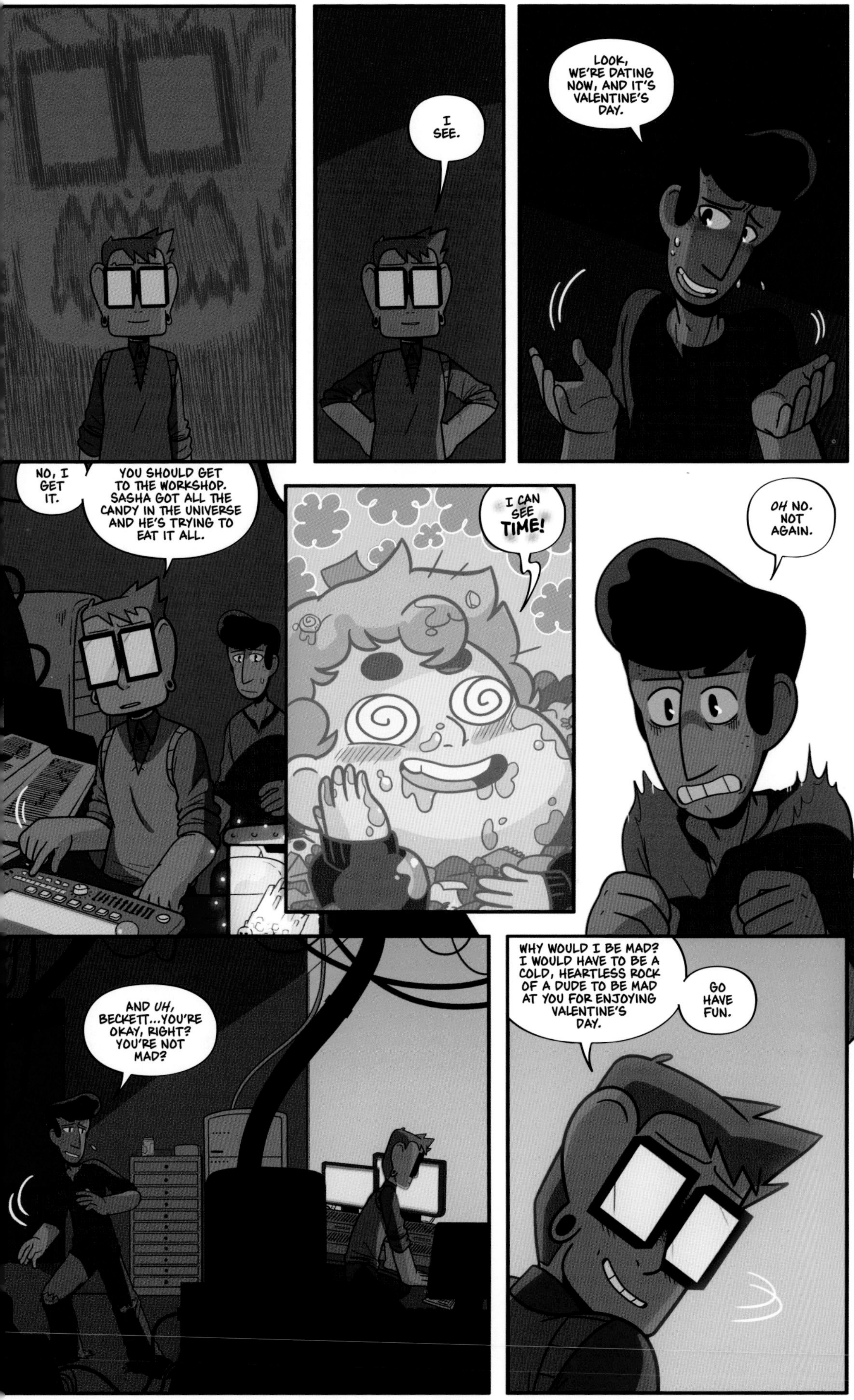
I SEE.
LOOK, WE'RE DATING NOW, AND IT'S VALENTINE'S DAY.
NO, I GET IT.
YOU SHOULD GET TO THE WORKSHOP. SASHA GOT ALL THE CANDY IN THE UNIVERSE AND HE'S TRYING TO EAT IT ALL.
I CAN SEE TIME!
OH NO. NOT AGAIN.
AND UH, BECKETT...YOU'RE OKAY, RIGHT? YOU'RE NOT MAD?
WHY WOULD I BE MAD? I WOULD HAVE TO BE A COLD, HEARTLESS ROCK OF A DUDE TO BE MAD AT YOU FOR ENJOYING VALENTINE'S DAY.
GO HAVE FUN.

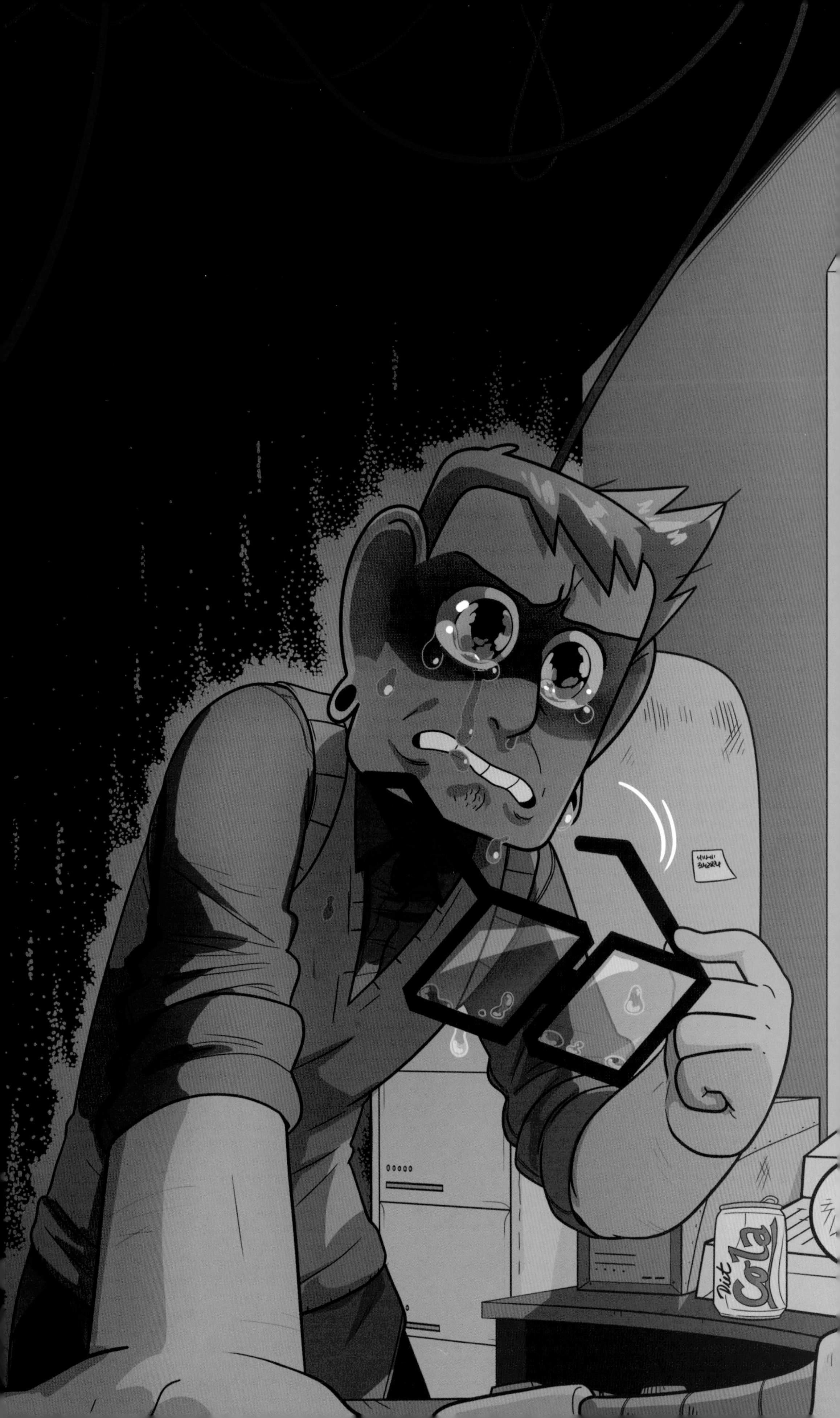
Diet Cola

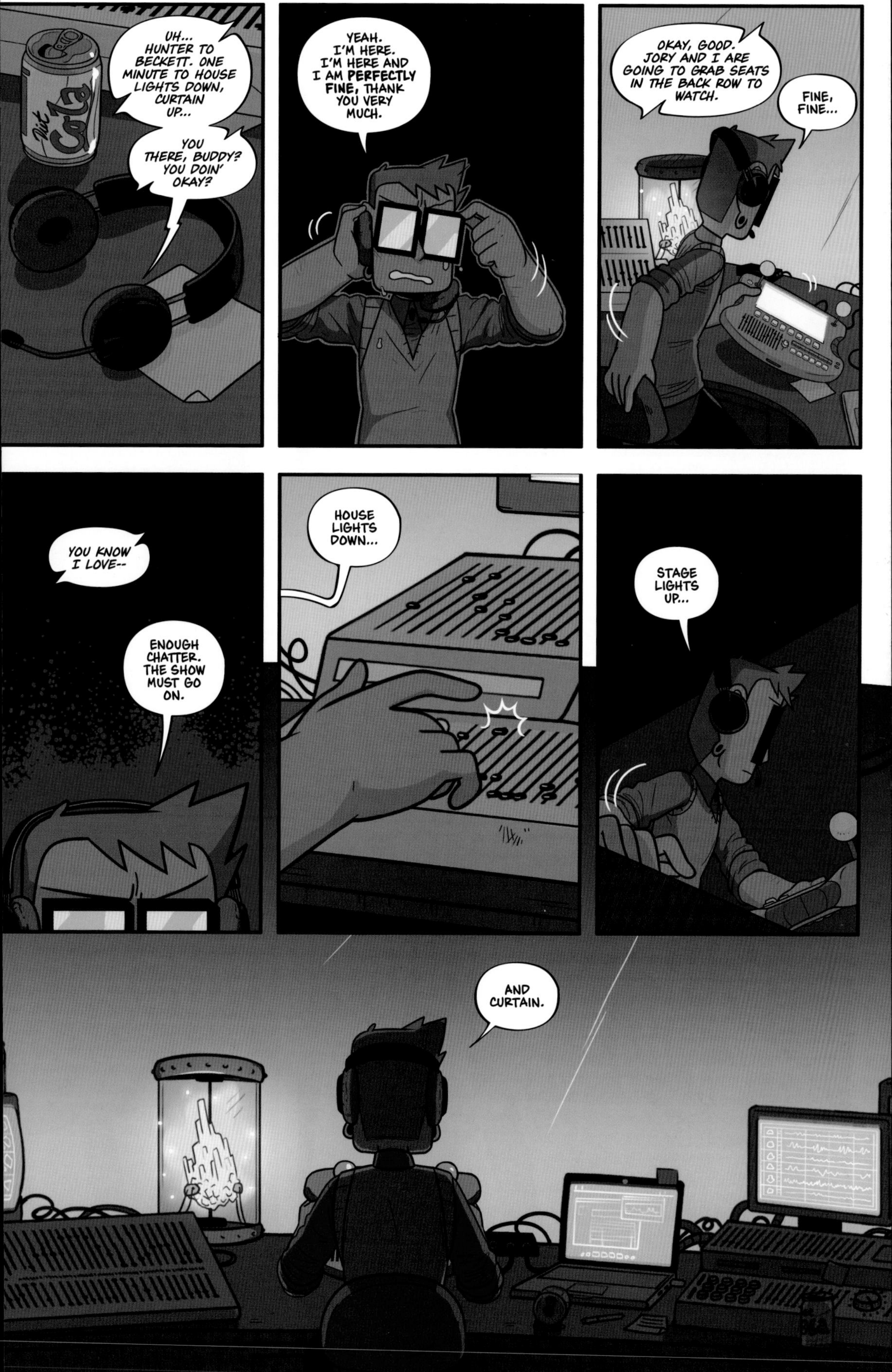
Diet Cola
UH... HUNTER TO BECKETT. ONE MINUTE TO HOUSE LIGHTS DOWN, CURTAIN UP...
YOU THERE, BUDDY? YOU DOIN' OKAY?
YEAH. I'M HERE. I'M HERE AND I AM PERFECTLY FINE, THANK YOU VERY MUCH.
OKAY, GOOD. JORY AND I ARE GOING TO GRAB SEATS IN THE BACK ROW TO WATCH.
FINE, FINE...
YOU KNOW I LOVE--
ENOUGH CHATTER. THE SHOW MUST GO ON.
HOUSE LIGHTS DOWN...
STAGE LIGHTS UP...
AND CURTAIN.

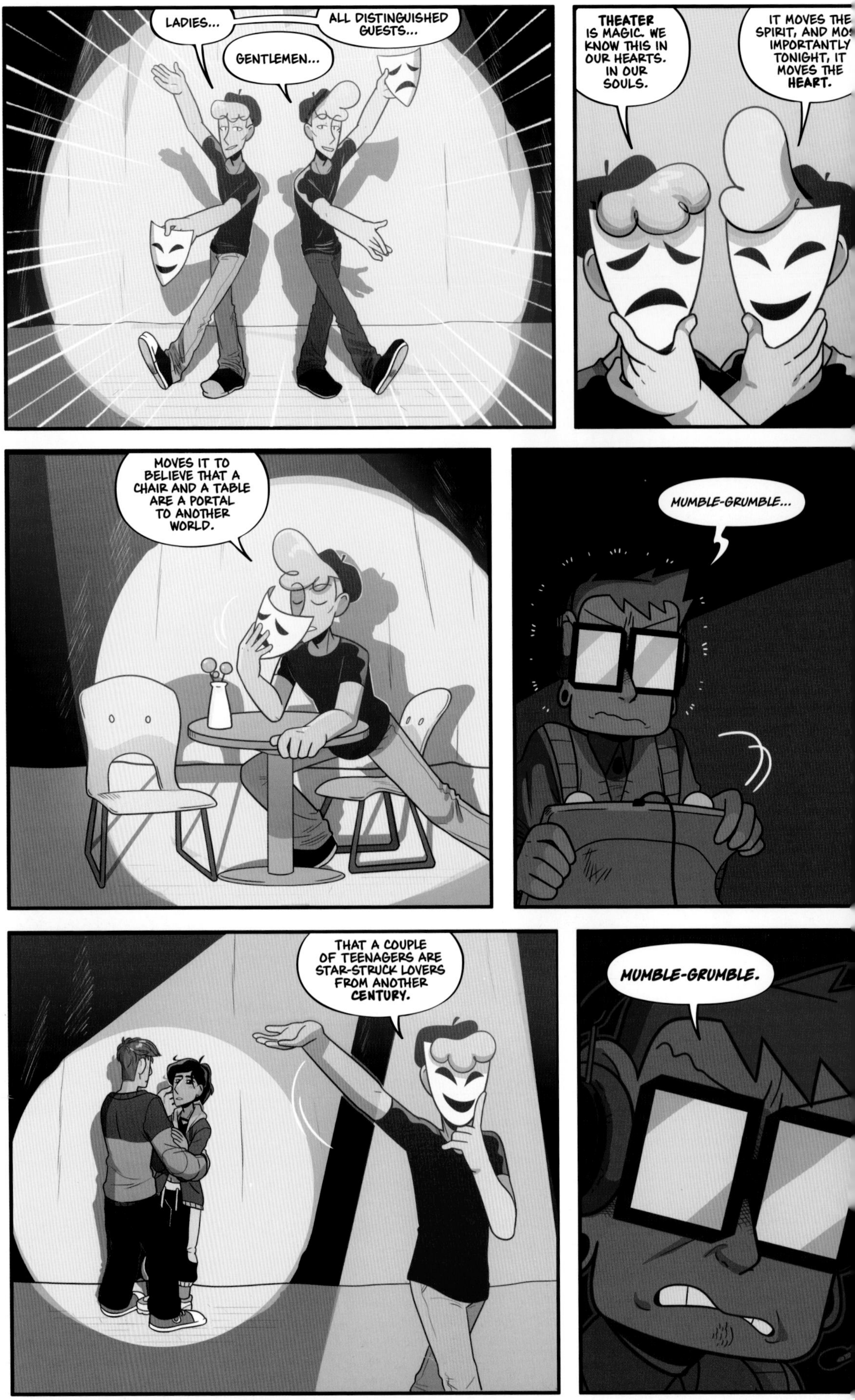
LADIES...
GENTLEMEN...
ALL DISTINGUISHED GUESTS...
THEATER IS MAGIC. WE KNOW THIS IN OUR HEARTS. IN OUR SOULS.
IT MOVES THE SPIRIT, AND MOS IMPORTANTLY TONIGHT, IT MOVES THE HEART.
MOVES IT TO BELIEVE THAT A CHAIR AND A TABLE ARE A PORTAL TO ANOTHER WORLD.
MUMBLE-GRUMBLE...
THAT A COUPLE OF TEENAGERS ARE STAR-STRUCK LOVERS FROM ANOTHER CENTURY.
MUMBLE-GRUMBLE.

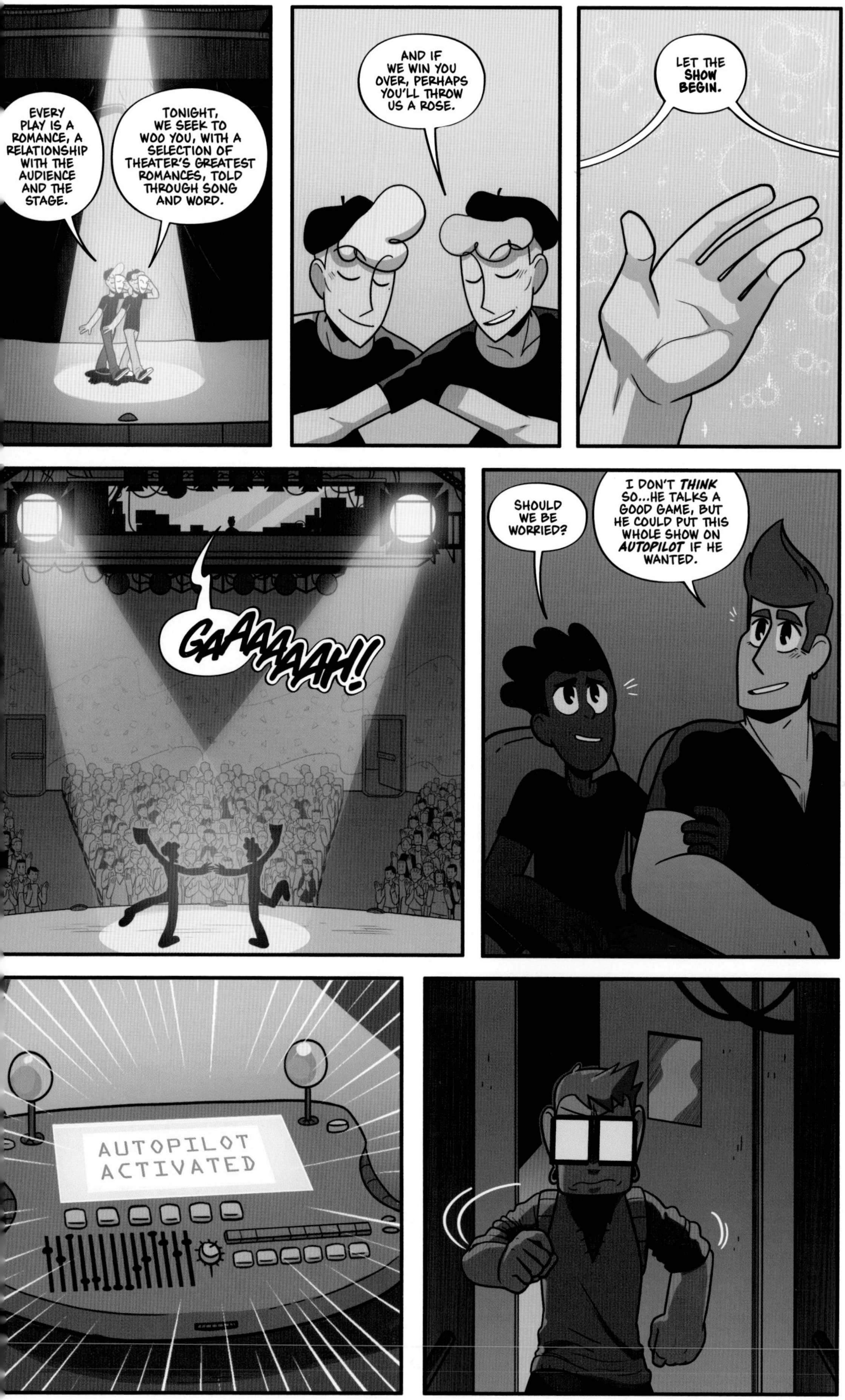
EVERY PLAY IS A ROMANCE, A RELATIONSHIP WITH THE AUDIENCE AND THE STAGE.
TONIGHT, WE SEEK TO WOO YOU, WITH A SELECTION OF THEATER'S GREATEST ROMANCES, TOLD THROUGH SONG AND WORD.
AND IF WE WIN YOU OVER, PERHAPS YOU'LL THROW US A ROSE.
LET THE SHOW BEGIN.
GAAAAAAH!!
SHOULD WE BE WORRIED?
I DON'T THINK SO...HE TALKS A GOOD GAME, BUT HE COULD PUT THIS WHOLE SHOW ON AUTOPILOT IF HE WANTED.
AUTOPILOT ACTIVATED

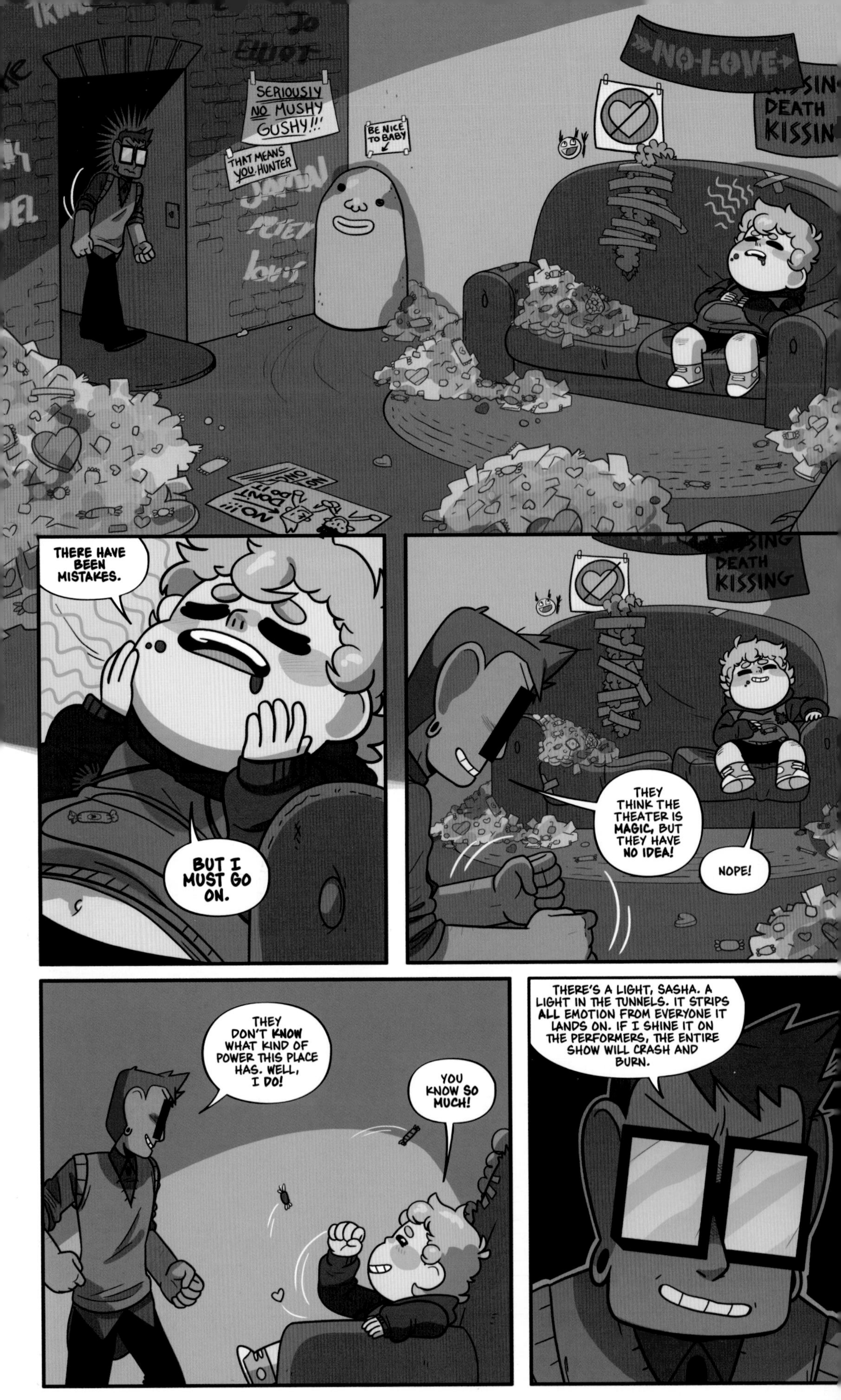
SERIOUSLY NO MUSHY GUSHY!!!
THAT MEANS YOU, HUNTER
BE NICE TO BABY
NO-LOVE
DEATH
THERE HAVE BEEN MISTAKES.
BUT I MUST GO ON.
THEY THINK THE THEATER IS MAGIC, BUT THEY HAVE NO IDEA!
NOPE!
DEATH KISSING
THEY DON'T KNOW WHAT KIND OF POWER THIS PLACE HAS. WELL, I DO!
YOU KNOW SO MUCH!
THERE'S A LIGHT, SASHA. A LIGHT IN THE TUNNELS. IT STRIPS ALL EMOTION FROM EVERYONE IT LANDS ON. IF I SHINE IT ON THE PERFORMERS, THE ENTIRE SHOW WILL CRASH AND BURN.

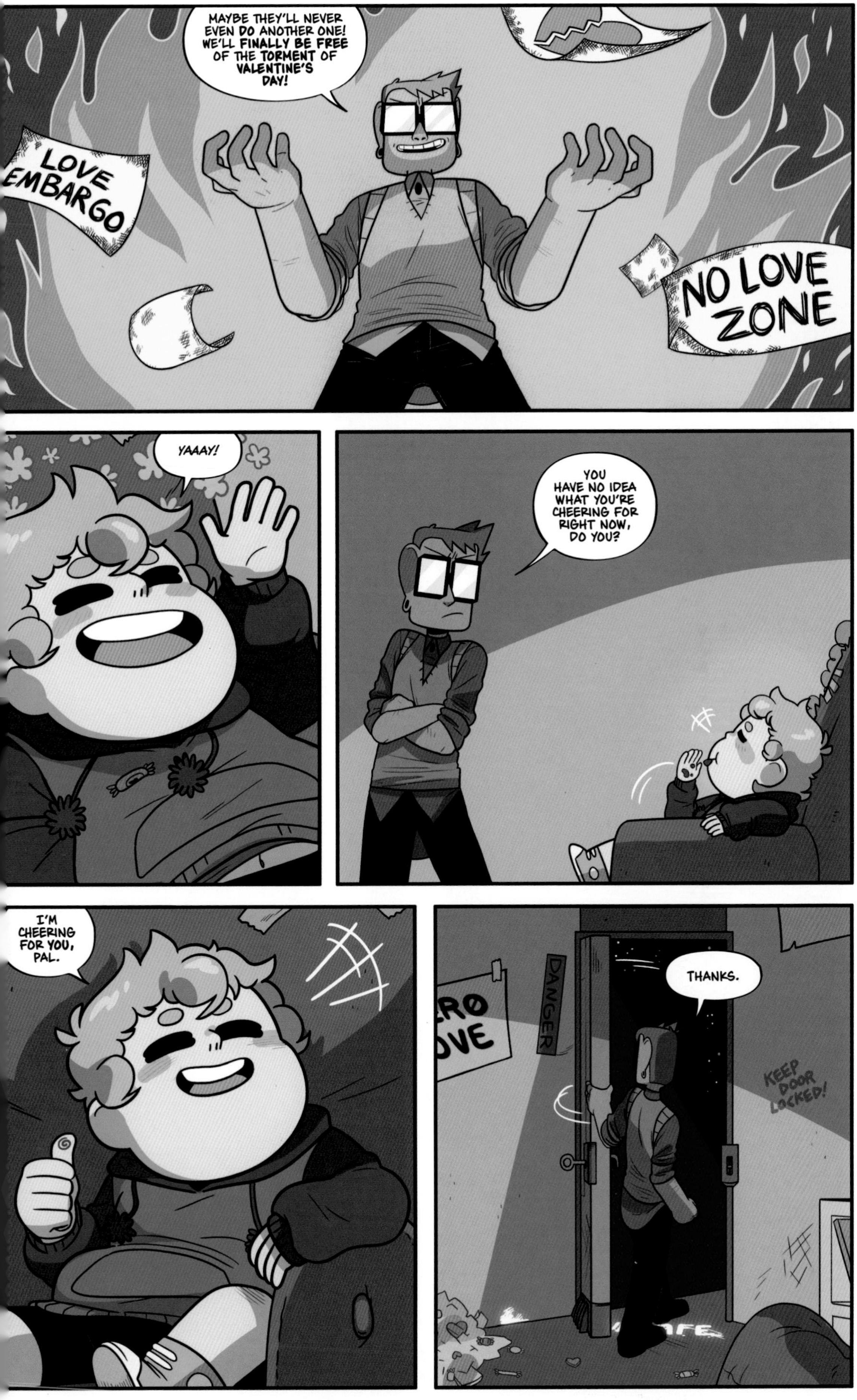
MAYBE THEY'LL NEVER EVEN DO ANOTHER ONE! WE'LL FINALLY BE FREE OF THE TORMENT OF VALENTINE'S DAY!
LOVE EMBARGO
NO LOVE ZONE
YAAAY!
YOU HAVE NO IDEA WHAT YOU'RE CHEERING FOR RIGHT NOW, DO YOU?
I'M CHEERING FOR YOU, PAL.
DANGER
THANKS.
KEEP DOOR LOCKED!

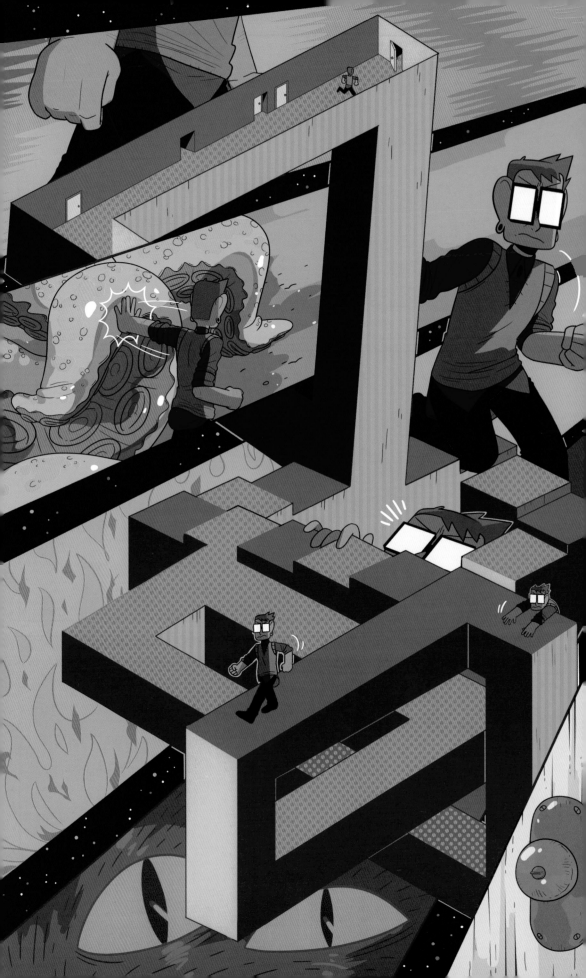

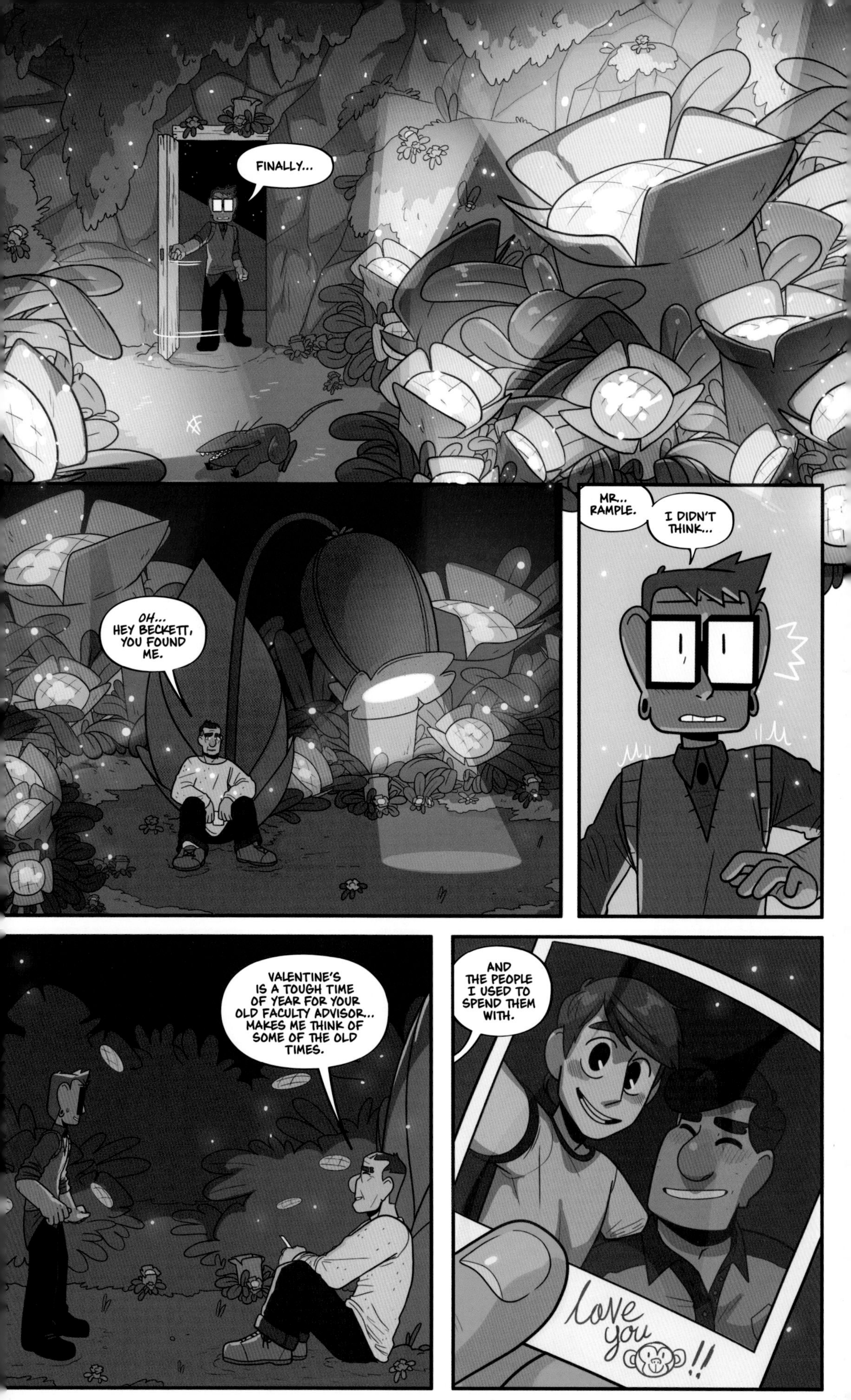
FINALLY...
OH... HEY BECKETT, YOU FOUND ME.
MR... RAMPLE.
I DIDN'T THINK...
VALENTINE'S IS A TOUGH TIME OF YEAR FOR YOUR OLD FACULTY ADVISOR... MAKES ME THINK OF SOME OF THE OLD TIMES.
AND THE PEOPLE I USED TO SPEND THEM WITH.
love you !!

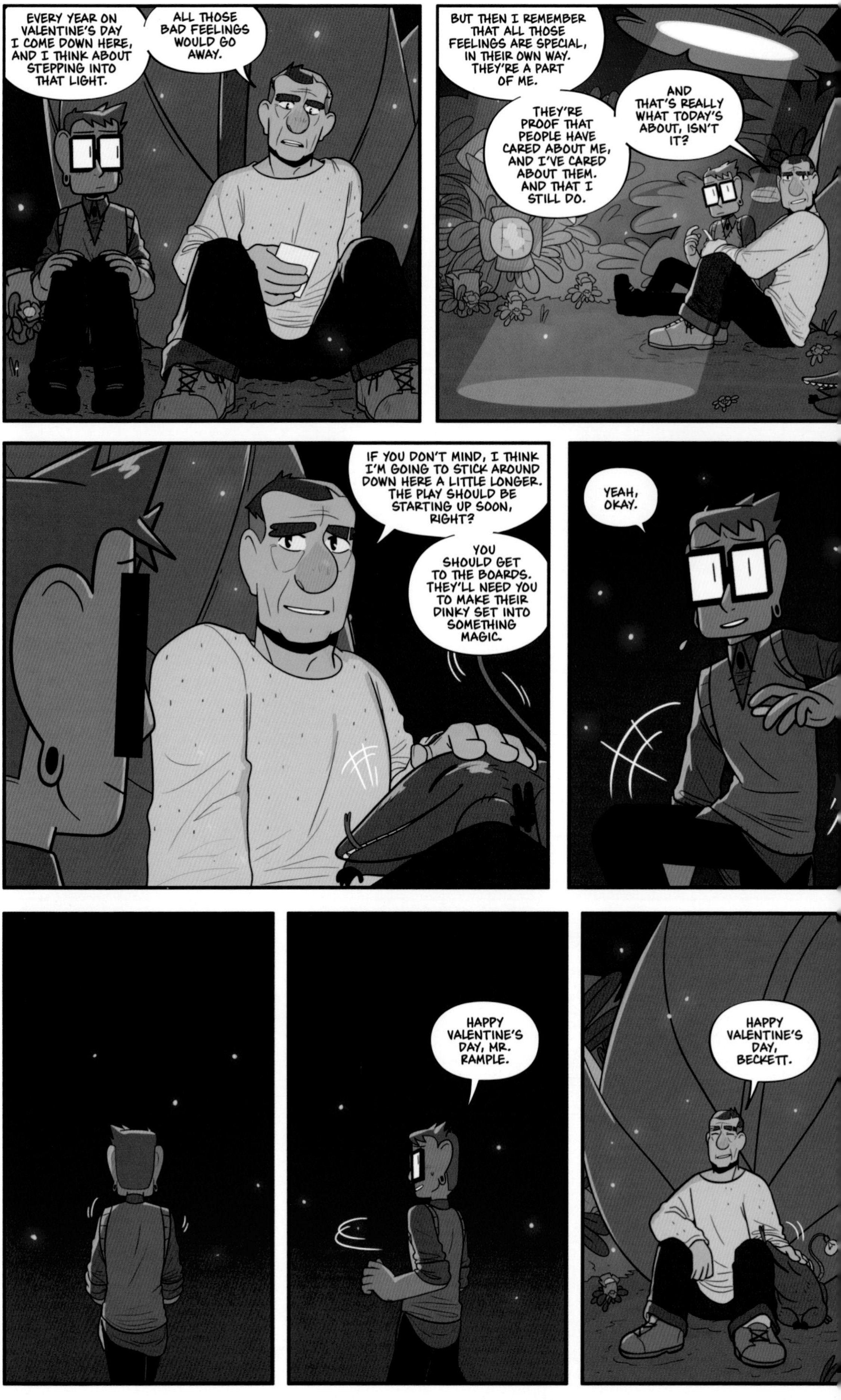

EVERY YEAR ON VALENTINE'S DAY I COME DOWN HERE, AND I THINK ABOUT STEPPING INTO THAT LIGHT.
ALL THOSE BAD FEELINGS WOULD GO AWAY.
BUT THEN I REMEMBER THAT ALL THOSE FEELINGS ARE SPECIAL, IN THEIR OWN WAY. THEY'RE A PART OF ME.
THEY'RE PROOF THAT PEOPLE HAVE CARED ABOUT ME, AND I'VE CARED ABOUT THEM. AND THAT I STILL DO.
AND THAT'S REALLY WHAT TODAY'S ABOUT, ISN'T IT?
IF YOU DON'T MIND, I THINK I'M GOING TO STICK AROUND DOWN HERE A LITTLE LONGER. THE PLAY SHOULD BE STARTING UP SOON, RIGHT?
YOU SHOULD GET TO THE BOARDS. THEY'LL NEED YOU TO MAKE THEIR DINKY SET INTO SOMETHING MAGIC.
YEAH, OKAY.
HAPPY VALENTINE'S DAY, MR. RAMPLE.
HAPPY VALENTINE'S DAY, BECKETT.

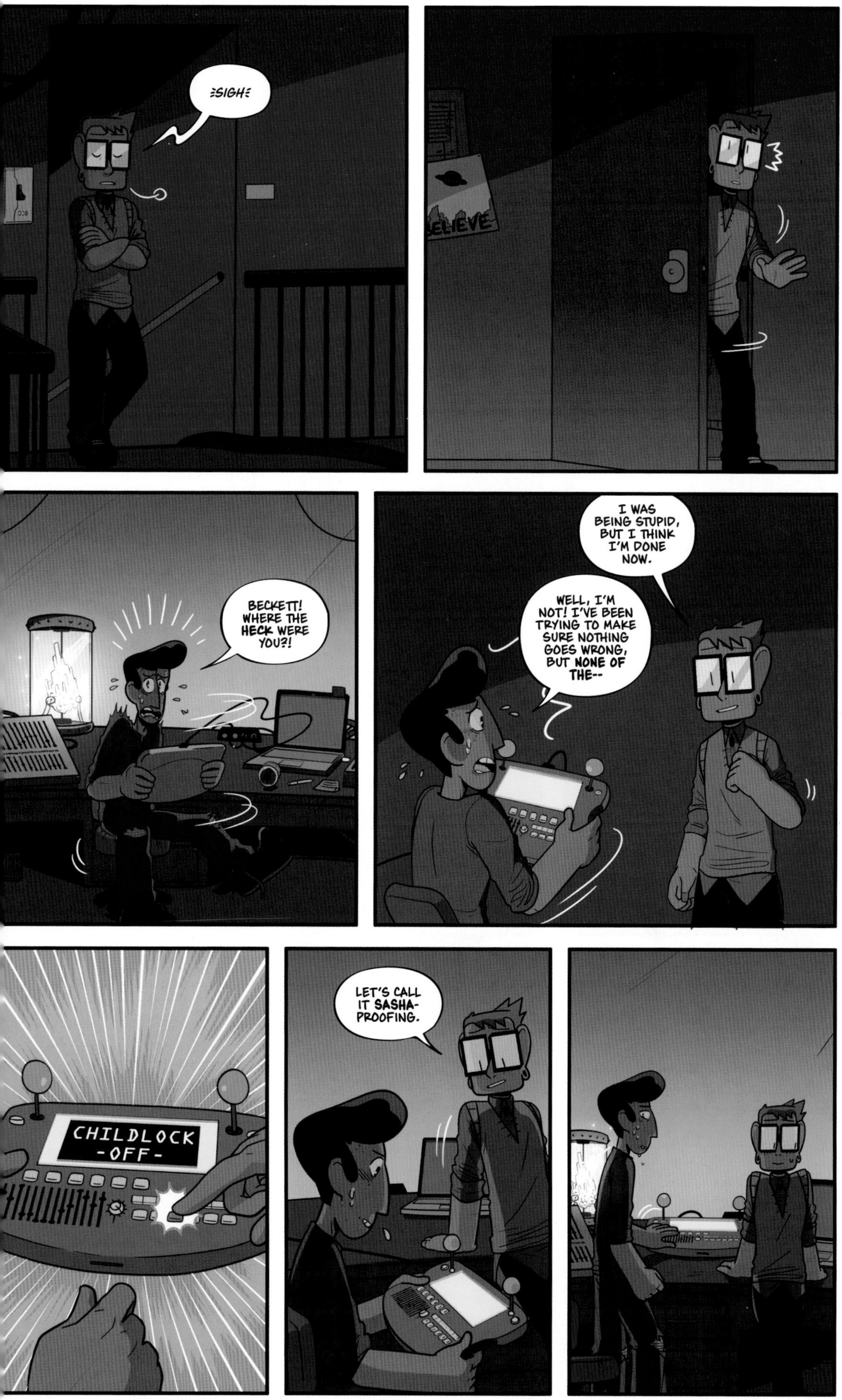
SIGH
BELIEVE
BECKETT! WHERE THE HECK WERE YOU?!
I WAS BEING STUPID, BUT I THINK I'M DONE NOW.
WELL, I'M NOT! I'VE BEEN TRYING TO MAKE SURE NOTHING GOES WRONG, BUT NONE OF THE--
CHILDLOCK -OFF-
LET'S CALL IT SASHA-PROOFING.

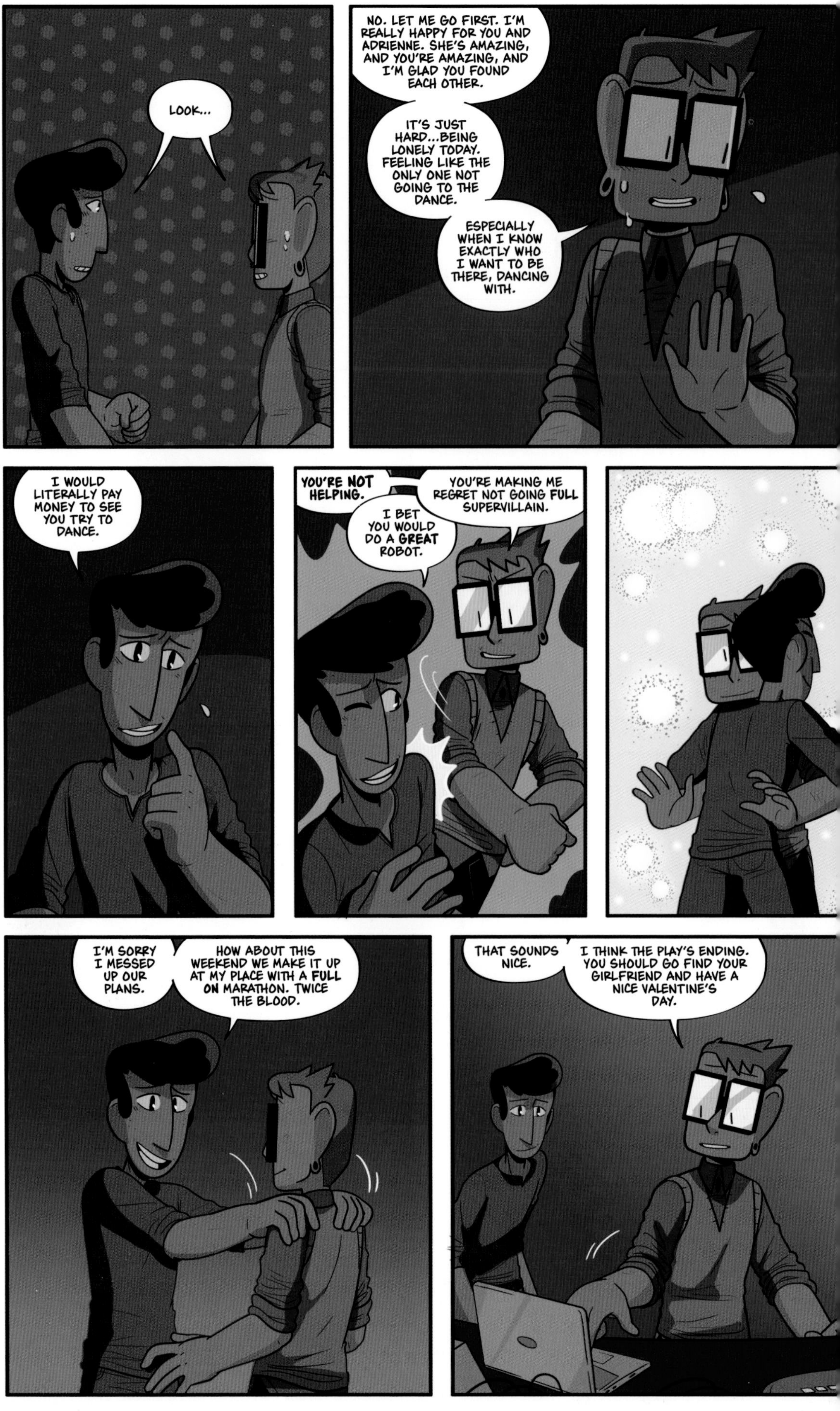
LOOK...
NO. LET ME GO FIRST. I'M REALLY HAPPY FOR YOU AND ADRIENNE. SHE'S AMAZING, AND YOU'RE AMAZING, AND I'M GLAD YOU FOUND EACH OTHER.
IT'S JUST HARD...BEING LONELY TODAY. FEELING LIKE THE ONLY ONE NOT GOING TO THE DANCE.
ESPECIALLY WHEN I KNOW EXACTLY WHO I WANT TO BE THERE, DANCING WITH.
I WOULD LITERALLY PAY MONEY TO SEE YOU TRY TO DANCE.
YOU'RE **NOT** HELPING.
I BET YOU WOULD DO A **GREAT** ROBOT.
YOU'RE MAKING ME REGRET NOT GOING **FULL** SUPERVILLAIN.
I'M SORRY I MESSED UP OUR PLANS.
HOW ABOUT THIS WEEKEND WE MAKE IT UP AT MY PLACE WITH A **FULL ON** MARATHON. TWICE THE BLOOD.
THAT SOUNDS NICE.
I THINK THE PLAY'S ENDING. YOU SHOULD GO FIND YOUR GIRLFRIEND AND HAVE A NICE VALENTINE'S DAY.

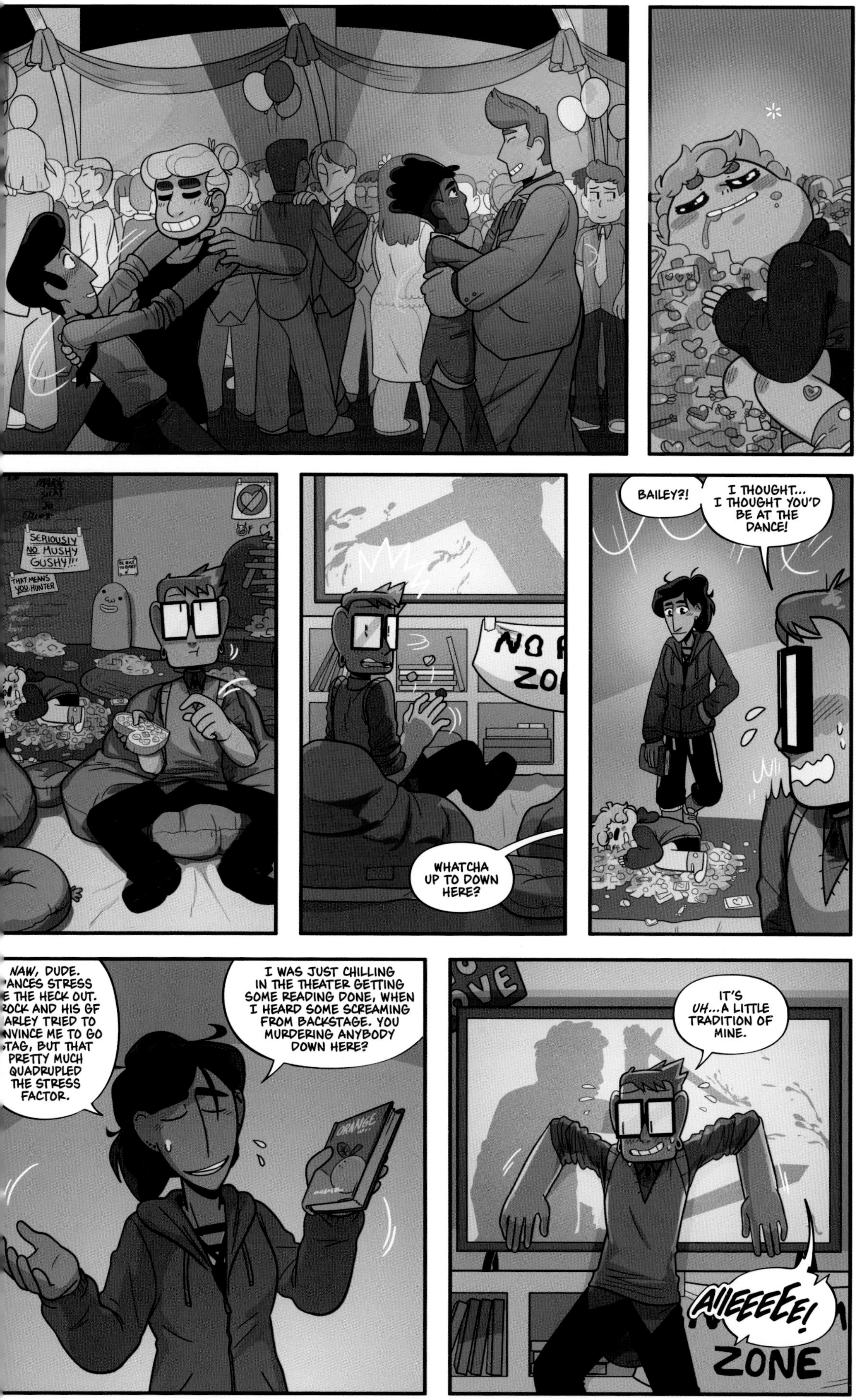

SERIOUSLY NO MUSHY GUSHY!!!
THAT MEANS YOU HUNTER
WHATCHA UP TO DOWN HERE?
BAILEY?!
I THOUGHT... I THOUGHT YOU'D BE AT THE DANCE!
NAW, DUDE. 'ANCES STRESS E THE HECK OUT. ROCK AND HIS GF ARLEY TRIED TO NVINCE ME TO GO STAG, BUT THAT PRETTY MUCH QUADRUPLED THE STRESS FACTOR.
I WAS JUST CHILLING IN THE THEATER GETTING SOME READING DONE, WHEN I HEARD SOME SCREAMING FROM BACKSTAGE. YOU MURDERING ANYBODY DOWN HERE?
ORANGE
IT'S UH...A LITTLE TRADITION OF MINE.
AIIEEEEE!
ZONE

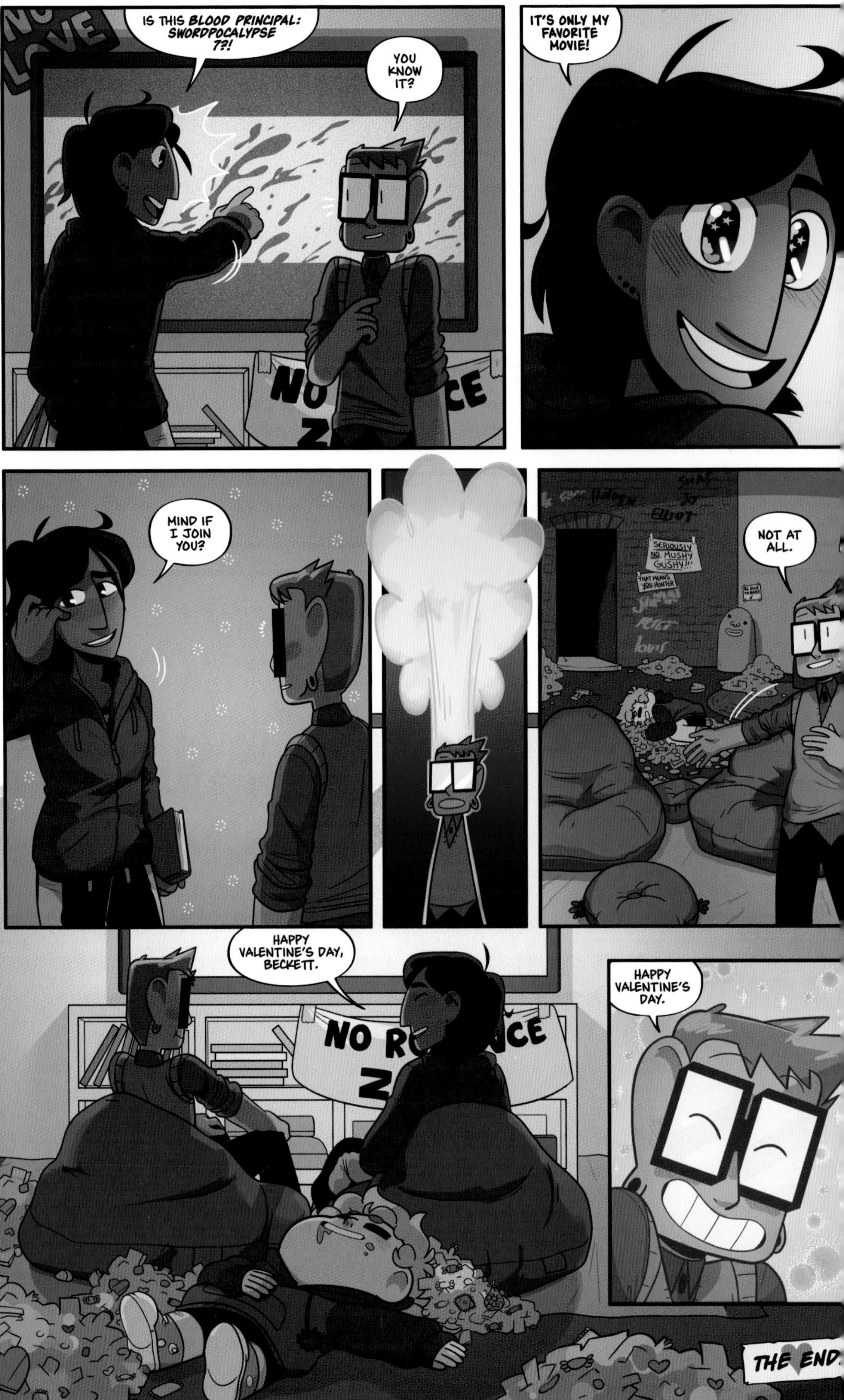

IS THIS BLOOD PRINCIPAL: SWORDPOCALYPSE 7?!
YOU KNOW IT?
IT'S ONLY MY FAVORITE MOVIE!
MIND IF I JOIN YOU?
SERIOUSLY NO MUSHY GUSHY!!!
THAT MEANS YOU, HUNTER
NOT AT ALL.
HAPPY VALENTINE'S DAY, BECKETT.
HAPPY VALENTINE'S DAY.
THE END.

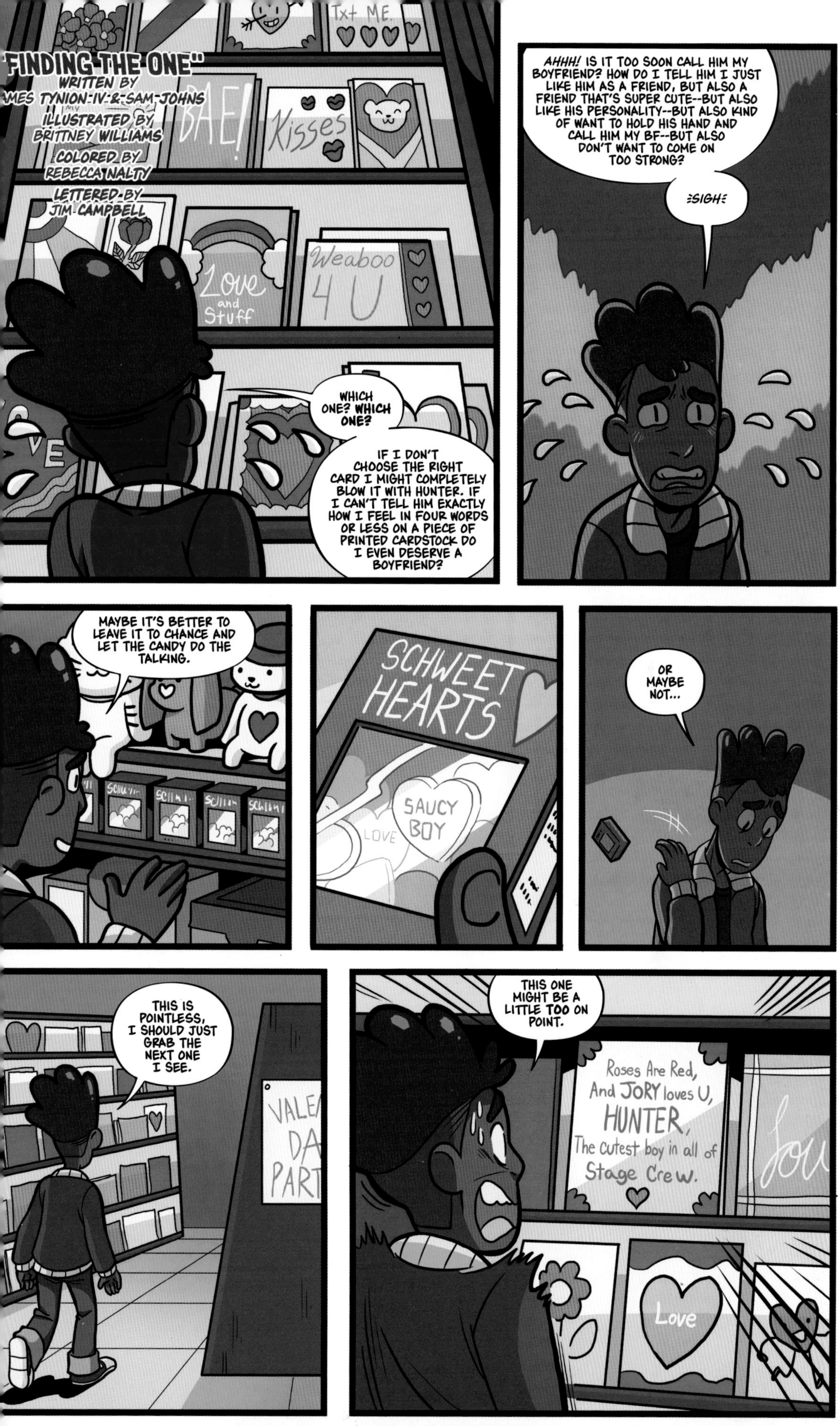

"FINDING THE ONE"
WRITTEN BY
MES TYNION IV & SAM JOHNS
ILLUSTRATED BY
BRITTNEY WILLIAMS
COLORED BY
REBECCA NALTY
LETTERED BY
JIM CAMPBELL
Txt ME.
BAE!
Kisses
Love and Stuff
Weaboo 4 U
WHICH ONE? WHICH ONE?
IF I DON'T CHOOSE THE RIGHT CARD I MIGHT COMPLETELY BLOW IT WITH HUNTER. IF I CAN'T TELL HIM EXACTLY HOW I FEEL IN FOUR WORDS OR LESS ON A PIECE OF PRINTED CARDSTOCK DO I EVEN DESERVE A BOYFRIEND?
AHHH! IS IT TOO SOON CALL HIM MY BOYFRIEND? HOW DO I TELL HIM I JUST LIKE HIM AS A FRIEND, BUT ALSO A FRIEND THAT'S SUPER CUTE--BUT ALSO LIKE HIS PERSONALITY--BUT ALSO KIND OF WANT TO HOLD HIS HAND AND CALL HIM MY BF--BUT ALSO DON'T WANT TO COME ON TOO STRONG?
SIGH
MAYBE IT'S BETTER TO LEAVE IT TO CHANCE AND LET THE CANDY DO THE TALKING.
SCHWEET HEARTS
SAUCY BOY
LOVE
OR MAYBE NOT...
THIS IS POINTLESS, I SHOULD JUST GRAB THE NEXT ONE I SEE.
THIS ONE MIGHT BE A LITTLE TOO ON POINT.
Roses Are Red, And JORY loves U, HUNTER, The cutest boy in all of Stage Crew.
Love

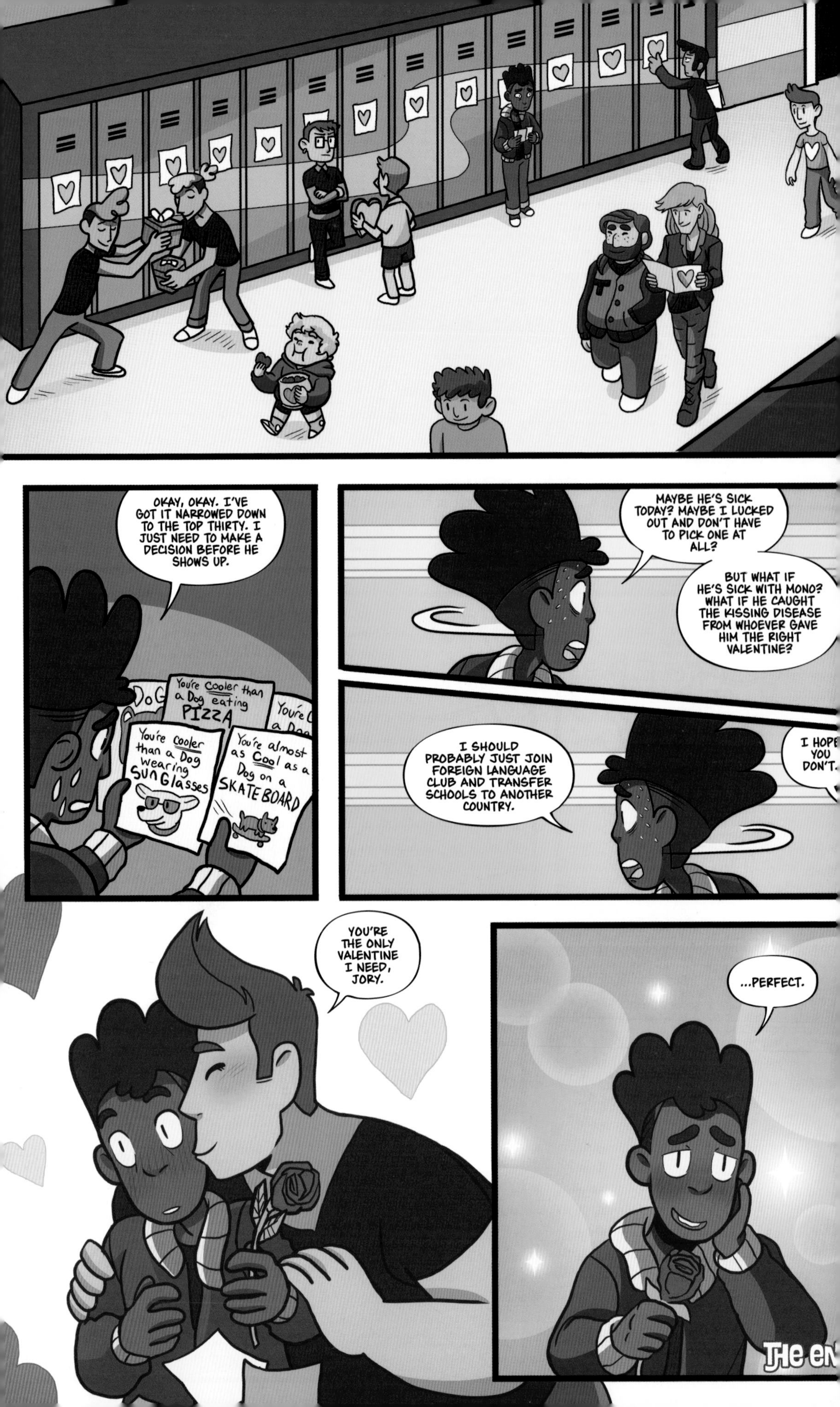
OKAY, OKAY. I'VE GOT IT NARROWED DOWN TO THE TOP THIRTY. I JUST NEED TO MAKE A DECISION BEFORE HE SHOWS UP.
You're cooler than a Dog eating PIZZA
You're cooler than a Dog wearing SunGlasses
You're almost as Cool as a Dog on a SKATEBOARD
MAYBE HE'S SICK TODAY? MAYBE I LUCKED OUT AND DON'T HAVE TO PICK ONE AT ALL?
BUT WHAT IF HE'S SICK WITH MONO? WHAT IF HE CAUGHT THE KISSING DISEASE FROM WHOEVER GAVE HIM THE RIGHT VALENTINE?
I SHOULD PROBABLY JUST JOIN FOREIGN LANGUAGE CLUB AND TRANSFER SCHOOLS TO ANOTHER COUNTRY.
I HOPE YOU DON'T.
YOU'RE THE ONLY VALENTINE I NEED, JORY.
...PERFECT.

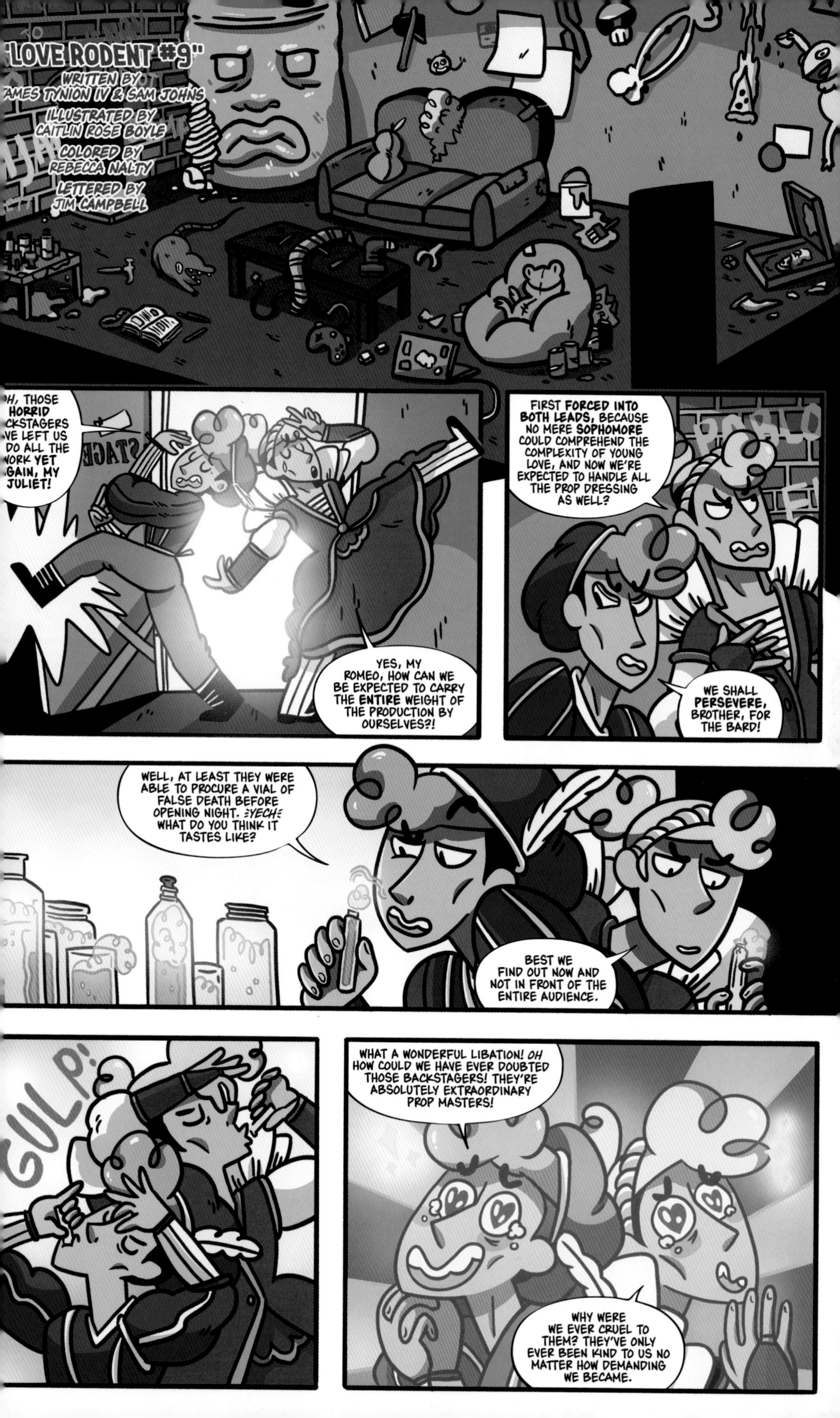

"LOVE RODENT #9"
WRITTEN BY
AMES TYNION IV & SAM JOHNS
ILLUSTRATED BY
CAITLIN ROSE BOYLE
COLORED BY
REBECCA NALTY
LETTERED BY
JIM CAMPBELL
H, THOSE HORRID CKSTAGERS VE LEFT US DO ALL THE WORK YET GAIN, MY JULIET!
YES, MY ROMEO, HOW CAN WE BE EXPECTED TO CARRY THE ENTIRE WEIGHT OF THE PRODUCTION BY OURSELVES?!
FIRST FORCED INTO BOTH LEADS, BECAUSE NO MERE SOPHOMORE COULD COMPREHEND THE COMPLEXITY OF YOUNG LOVE, AND NOW WE'RE EXPECTED TO HANDLE ALL THE PROP DRESSING AS WELL?
WE SHALL PERSEVERE, BROTHER, FOR THE BARD!
WELL, AT LEAST THEY WERE ABLE TO PROCURE A VIAL OF FALSE DEATH BEFORE OPENING NIGHT. YECH! WHAT DO YOU THINK IT TASTES LIKE?
BEST WE FIND OUT NOW AND NOT IN FRONT OF THE ENTIRE AUDIENCE.
GULP!
WHAT A WONDERFUL LIBATION! OH HOW COULD WE HAVE EVER DOUBTED THOSE BACKSTAGERS! THEY'RE ABSOLUTELY EXTRAORDINARY PROP MASTERS!
WHY WERE WE EVER CRUEL TO THEM? THEY'VE ONLY EVER BEEN KIND TO US NO MATTER HOW DEMANDING WE BECAME.

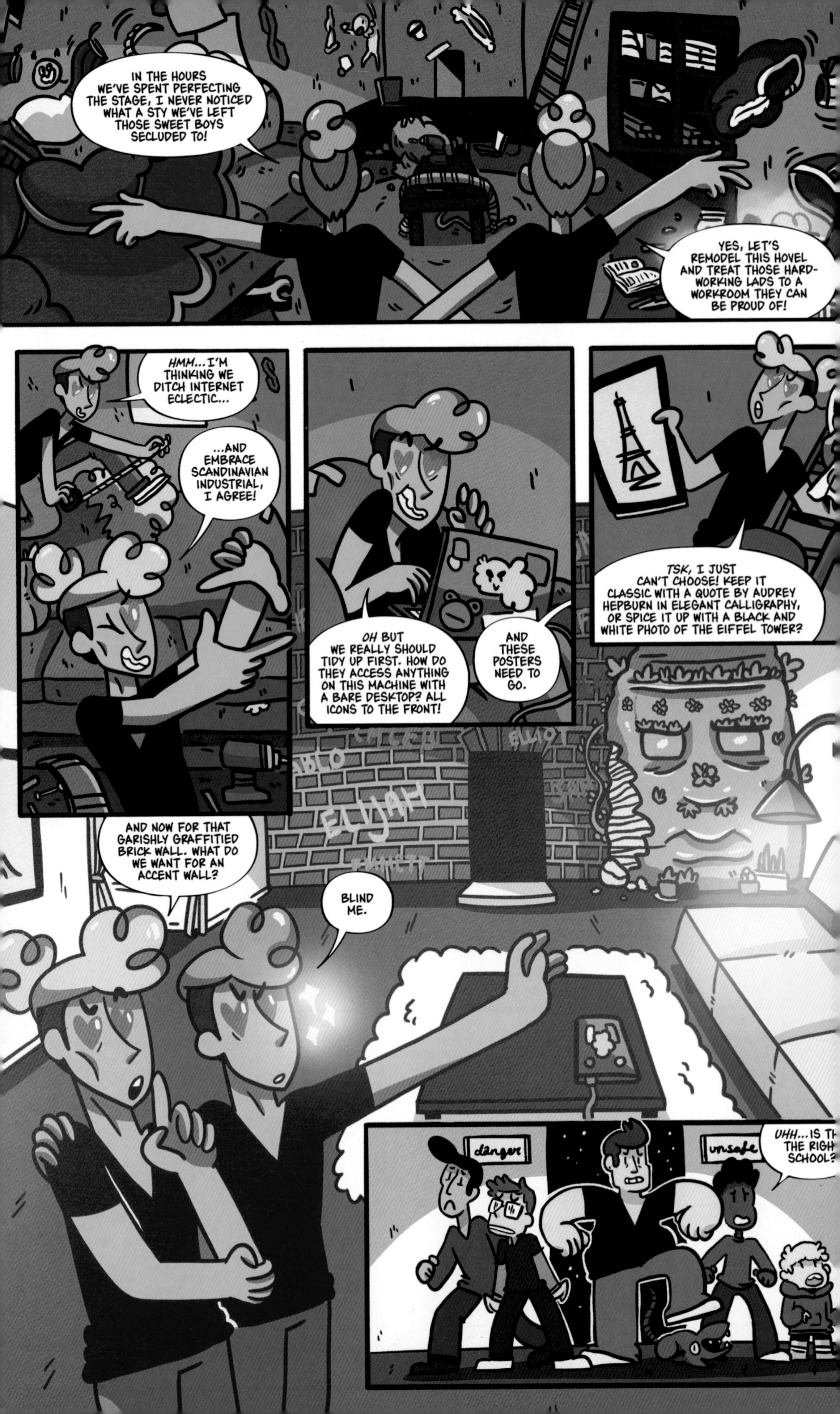
IN THE HOURS WE'VE SPENT PERFECTING THE STAGE, I NEVER NOTICED WHAT A STY WE'VE LEFT THOSE SWEET BOYS SECLUDED TO!
YES, LET'S REMODEL THIS HOVEL AND TREAT THOSE HARD-WORKING LADS TO A WORKROOM THEY CAN BE PROUD OF!
HMM... I'M THINKING WE DITCH INTERNET ECLECTIC...
...AND EMBRACE SCANDINAVIAN INDUSTRIAL, I AGREE!
OH BUT WE REALLY SHOULD TIDY UP FIRST. HOW DO THEY ACCESS ANYTHING ON THIS MACHINE WITH A BARE DESKTOP? ALL ICONS TO THE FRONT!
AND THESE POSTERS NEED TO GO.
TSK, I JUST CAN'T CHOOSE! KEEP IT CLASSIC WITH A QUOTE BY AUDREY HEPBURN IN ELEGANT CALLIGRAPHY, OR SPICE IT UP WITH A BLACK AND WHITE PHOTO OF THE EIFFEL TOWER?
ELIJAH
AND NOW FOR THAT GARISHLY GRAFFITIED BRICK WALL. WHAT DO WE WANT FOR AN ACCENT WALL?
BLIND ME.
danger
unsafe
UHH... IS TH THE RIGH SCHOOL?

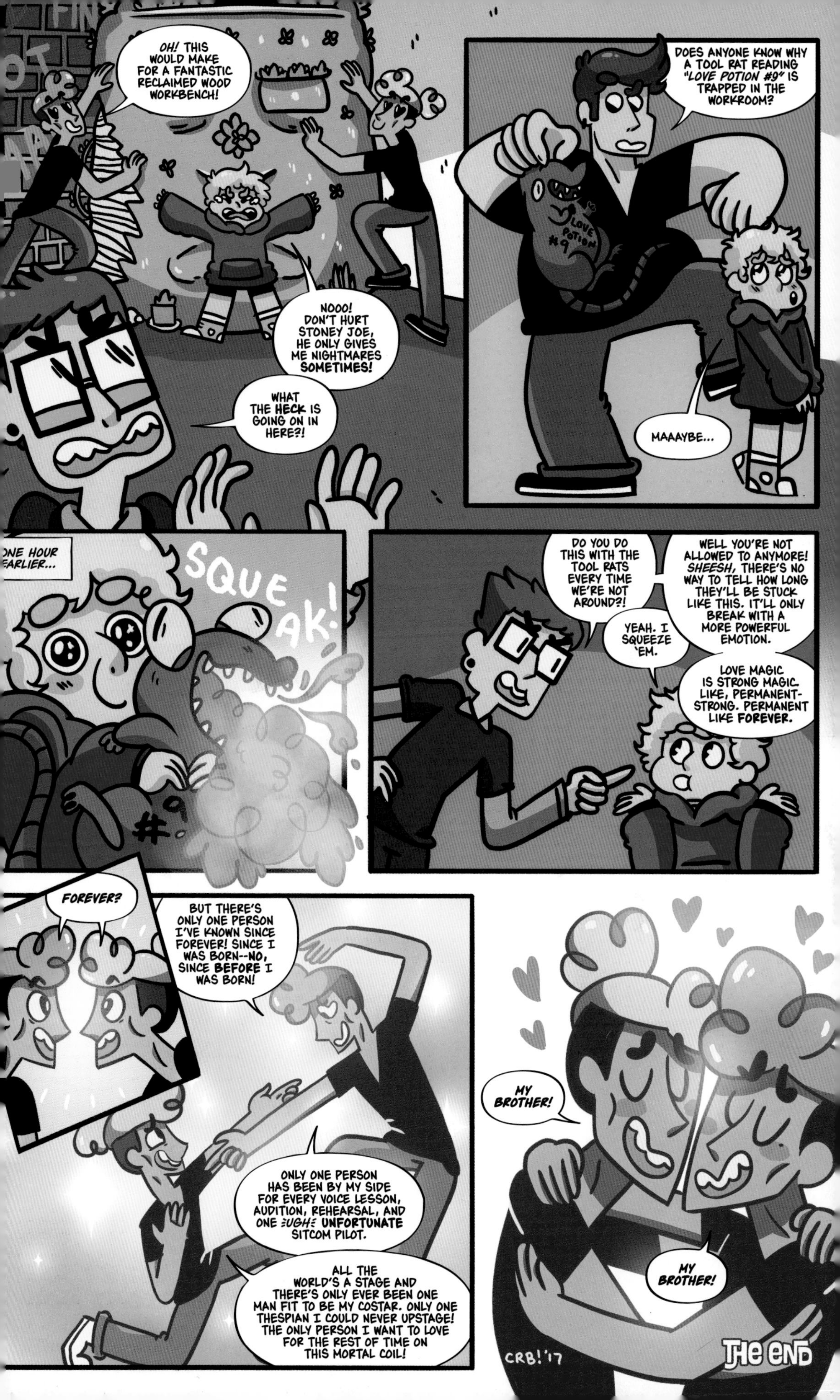
OH! THIS WOULD MAKE FOR A FANTASTIC RECLAIMED WOOD WORKBENCH!
NOOO! DON'T HURT STONEY JOE, HE ONLY GIVES ME NIGHTMARES SOMETIMES!
WHAT THE HECK IS GOING ON IN HERE?!
DOES ANYONE KNOW WHY A TOOL RAT READING "LOVE POTION #9" IS TRAPPED IN THE WORKROOM?
LOVE POTION #9
MAAAYBE...
ONE HOUR EARLIER...
SQUEAK!
#9
DO YOU DO THIS WITH THE TOOL RATS EVERY TIME WE'RE NOT AROUND?!
YEAH. I SQUEEZE 'EM.
WELL YOU'RE NOT ALLOWED TO ANYMORE! SHEESH, THERE'S NO WAY TO TELL HOW LONG THEY'LL BE STUCK LIKE THIS. IT'LL ONLY BREAK WITH A MORE POWERFUL EMOTION.
LOVE MAGIC IS STRONG MAGIC. LIKE, PERMANENT-STRONG. PERMANENT LIKE FOREVER.
FOREVER?
BUT THERE'S ONLY ONE PERSON I'VE KNOWN SINCE FOREVER! SINCE I WAS BORN--NO, SINCE BEFORE I WAS BORN!
ONLY ONE PERSON HAS BEEN BY MY SIDE FOR EVERY VOICE LESSON, AUDITION, REHEARSAL, AND ONE *UGH* UNFORTUNATE SITCOM PILOT.
ALL THE WORLD'S A STAGE AND THERE'S ONLY EVER BEEN ONE MAN FIT TO BE MY COSTAR. ONLY ONE THESPIAN I COULD NEVER UPSTAGE! THE ONLY PERSON I WANT TO LOVE FOR THE REST OF TIME ON THIS MORTAL COIL!
MY BROTHER!
MY BROTHER!
CRB! '17
THE END

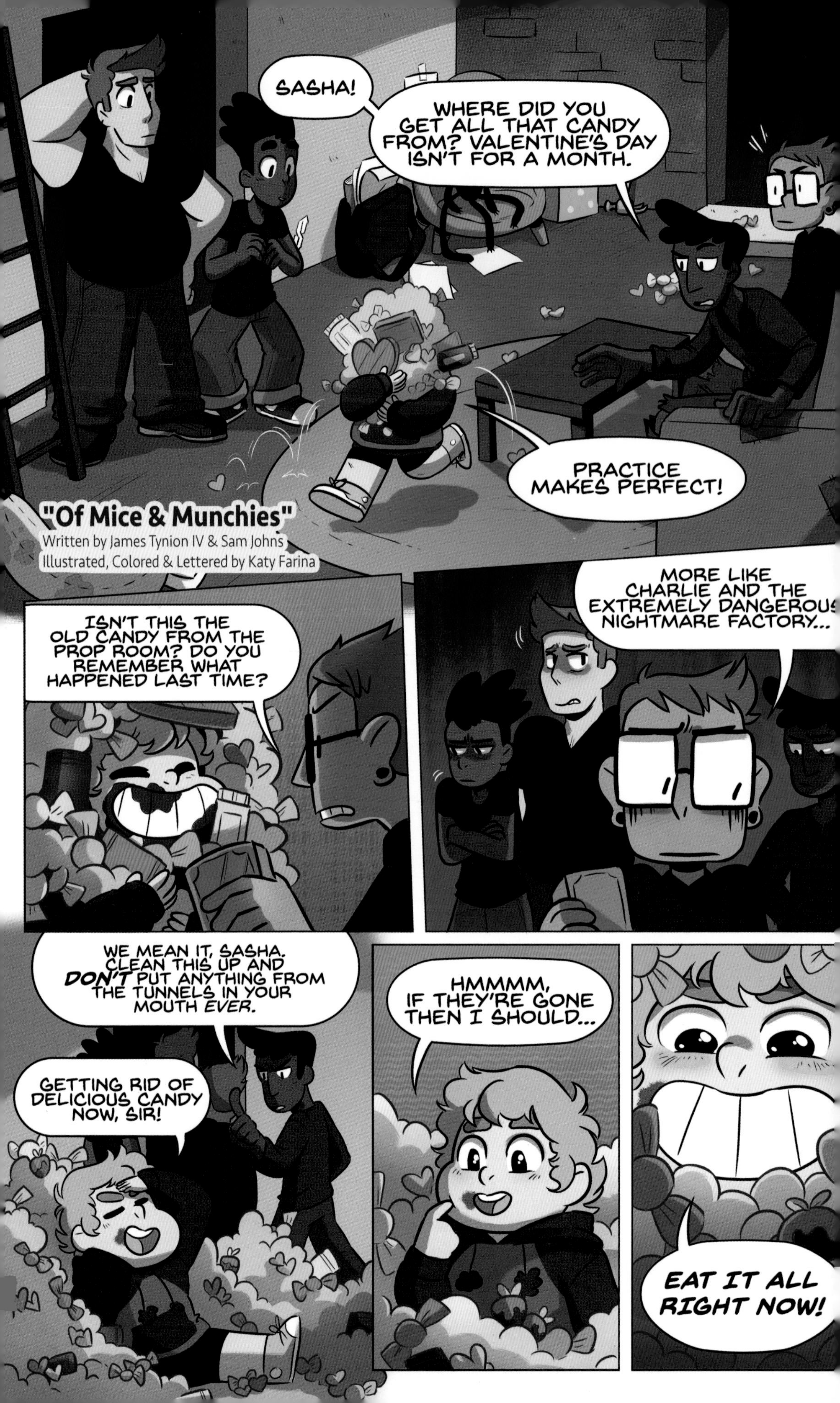
SASHA!
WHERE DID YOU GET ALL THAT CANDY FROM? VALENTINE'S DAY ISN'T FOR A MONTH.
PRACTICE MAKES PERFECT!
"Of Mice & Munchies"
Written by James Tynion IV & Sam Johns
Illustrated, Colored & Lettered by Katy Farina
ISN'T THIS THE OLD CANDY FROM THE PROP ROOM? DO YOU REMEMBER WHAT HAPPENED LAST TIME?
MORE LIKE CHARLIE AND THE EXTREMELY DANGEROUS NIGHTMARE FACTORY...
WE MEAN IT, SASHA. CLEAN THIS UP AND *DON'T* PUT ANYTHING FROM THE TUNNELS IN YOUR MOUTH *EVER*.
GETTING RID OF DELICIOUS CANDY NOW, SIR!
HMMMM, IF THEY'RE GONE THEN I SHOULD...
EAT IT ALL RIGHT NOW!

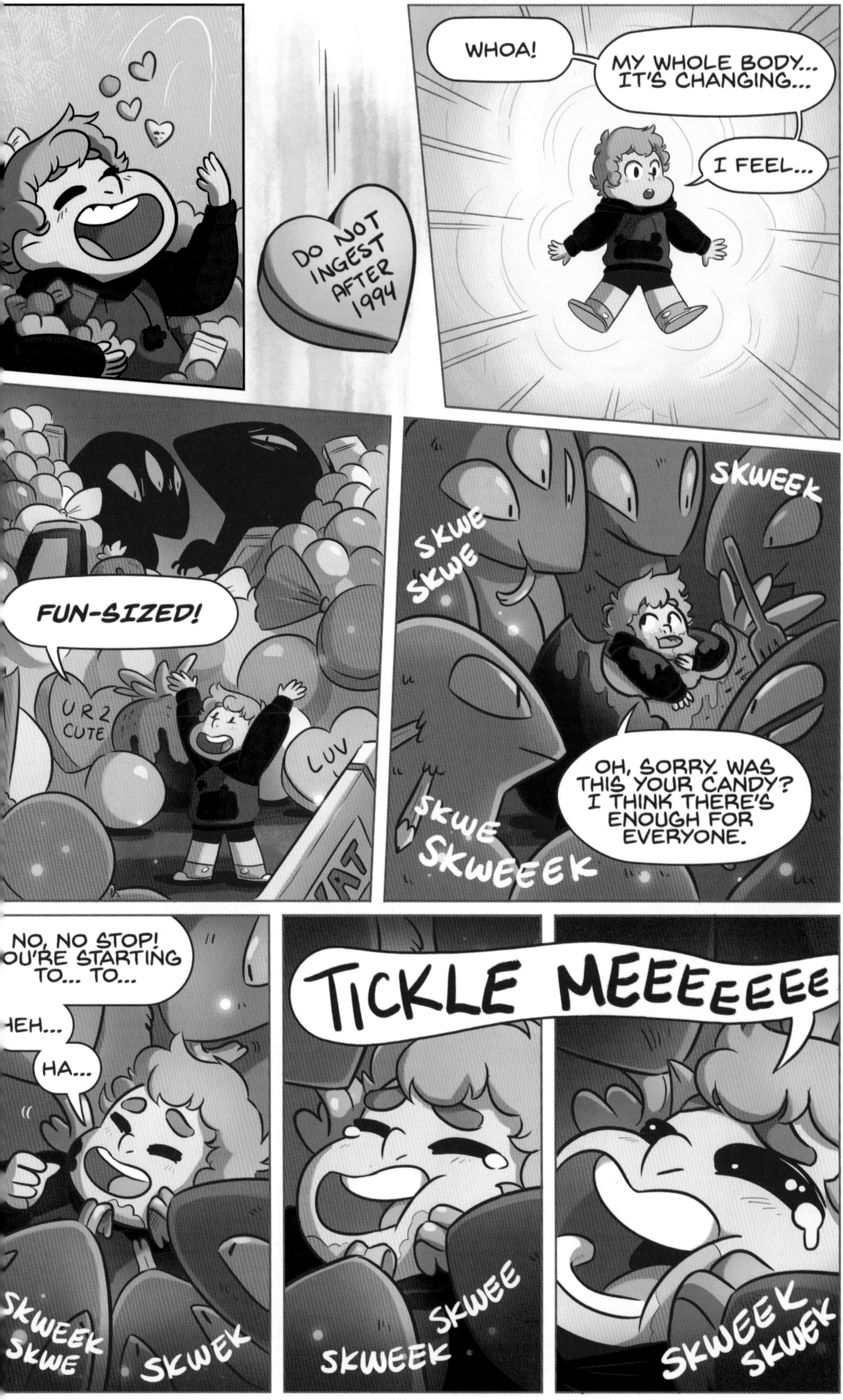
DO NOT INGEST AFTER 1994
WHOA!
MY WHOLE BODY... IT'S CHANGING...
I FEEL...
FUN-SIZED!
UR 2 CUTE
LUV
SKWEEK
SKWE SKWE
OH, SORRY. WAS THIS YOUR CANDY? I THINK THERE'S ENOUGH FOR EVERYONE.
SKWE SKWEEEK
NO, NO STOP! OU'RE STARTING TO... TO...
HEH...
HA...
SKWEEK SKWE
SKWEK
TICKLE MEEEEEEE
SKWEEK SKWEE
SKWEEK SKWEK

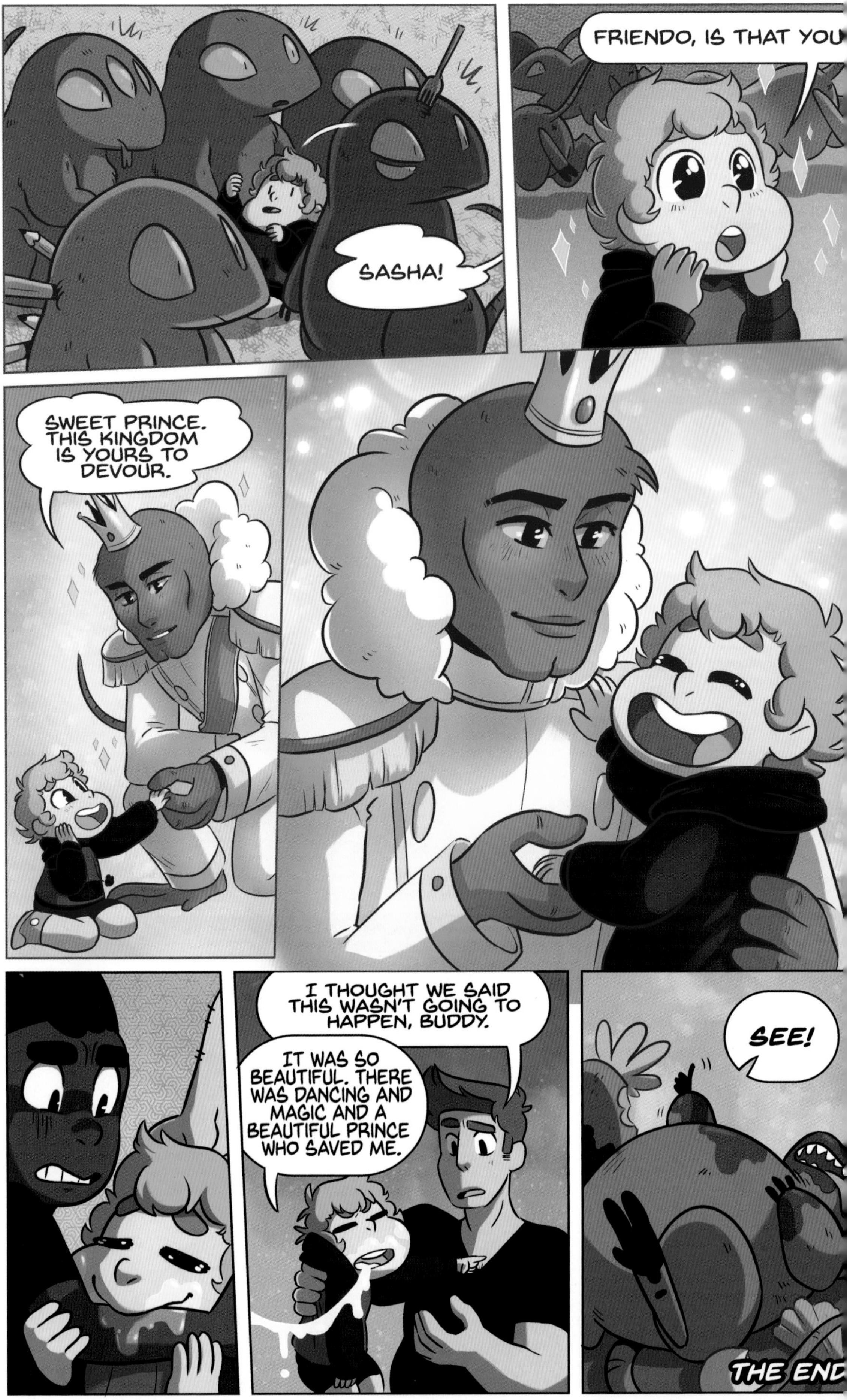

SASHA!
FRIENDO, IS THAT YOU
SWEET PRINCE. THIS KINGDOM IS YOURS TO DEVOUR.
I THOUGHT WE SAID THIS WASN'T GOING TO HAPPEN, BUDDY.
IT WAS SO BEAUTIFUL. THERE WAS DANCING AND MAGIC AND A BEAUTIFUL PRINCE WHO SAVED ME.
SEE!
THE END

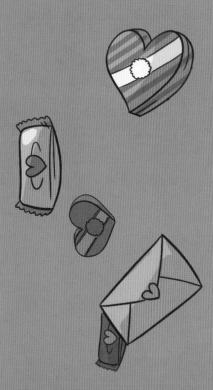

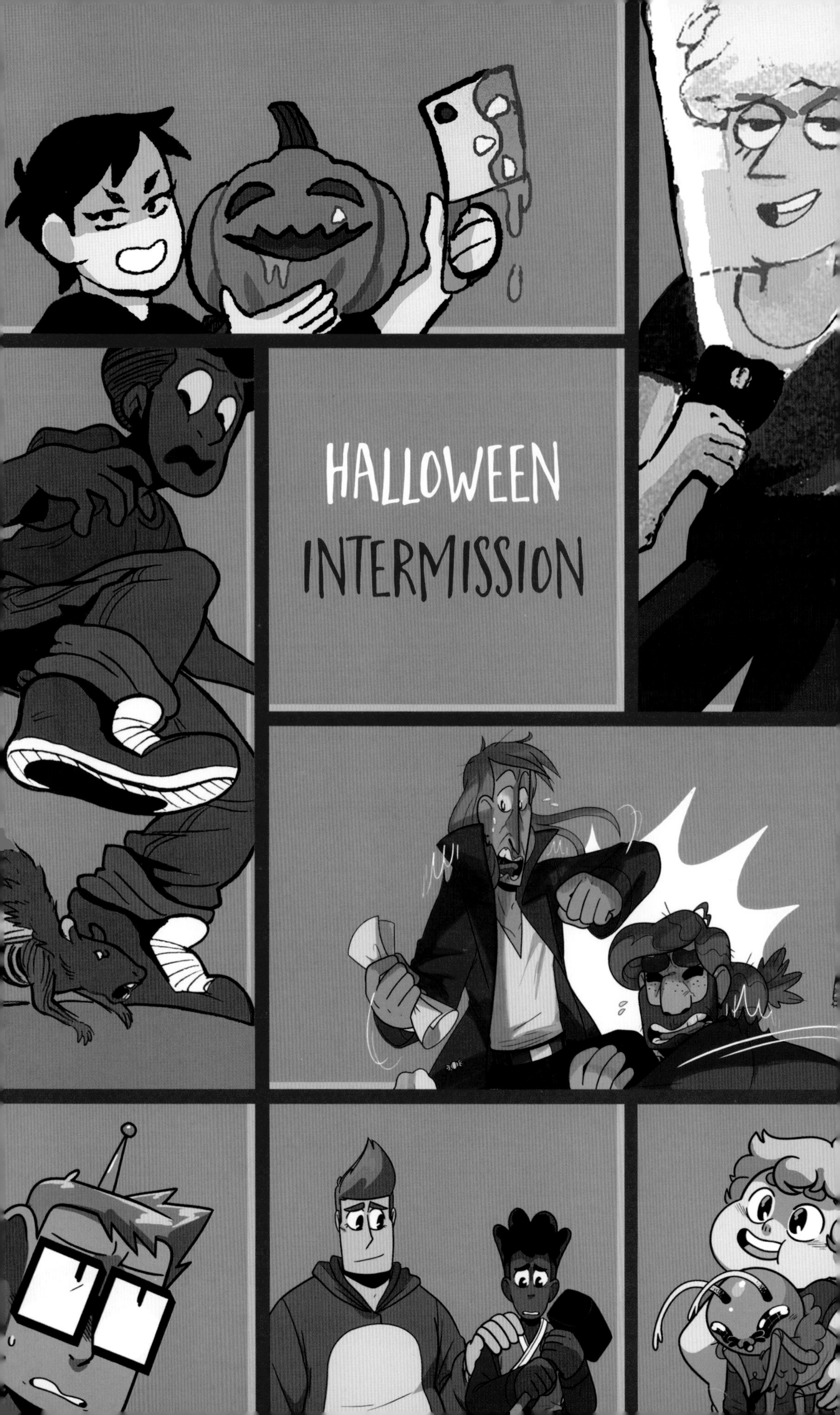
HALLOWEEN
INTERMISSION

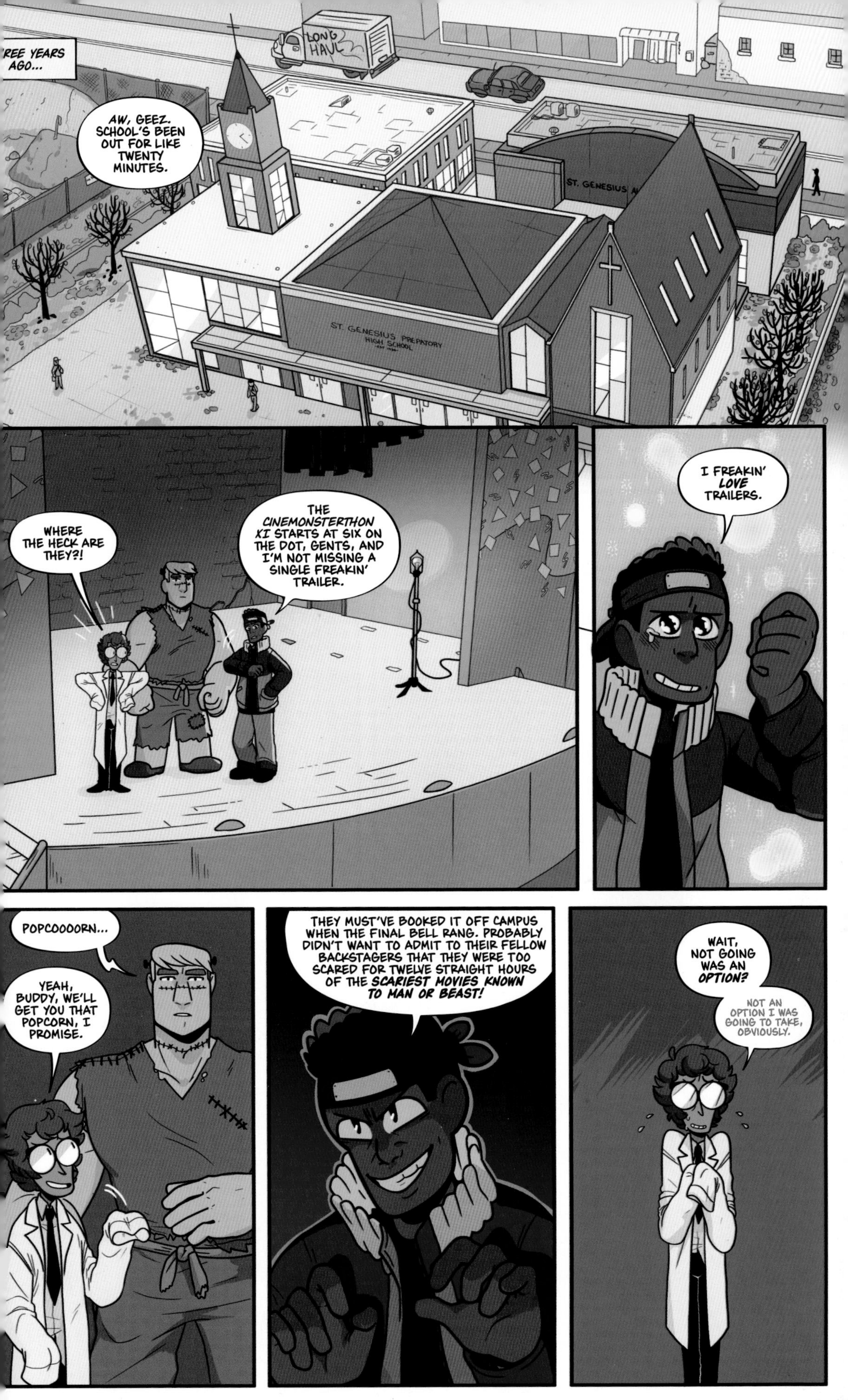

REE YEARS AGO...
LONG HAUL
AW, GEEZ. SCHOOL'S BEEN OUT FOR LIKE TWENTY MINUTES.
ST. GENESIUS PREPATORY HIGH SCHOOL
WHERE THE HECK ARE THEY?!
THE *CINEMONSTERTHON XI* STARTS AT SIX ON THE DOT, GENTS, AND I'M NOT MISSING A SINGLE FREAKIN' TRAILER.
I FREAKIN' ***LOVE*** TRAILERS.
POPCOOOORN...
YEAH, BUDDY, WE'LL GET YOU THAT POPCORN, I PROMISE.
THEY MUST'VE BOOKED IT OFF CAMPUS WHEN THE FINAL BELL RANG. PROBABLY DIDN'T WANT TO ADMIT TO THEIR FELLOW BACKSTAGERS THAT THEY WERE TOO SCARED FOR TWELVE STRAIGHT HOURS OF THE ***SCARIEST MOVIES KNOWN TO MAN OR BEAST!***
WAIT, NOT GOING WAS AN ***OPTION?***
NOT AN OPTION I WAS GOING TO TAKE, OBVIOUSLY.

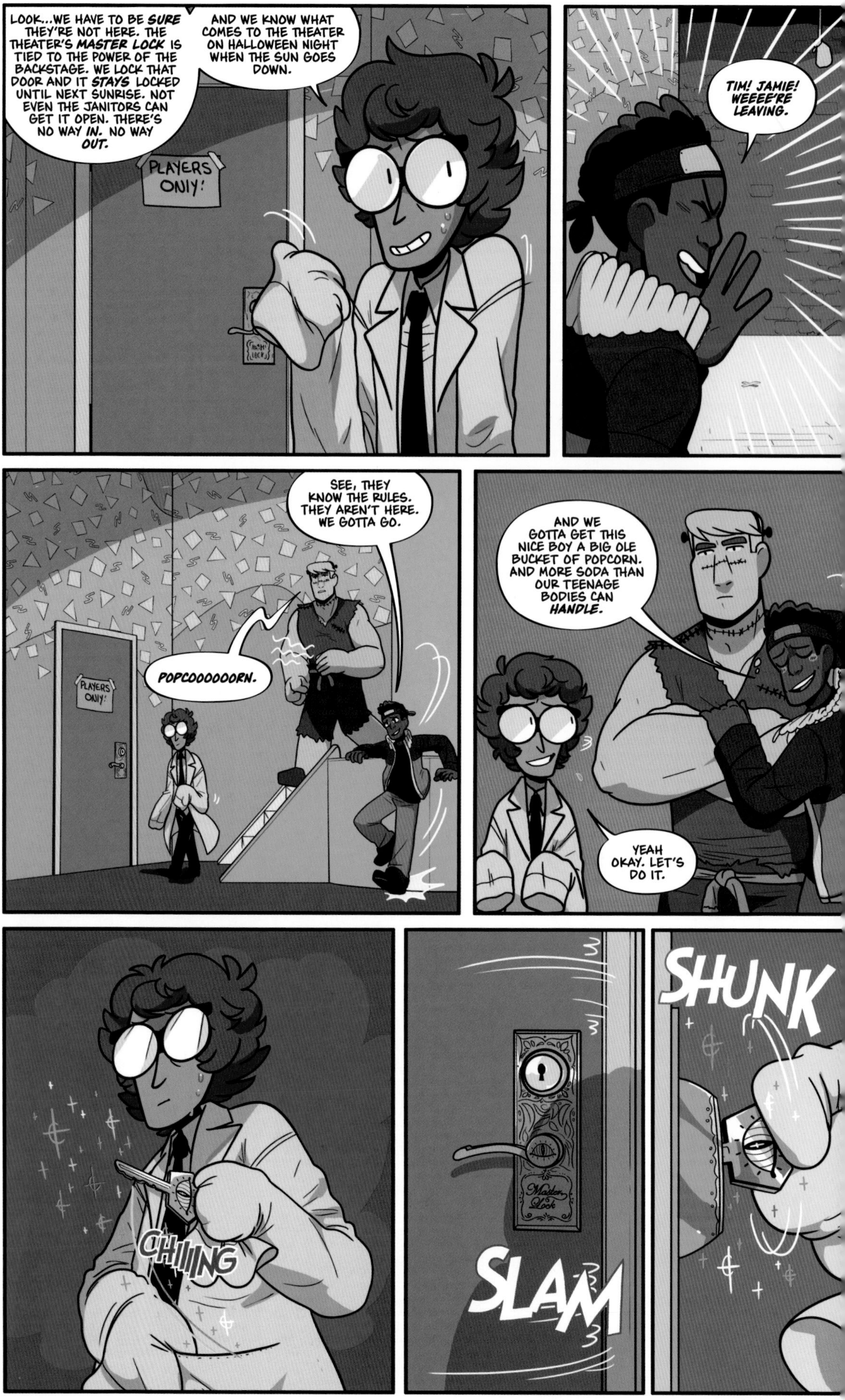
LOOK...WE HAVE TO BE SURE THEY'RE NOT HERE. THE THEATER'S MASTER LOCK IS TIED TO THE POWER OF THE BACKSTAGE. WE LOCK THAT DOOR AND IT STAYS LOCKED UNTIL NEXT SUNRISE. NOT EVEN THE JANITORS CAN GET IT OPEN. THERE'S NO WAY IN. NO WAY OUT.
AND WE KNOW WHAT COMES TO THE THEATER ON HALLOWEEN NIGHT WHEN THE SUN GOES DOWN.
PLAYERS ONLY!
TIM! JAMIE! WEEEE'RE LEAVING.
SEE, THEY KNOW THE RULES. THEY AREN'T HERE. WE GOTTA GO.
PLAYERS ONLY!
POPCOOOOOORN.
AND WE GOTTA GET THIS NICE BOY A BIG OLE BUCKET OF POPCORN. AND MORE SODA THAN OUR TEENAGE BODIES CAN HANDLE.
YEAH OKAY. LET'S DO IT.
CHIIIING
Master Lock
SLAM
SHUNK

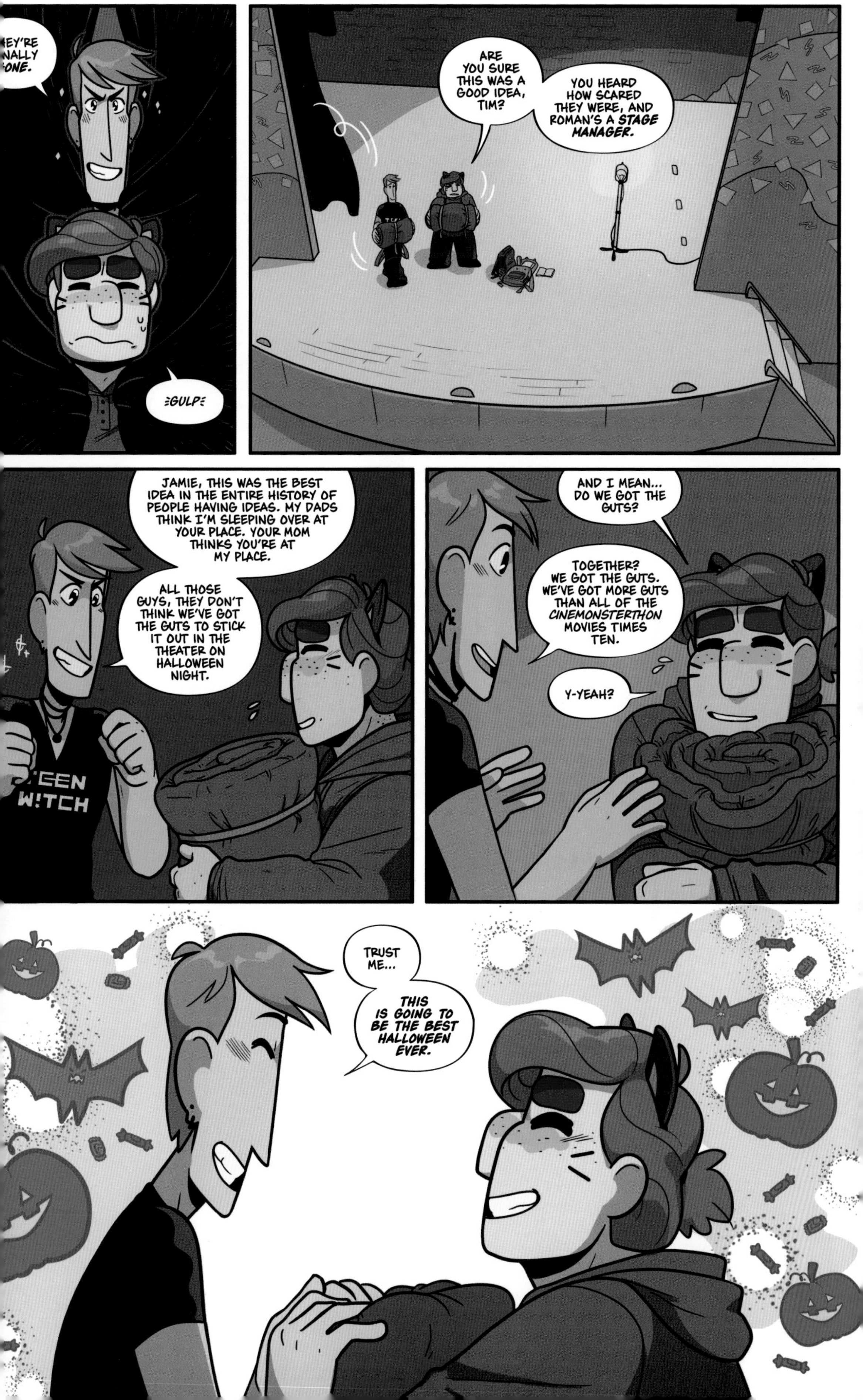

EY'RE
NALLY
ONE.
≡GULP≡
ARE YOU SURE THIS WAS A GOOD IDEA, TIM?
YOU HEARD HOW SCARED THEY WERE, AND ROMAN'S A STAGE MANAGER.
JAMIE, THIS WAS THE BEST IDEA IN THE ENTIRE HISTORY OF PEOPLE HAVING IDEAS. MY DADS THINK I'M SLEEPING OVER AT YOUR PLACE. YOUR MOM THINKS YOU'RE AT MY PLACE.
ALL THOSE GUYS, THEY DON'T THINK WE'VE GOT THE GUTS TO STICK IT OUT IN THE THEATER ON HALLOWEEN NIGHT.
TEEN W!TCH
AND I MEAN... DO WE GOT THE GUTS?
TOGETHER? WE GOT THE GUTS. WE'VE GOT MORE GUTS THAN ALL OF THE CINEMONSTERTHON MOVIES TIMES TEN.
Y-YEAH?
TRUST ME...
THIS IS GOING TO BE THE BEST HALLOWEEN EVER.

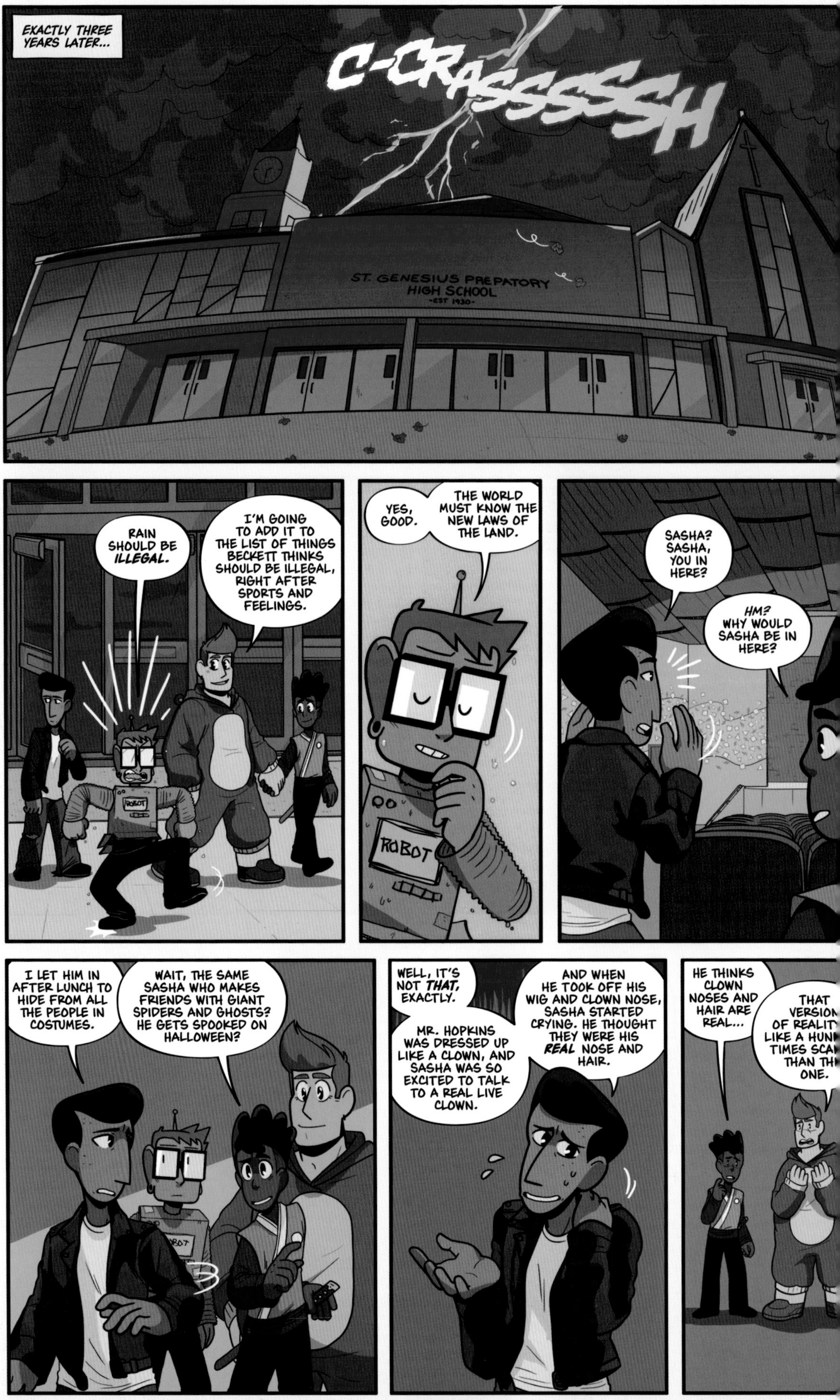
EXACTLY THREE YEARS LATER...
C-CRASSSSSH
ST. GENESIUS PREPATORY HIGH SCHOOL
~EST 1930~
RAIN SHOULD BE *ILLEGAL.*
I'M GOING TO ADD IT TO THE LIST OF THINGS BECKETT THINKS SHOULD BE ILLEGAL, RIGHT AFTER SPORTS AND FEELINGS.
YES, GOOD.
THE WORLD MUST KNOW THE NEW LAWS OF THE LAND.
ROBOT
SASHA? SASHA, YOU IN HERE?
HM? WHY WOULD SASHA BE IN HERE?
I LET HIM IN AFTER LUNCH TO HIDE FROM ALL THE PEOPLE IN COSTUMES.
WAIT, THE SAME SASHA WHO MAKES FRIENDS WITH GIANT SPIDERS AND GHOSTS? HE GETS SPOOKED ON HALLOWEEN?
WELL, IT'S NOT *THAT,* EXACTLY.
MR. HOPKINS WAS DRESSED UP LIKE A CLOWN, AND SASHA WAS SO EXCITED TO TALK TO A REAL LIVE CLOWN.
AND WHEN HE TOOK OFF HIS WIG AND CLOWN NOSE, SASHA STARTED CRYING. HE THOUGHT THEY WERE HIS *REAL* NOSE AND HAIR.
HE THINKS CLOWN NOSES AND HAIR ARE REAL...

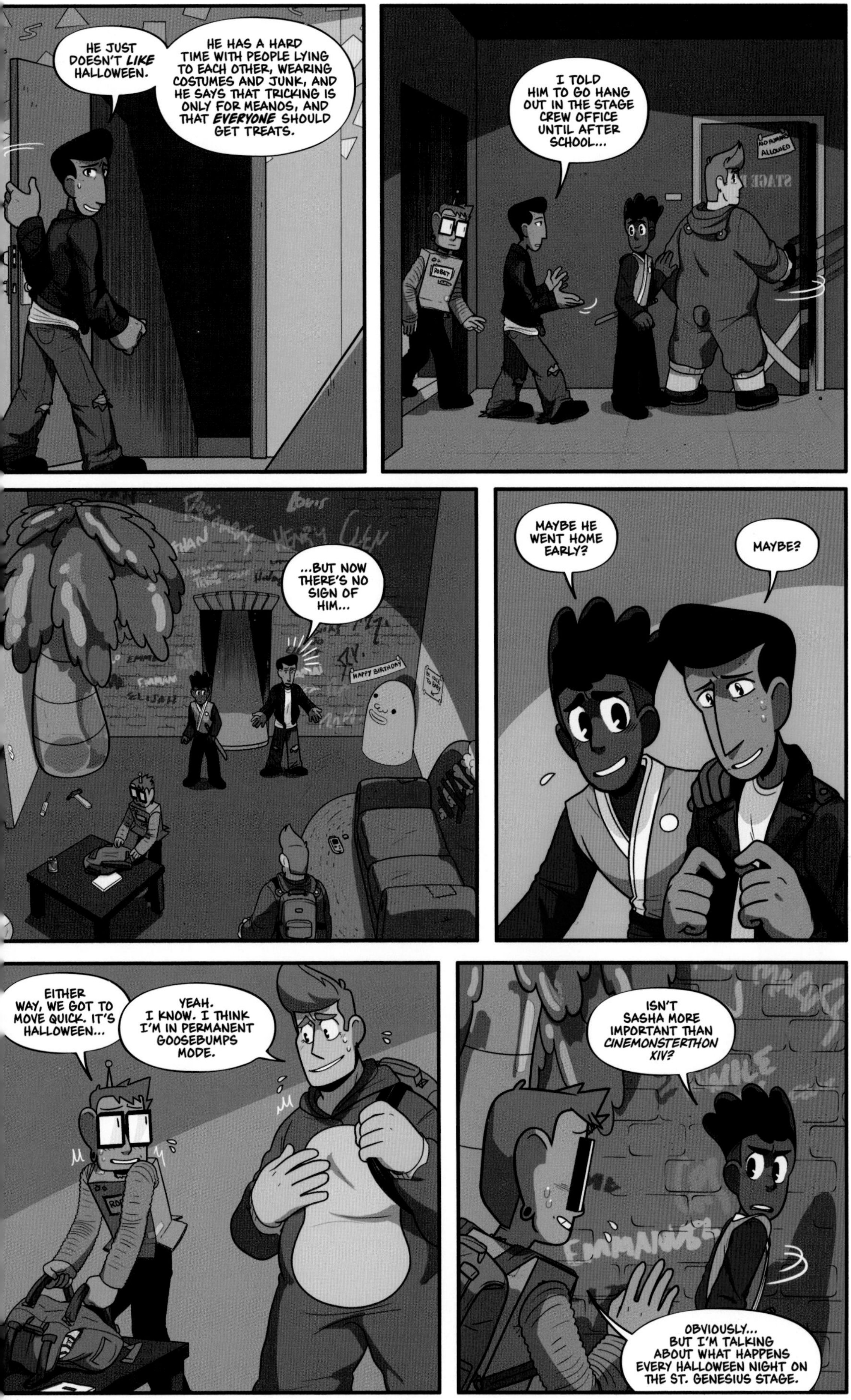
HE JUST DOESN'T *LIKE* HALLOWEEN.
HE HAS A HARD TIME WITH PEOPLE LYING TO EACH OTHER, WEARING COSTUMES AND JUNK, AND HE SAYS THAT TRICKING IS ONLY FOR MEANOS, AND THAT *EVERYONE* SHOULD GET TREATS.
I TOLD HIM TO GO HANG OUT IN THE STAGE CREW OFFICE UNTIL AFTER SCHOOL...
ROBOT
...BUT NOW THERE'S NO SIGN OF HIM...
HAPPY BIRTHDAY
MAYBE HE WENT HOME EARLY?
MAYBE?
EITHER WAY, WE GOT TO MOVE QUICK. IT'S HALLOWEEN...
YEAH. I KNOW. I THINK I'M IN PERMANENT GOOSEBUMPS MODE.
ISN'T SASHA MORE IMPORTANT THAN *CINEMONSTERTHON XIV?*
OBVIOUSLY... BUT I'M TALKING ABOUT WHAT HAPPENS EVERY HALLOWEEN NIGHT ON THE ST. GENESIUS STAGE.

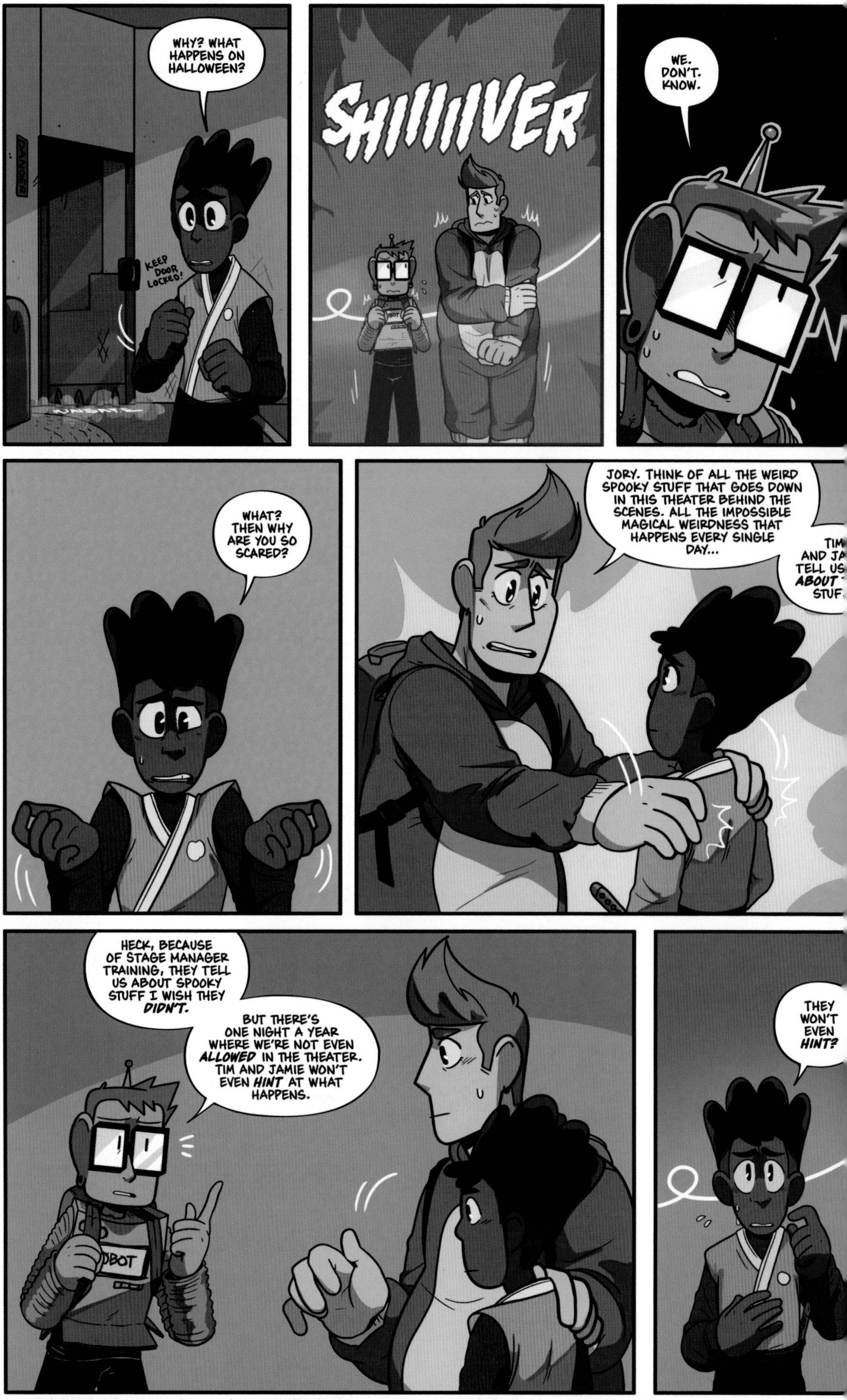

WHY? WHAT HAPPENS ON HALLOWEEN?
DANGER
KEEP DOOR LOCKED!
SHIIIIIVER
WE. DON'T. KNOW.
WHAT? THEN WHY ARE YOU SO SCARED?
JORY. THINK OF ALL THE WEIRD SPOOKY STUFF THAT GOES DOWN IN THIS THEATER BEHIND THE SCENES. ALL THE IMPOSSIBLE MAGICAL WEIRDNESS THAT HAPPENS EVERY SINGLE DAY...
TIM
AND JA
TELL US
ABOUT
STUF
HECK, BECAUSE OF STAGE MANAGER TRAINING, THEY TELL US ABOUT SPOOKY STUFF I WISH THEY DIDN'T.
BUT THERE'S ONE NIGHT A YEAR WHERE WE'RE NOT EVEN ALLOWED IN THE THEATER. TIM AND JAMIE WON'T EVEN HINT AT WHAT HAPPENS.
THEY WON'T EVEN HINT?

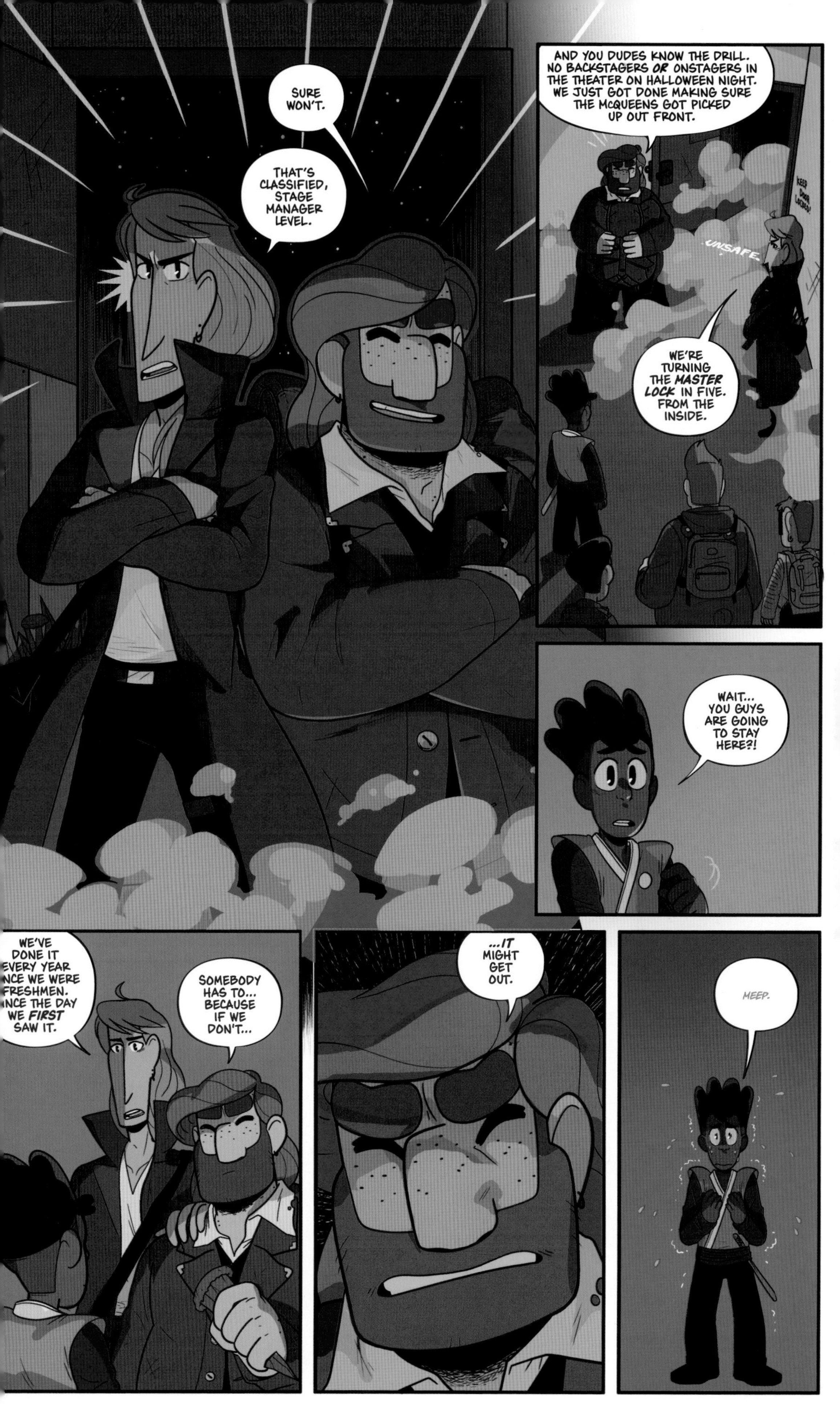
SURE WON'T.
THAT'S CLASSIFIED, STAGE MANAGER LEVEL.
AND YOU DUDES KNOW THE DRILL. NO BACKSTAGERS OR ONSTAGERS IN THE THEATER ON HALLOWEEN NIGHT. WE JUST GOT DONE MAKING SURE THE McQUEENS GOT PICKED UP OUT FRONT.
KEEP DOOR LOCKED!
UNSAFE.
WE'RE TURNING THE MASTER LOCK IN FIVE. FROM THE INSIDE.
WAIT... YOU GUYS ARE GOING TO STAY HERE?!
WE'VE DONE IT EVERY YEAR NCE WE WERE FRESHMEN. NCE THE DAY WE FIRST SAW IT.
SOMEBODY HAS TO... BECAUSE IF WE DON'T...
...IT MIGHT GET OUT.
MEEP.

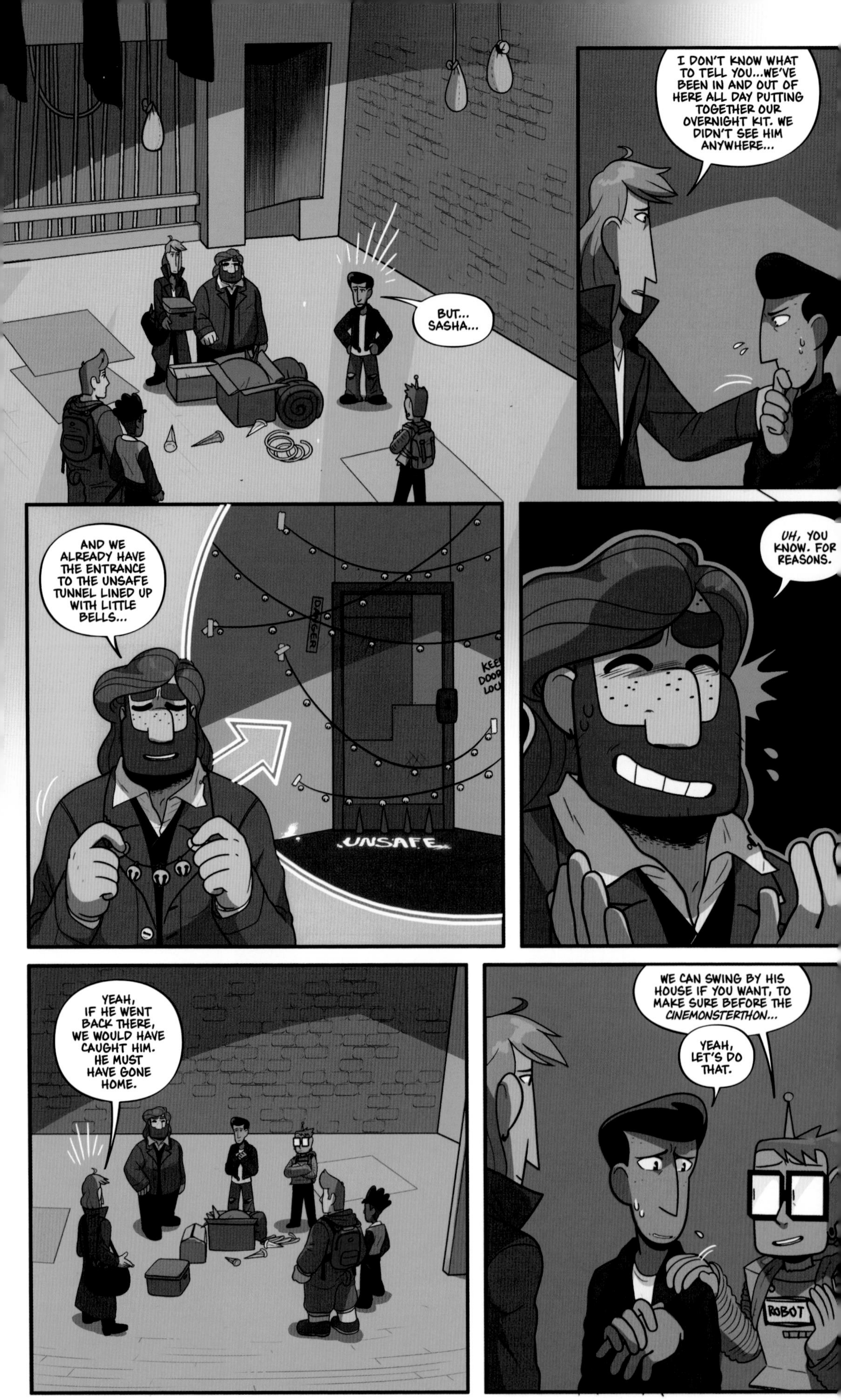
BUT... SASHA...
I DON'T KNOW WHAT TO TELL YOU...WE'VE BEEN IN AND OUT OF HERE ALL DAY PUTTING TOGETHER OUR OVERNIGHT KIT. WE DIDN'T SEE HIM ANYWHERE...
AND WE ALREADY HAVE THE ENTRANCE TO THE UNSAFE TUNNEL LINED UP WITH LITTLE BELLS...
DANGER
UNSAFE
UH, YOU KNOW. FOR REASONS.
YEAH, IF HE WENT BACK THERE, WE WOULD HAVE CAUGHT HIM. HE MUST HAVE GONE HOME.
WE CAN SWING BY HIS HOUSE IF YOU WANT, TO MAKE SURE BEFORE THE *CINEMONSTERTHON*...
YEAH, LET'S DO THAT.
ROBOT

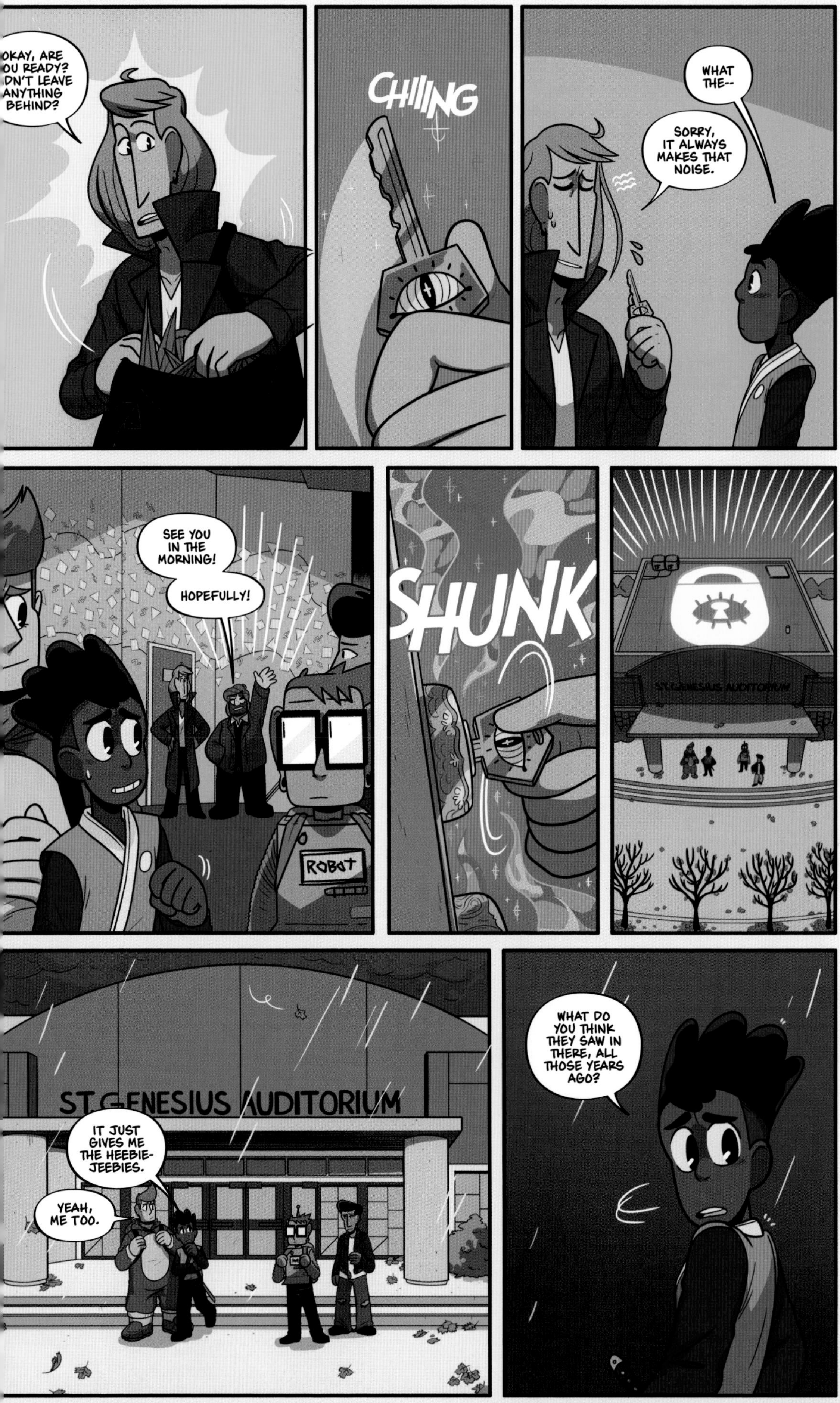
OKAY, ARE
OU READY?
DN'T LEAVE
ANYTHING
BEHIND?
CHIIING
WHAT THE--
SORRY, IT ALWAYS MAKES THAT NOISE.
SEE YOU IN THE MORNING!
HOPEFULLY!
ROBOT
SHUNK
ST. GENESIUS AUDITORIUM
ST. GENESIUS AUDITORIUM
IT JUST GIVES ME THE HEEBIE-JEEBIES.
YEAH, ME TOO.
WHAT DO YOU THINK THEY SAW IN THERE, ALL THOSE YEARS AGO?

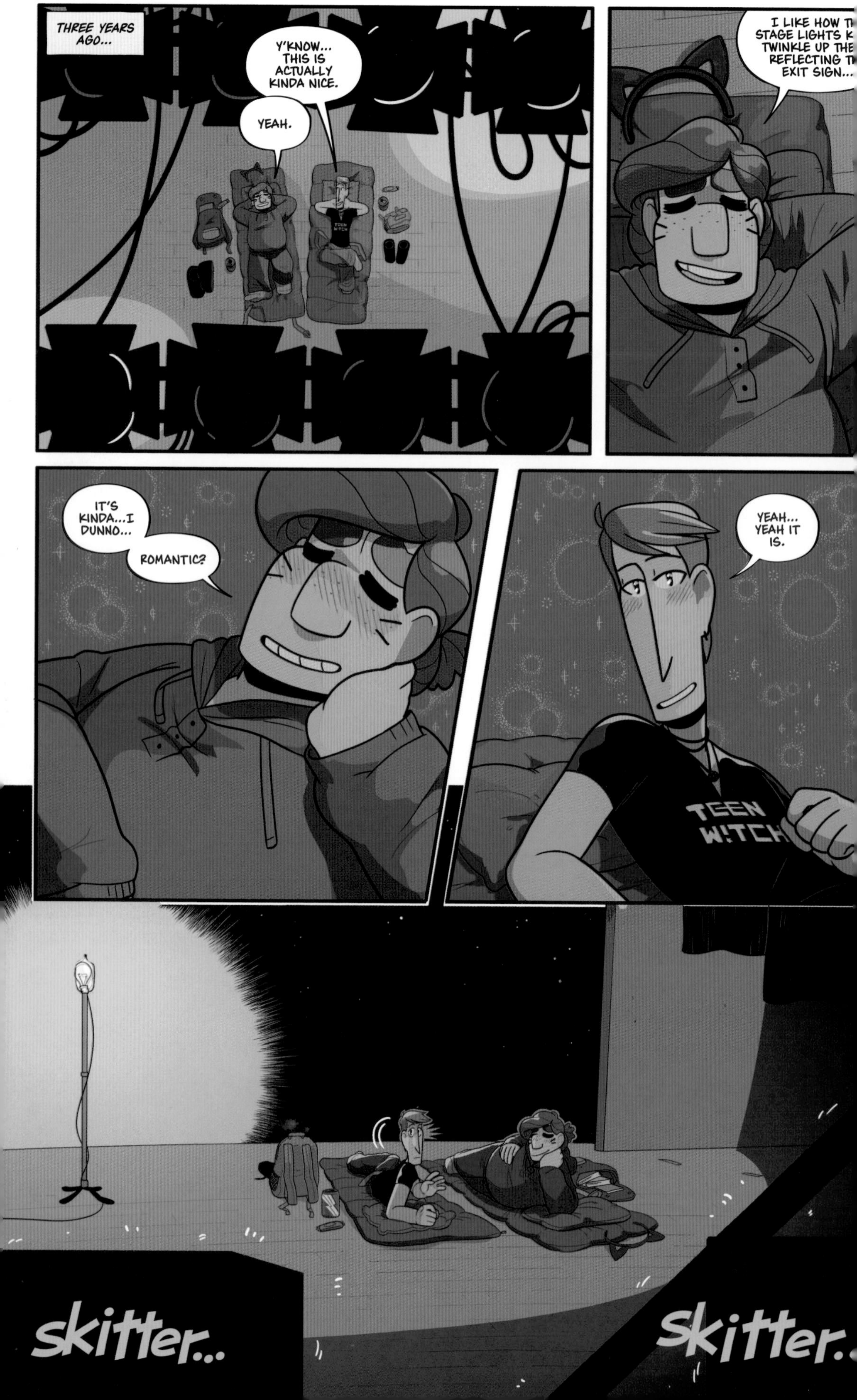

THREE YEARS AGO...
Y'KNOW... THIS IS ACTUALLY KINDA NICE.
YEAH.
I LIKE HOW T STAGE LIGHTS K TWINKLE UP THE REFLECTING T EXIT SIGN...
IT'S KINDA...I DUNNO...
ROMANTIC?
YEAH... YEAH IT IS.
TEEN W!TCH
skitter..
skitter..

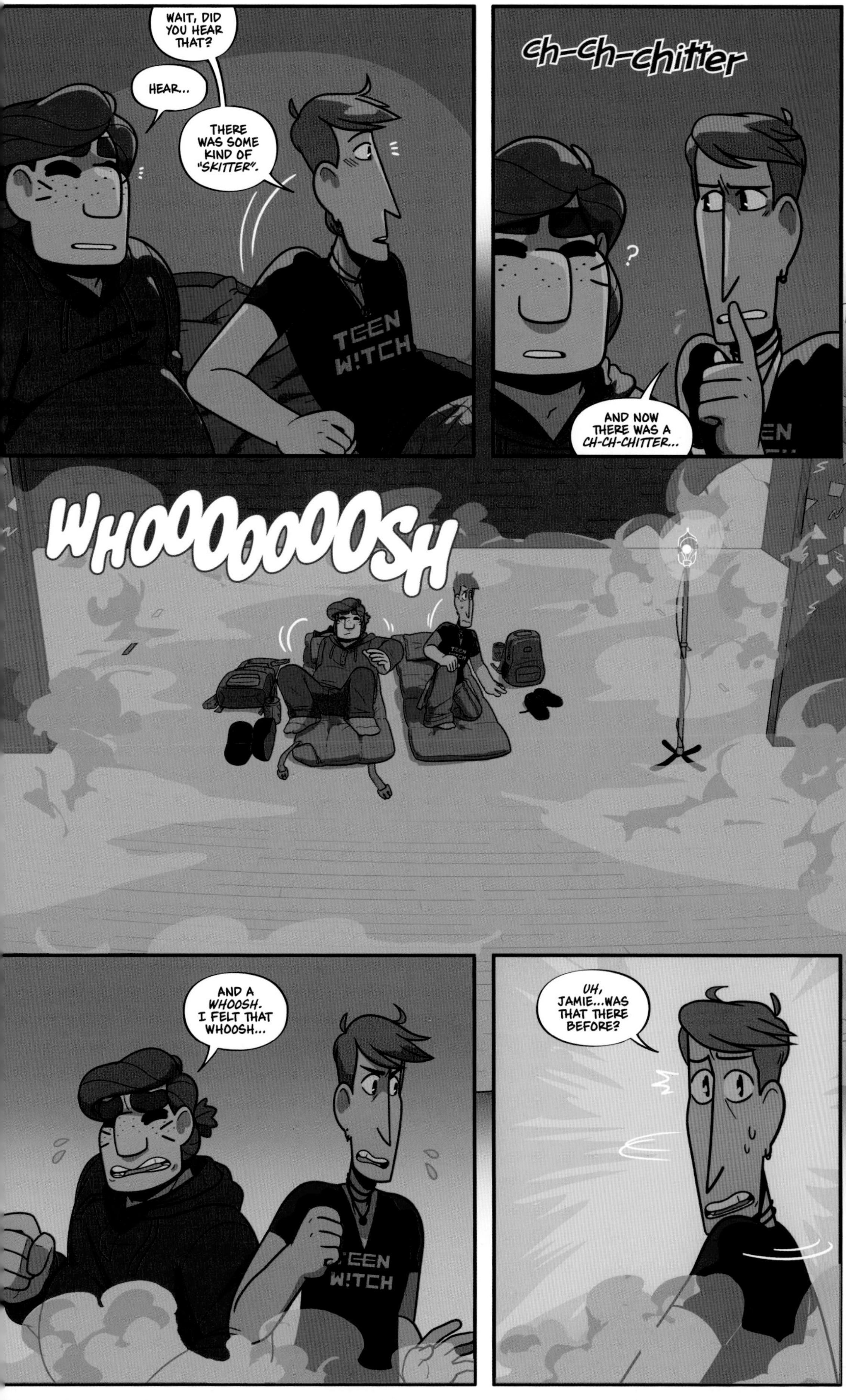
WAIT, DID YOU HEAR THAT?
HEAR...
THERE WAS SOME KIND OF "SKITTER".
ch-ch-chitter
AND NOW THERE WAS A CH-CH-CHITTER...
WHOOOOOOOOSH
AND A WHOOSH. I FELT THAT WHOOSH...
UH, JAMIE...WAS THAT THERE BEFORE?

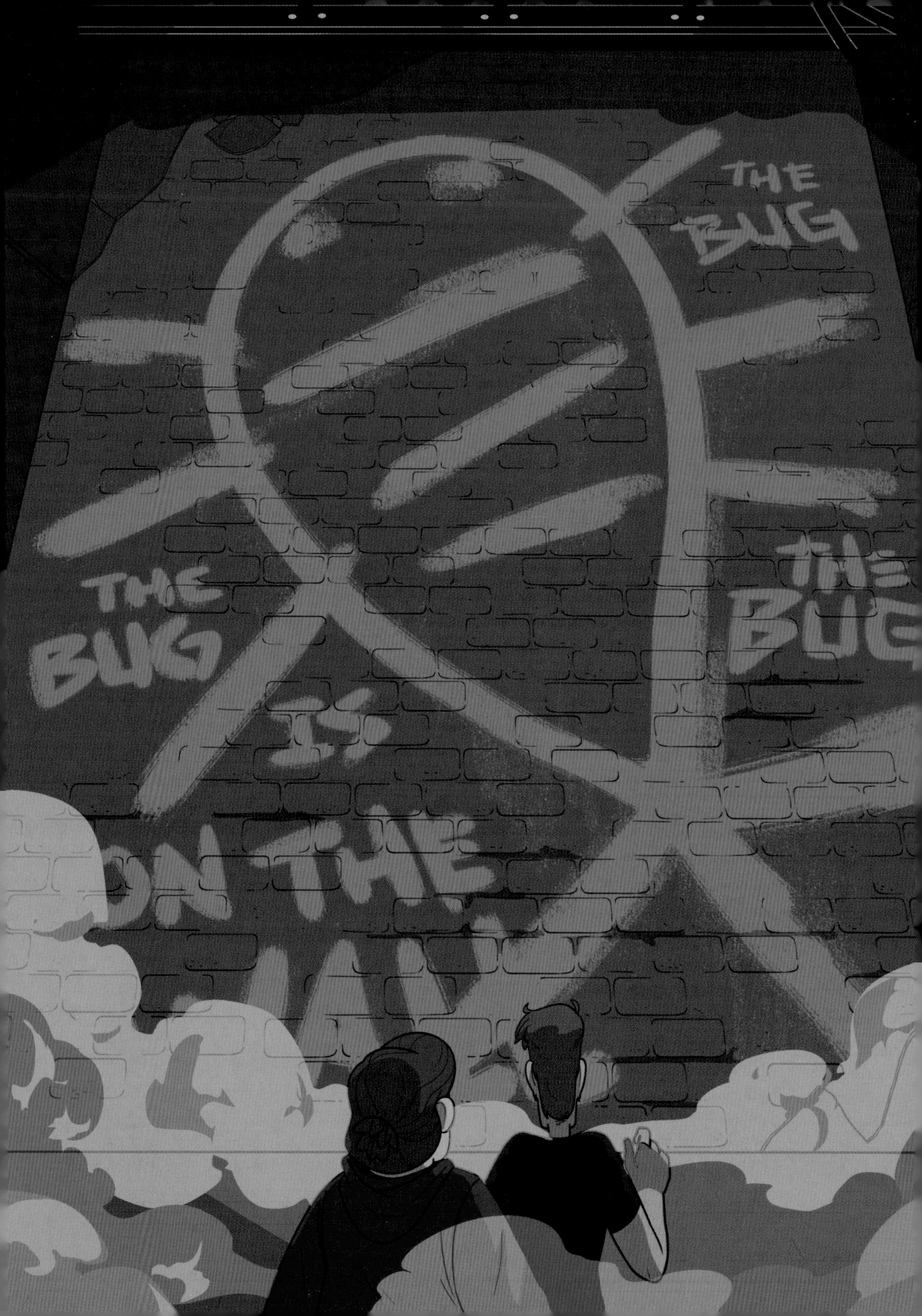
THE BUG
THE BUG
IS
ON THE

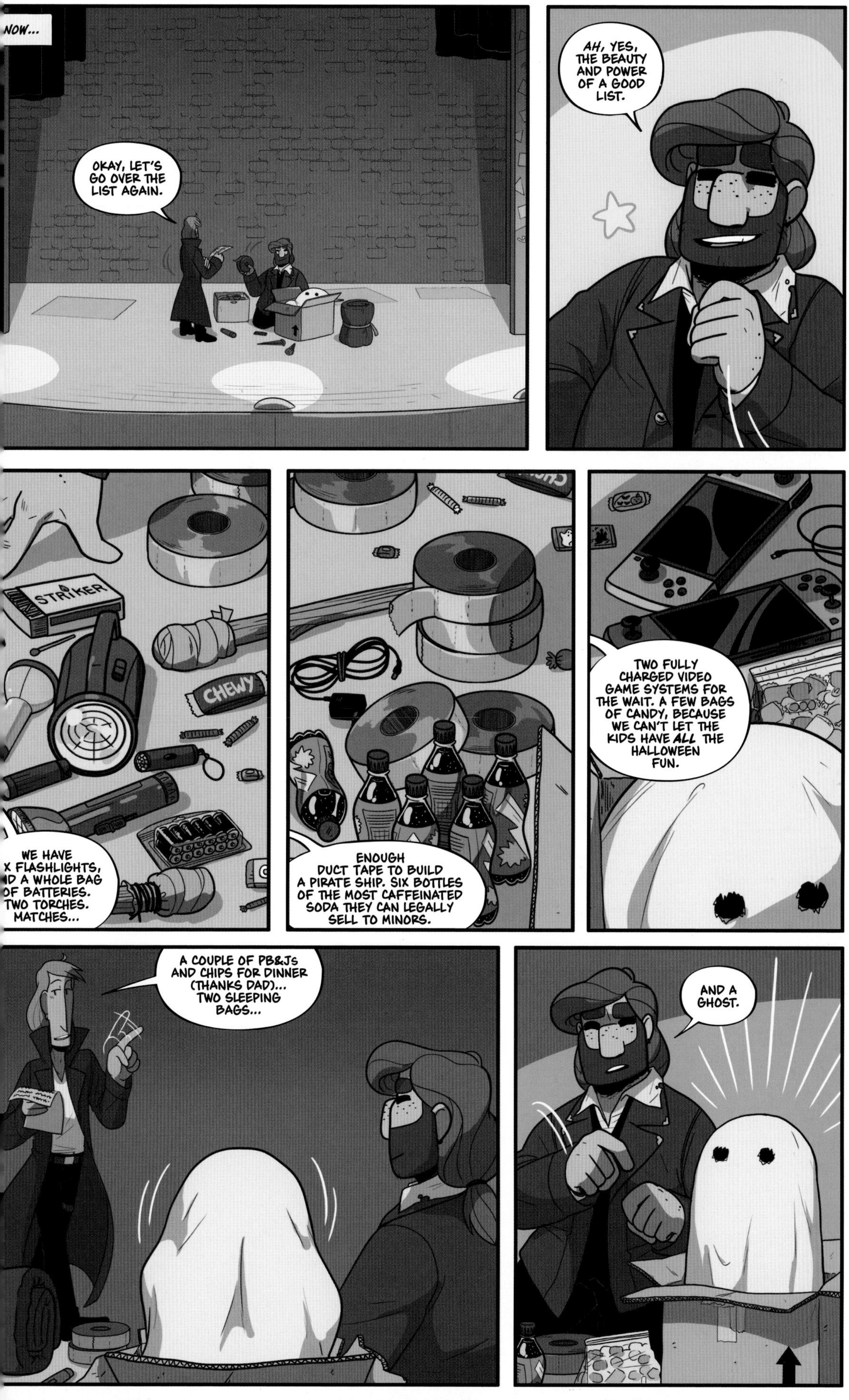
NOW...
OKAY, LET'S GO OVER THE LIST AGAIN.
AH, YES, THE BEAUTY AND POWER OF A GOOD LIST.
STRIKER
CHEWY
WE HAVE X FLASHLIGHTS, ID A WHOLE BAG OF BATTERIES. TWO TORCHES. MATCHES...
ENOUGH DUCT TAPE TO BUILD A PIRATE SHIP. SIX BOTTLES OF THE MOST CAFFEINATED SODA THEY CAN LEGALLY SELL TO MINORS.
TWO FULLY CHARGED VIDEO GAME SYSTEMS FOR THE WAIT. A FEW BAGS OF CANDY, BECAUSE WE CAN'T LET THE KIDS HAVE ALL THE HALLOWEEN FUN.
A COUPLE OF PB&JS AND CHIPS FOR DINNER (THANKS DAD)... TWO SLEEPING BAGS...
AND A GHOST.

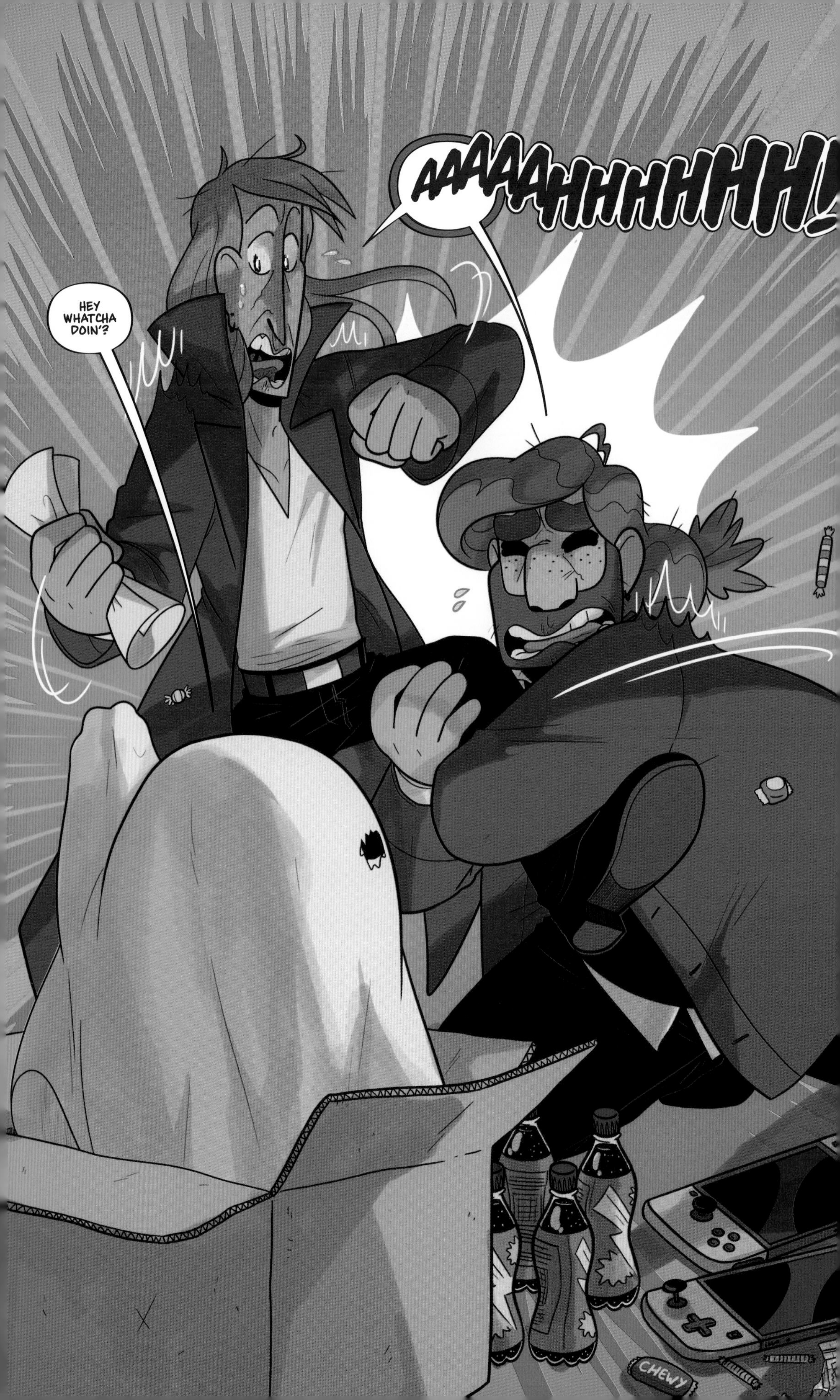
HEY WHATCHA DOIN'?
AAAAAHHHHHHH!
CHEWY

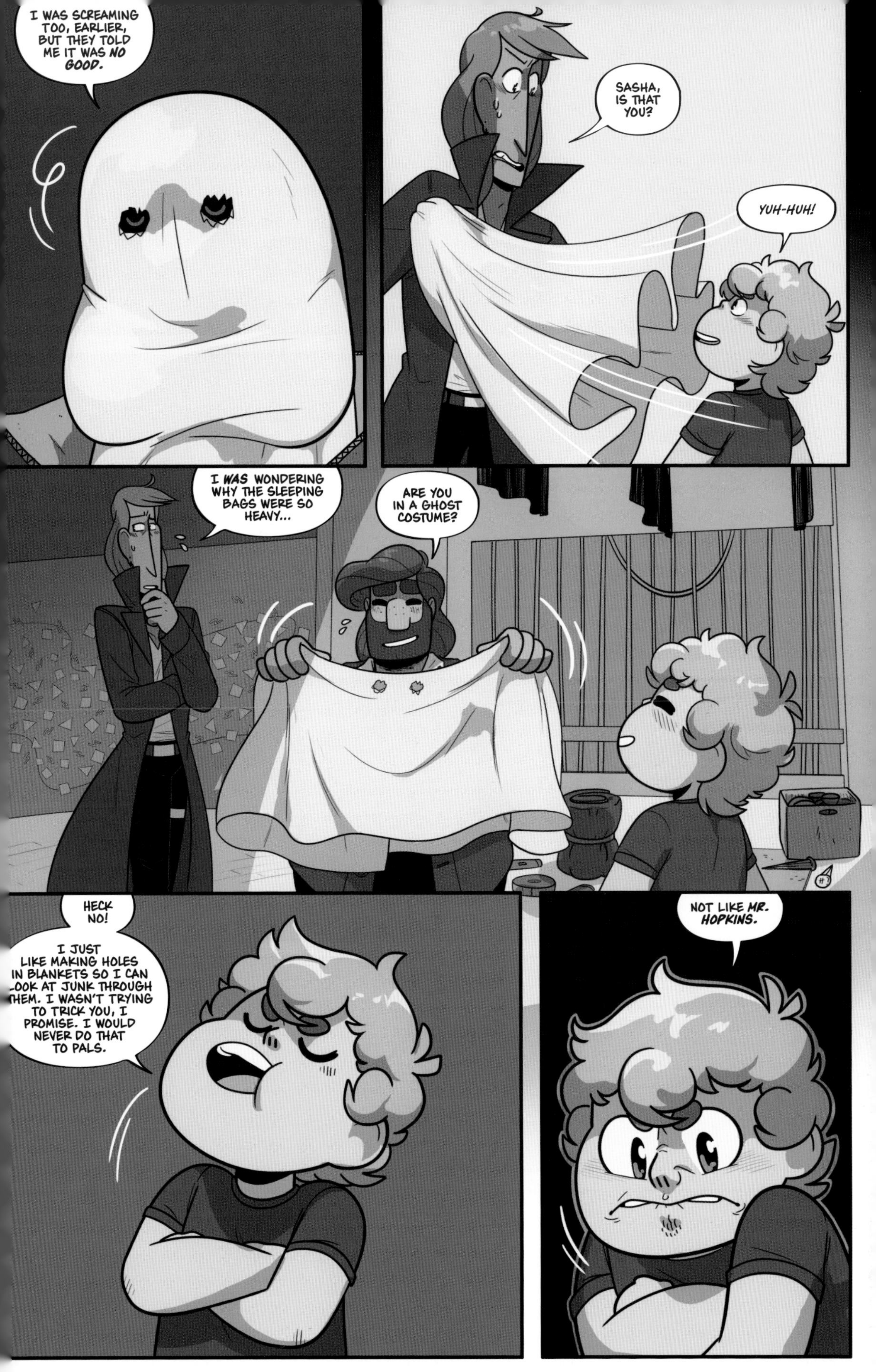
I WAS SCREAMING TOO, EARLIER, BUT THEY TOLD ME IT WAS *NO GOOD*.
SASHA, IS THAT YOU?
YUH-HUH!
I *WAS* WONDERING WHY THE SLEEPING BAGS WERE SO HEAVY...
ARE YOU IN A GHOST COSTUME?
HECK NO!
I JUST LIKE MAKING HOLES IN BLANKETS SO I CAN LOOK AT JUNK THROUGH THEM. I WASN'T TRYING TO TRICK YOU, I PROMISE. I WOULD NEVER DO THAT TO PALS.
NOT LIKE *MR. HOPKINS*.

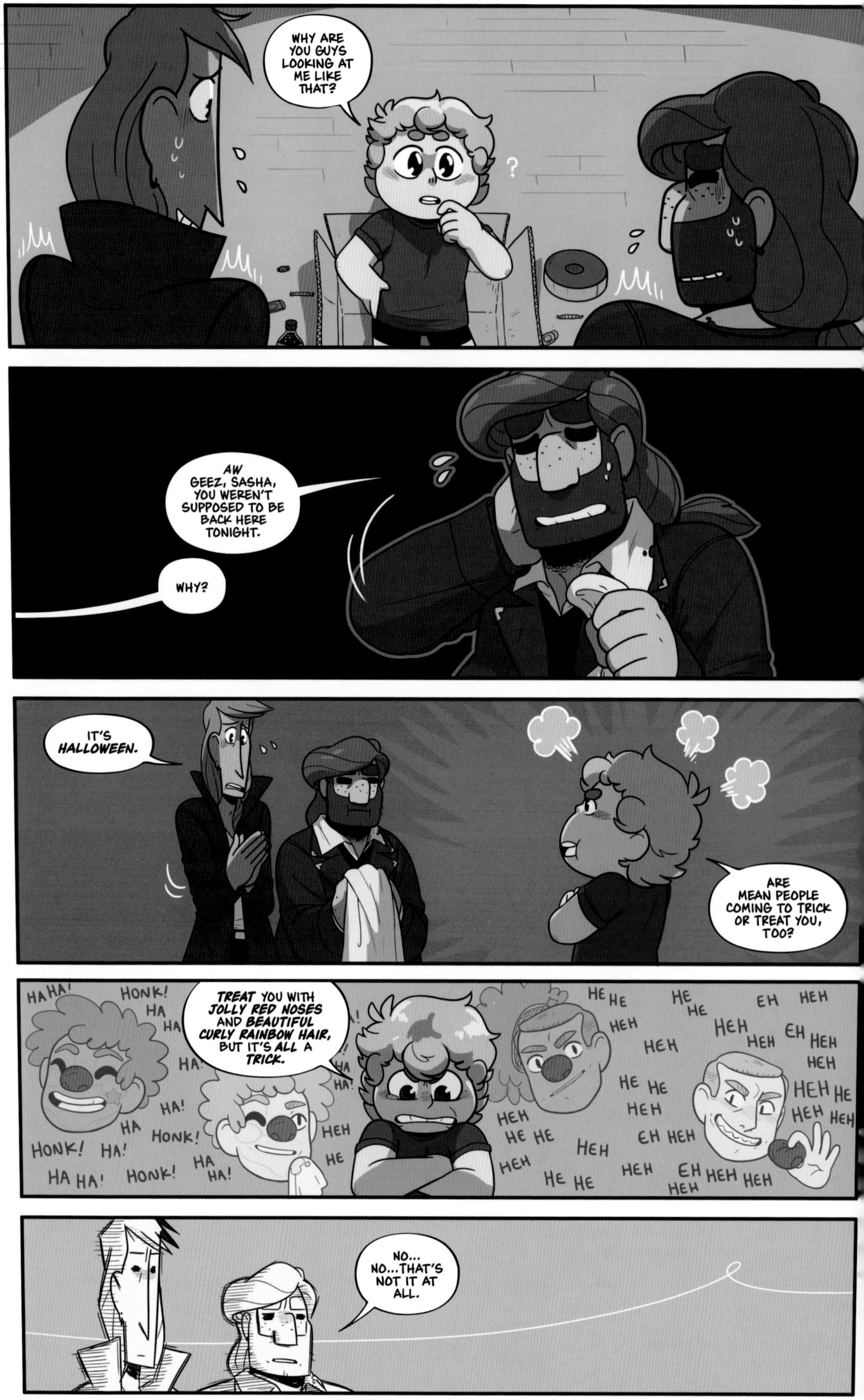

WHY ARE YOU GUYS LOOKING AT ME LIKE THAT?
?
AW GEEZ, SASHA, YOU WEREN'T SUPPOSED TO BE BACK HERE TONIGHT.
WHY?
IT'S HALLOWEEN.
ARE MEAN PEOPLE COMING TO TRICK OR TREAT YOU, TOO?
HA HA! HONK! HA HA HA!
HONK! HA! HA HA! HONK! HA HA!
TREAT YOU WITH JOLLY RED NOSES AND BEAUTIFUL CURLY RAINBOW HAIR, BUT IT'S ALL A TRICK.
HE HE HE HE EH HEH HEH HEH HEH EH HEH
NO... NO...THAT'S NOT IT AT ALL.

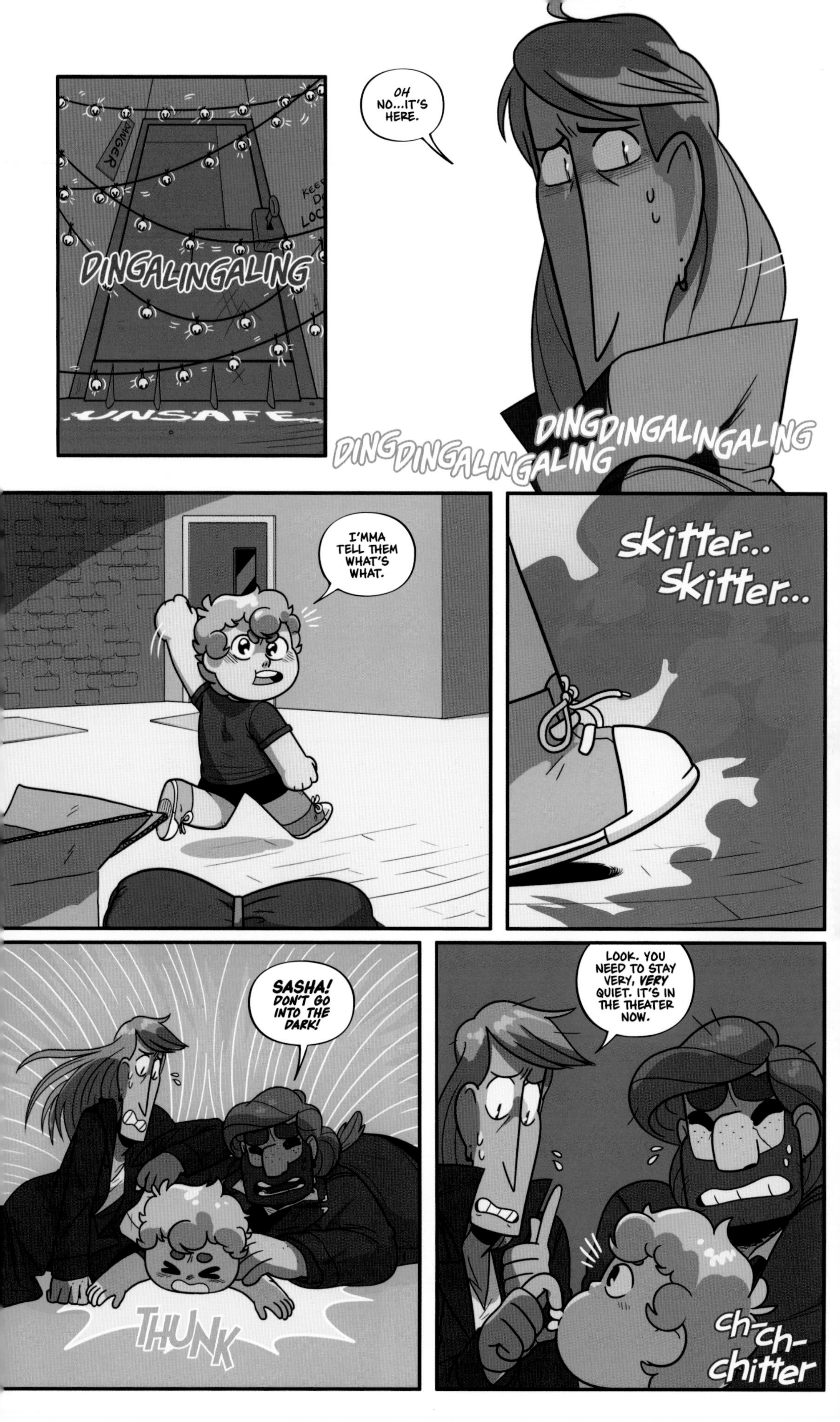
DANGER
DINGALINGALING
UNSAFE
OH NO...IT'S HERE.
DINGDINGALINGALING
DINGDINGALINGALING
I'MMA TELL THEM WHAT'S WHAT.
skitter.. skitter...
SASHA! DON'T GO INTO THE DARK!
THUNK
LOOK. YOU NEED TO STAY VERY, VERY QUIET. IT'S IN THE THEATER NOW.
ch-ch-chitter

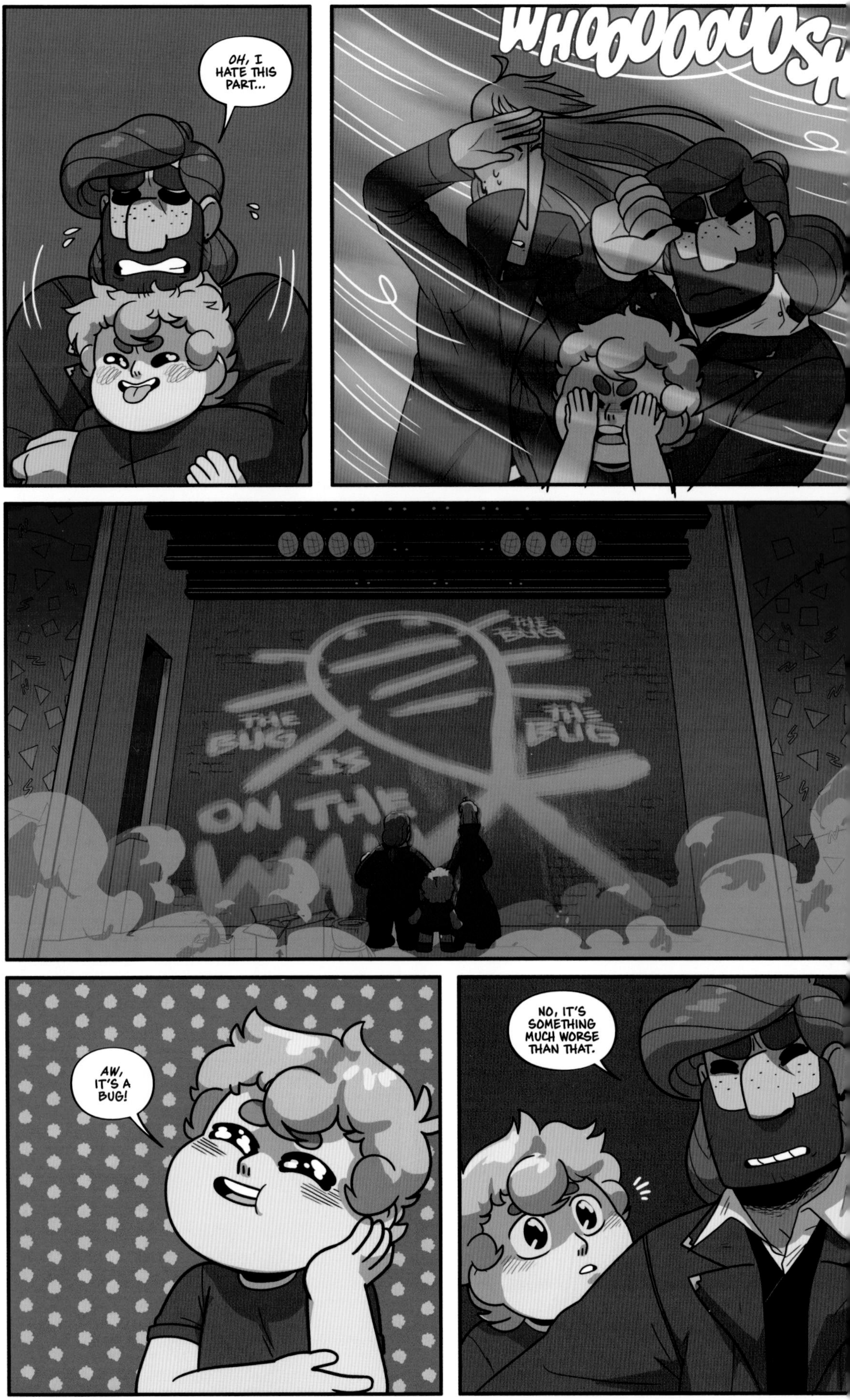
OH, I HATE THIS PART...
WHOOOOOOOSH
THE BUG
THE BUG IS ON THE
THE BUG
AW, IT'S A BUG!
NO, IT'S SOMETHING MUCH WORSE THAN THAT.

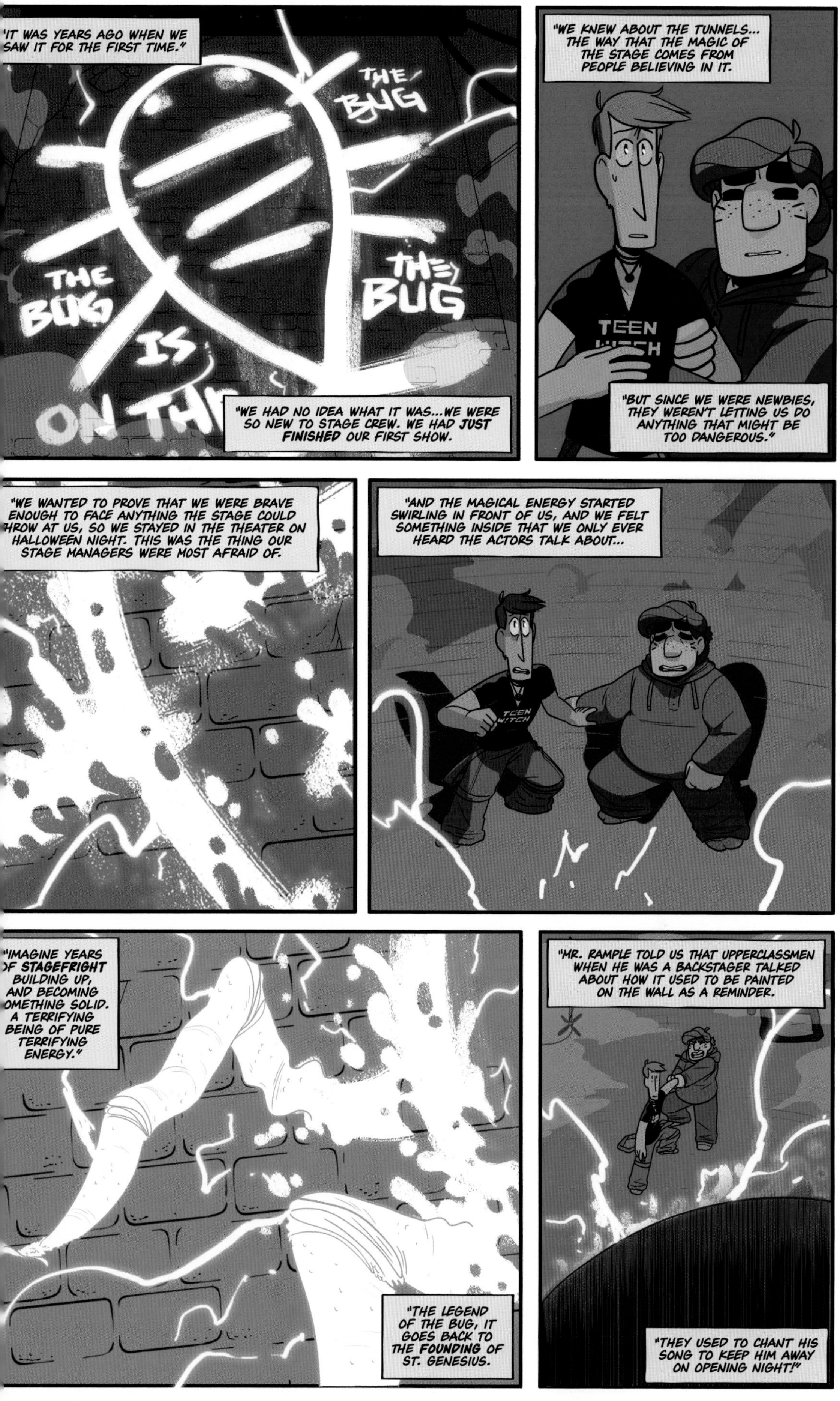
"IT WAS YEARS AGO WHEN WE SAW IT FOR THE FIRST TIME."
THE BUG
THE BUG
THE BUG IS ON THE
"WE HAD NO IDEA WHAT IT WAS...WE WERE SO NEW TO STAGE CREW. WE HAD JUST FINISHED OUR FIRST SHOW.
"WE KNEW ABOUT THE TUNNELS... THE WAY THAT THE MAGIC OF THE STAGE COMES FROM PEOPLE BELIEVING IN IT.
"BUT SINCE WE WERE NEWBIES, THEY WEREN'T LETTING US DO ANYTHING THAT MIGHT BE TOO DANGEROUS."
"WE WANTED TO PROVE THAT WE WERE BRAVE ENOUGH TO FACE ANYTHING THE STAGE COULD THROW AT US, SO WE STAYED IN THE THEATER ON HALLOWEEN NIGHT. THIS WAS THE THING OUR STAGE MANAGERS WERE MOST AFRAID OF.
"AND THE MAGICAL ENERGY STARTED SWIRLING IN FRONT OF US, AND WE FELT SOMETHING INSIDE THAT WE ONLY EVER HEARD THE ACTORS TALK ABOUT...
"IMAGINE YEARS OF STAGEFRIGHT BUILDING UP, AND BECOMING SOMETHING SOLID. A TERRIFYING BEING OF PURE TERRIFYING ENERGY."
"THE LEGEND OF THE BUG, IT GOES BACK TO THE FOUNDING OF ST. GENESIUS.
"MR. RAMPLE TOLD US THAT UPPERCLASSMEN WHEN HE WAS A BACKSTAGER TALKED ABOUT HOW IT USED TO BE PAINTED ON THE WALL AS A REMINDER.
"THEY USED TO CHANT HIS SONG TO KEEP HIM AWAY ON OPENING NIGHT!"

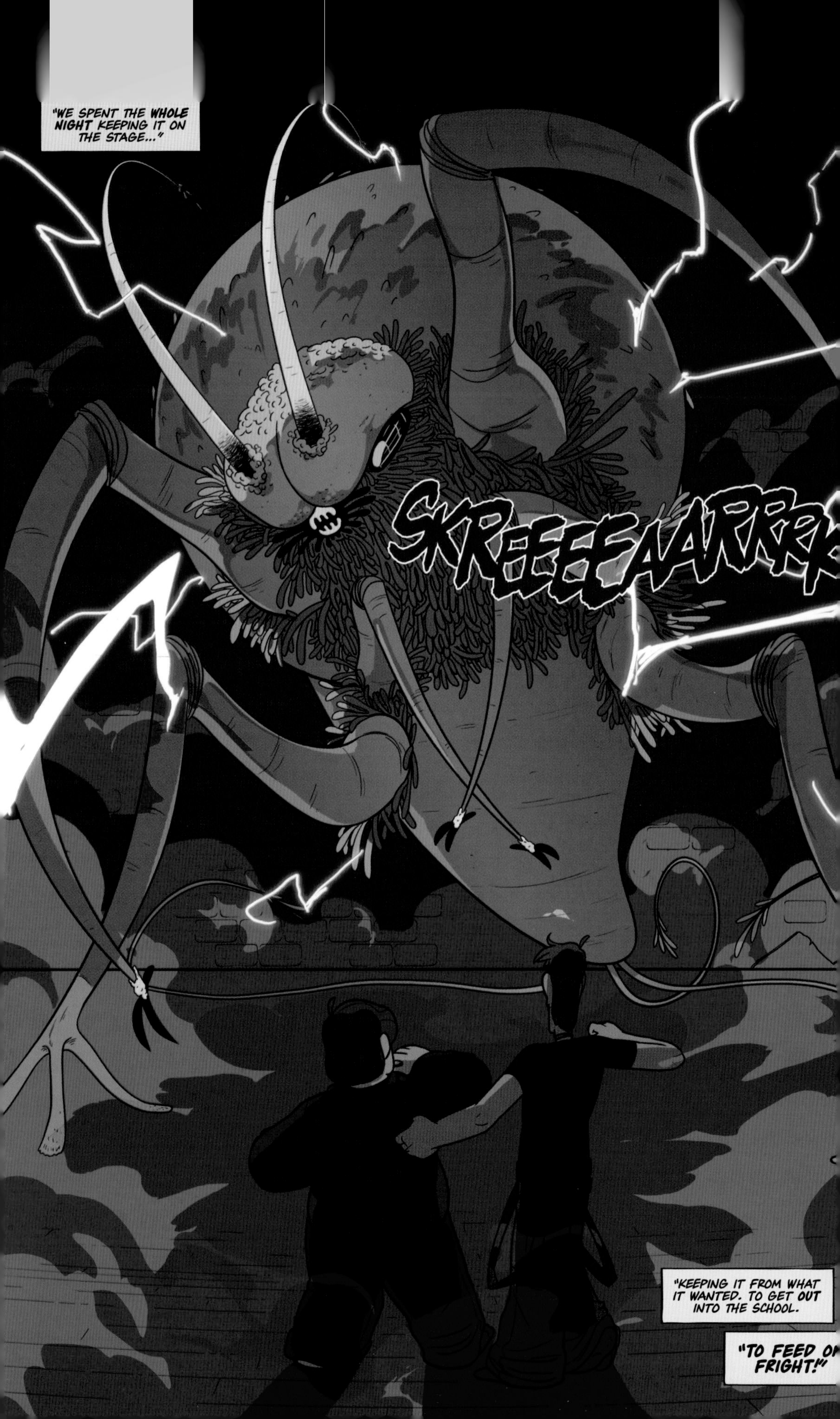
"WE SPENT THE WHOLE NIGHT KEEPING IT ON THE STAGE..."
SKREEEEAARRRK
"KEEPING IT FROM WHAT IT WANTED. TO GET OUT INTO THE SCHOOL.
"TO FEED O
FRIGHT!"

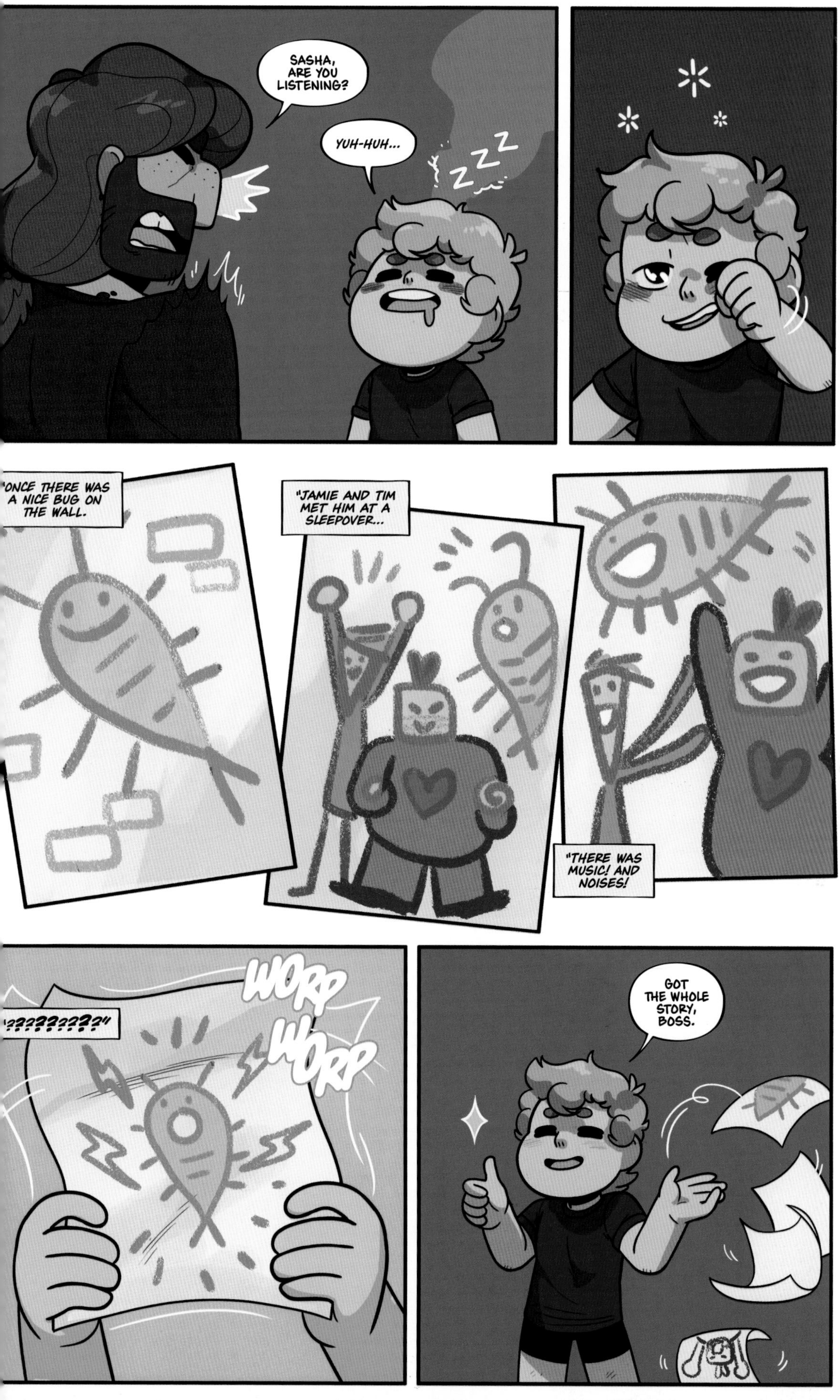
SASHA, ARE YOU LISTENING?
YUH-HUH...
ZZZ
"ONCE THERE WAS A NICE BUG ON THE WALL.
"JAMIE AND TIM MET HIM AT A SLEEPOVER...
"THERE WAS MUSIC! AND NOISES!
WORP WORP
"?????????"
GOT THE WHOLE STORY, BOSS.

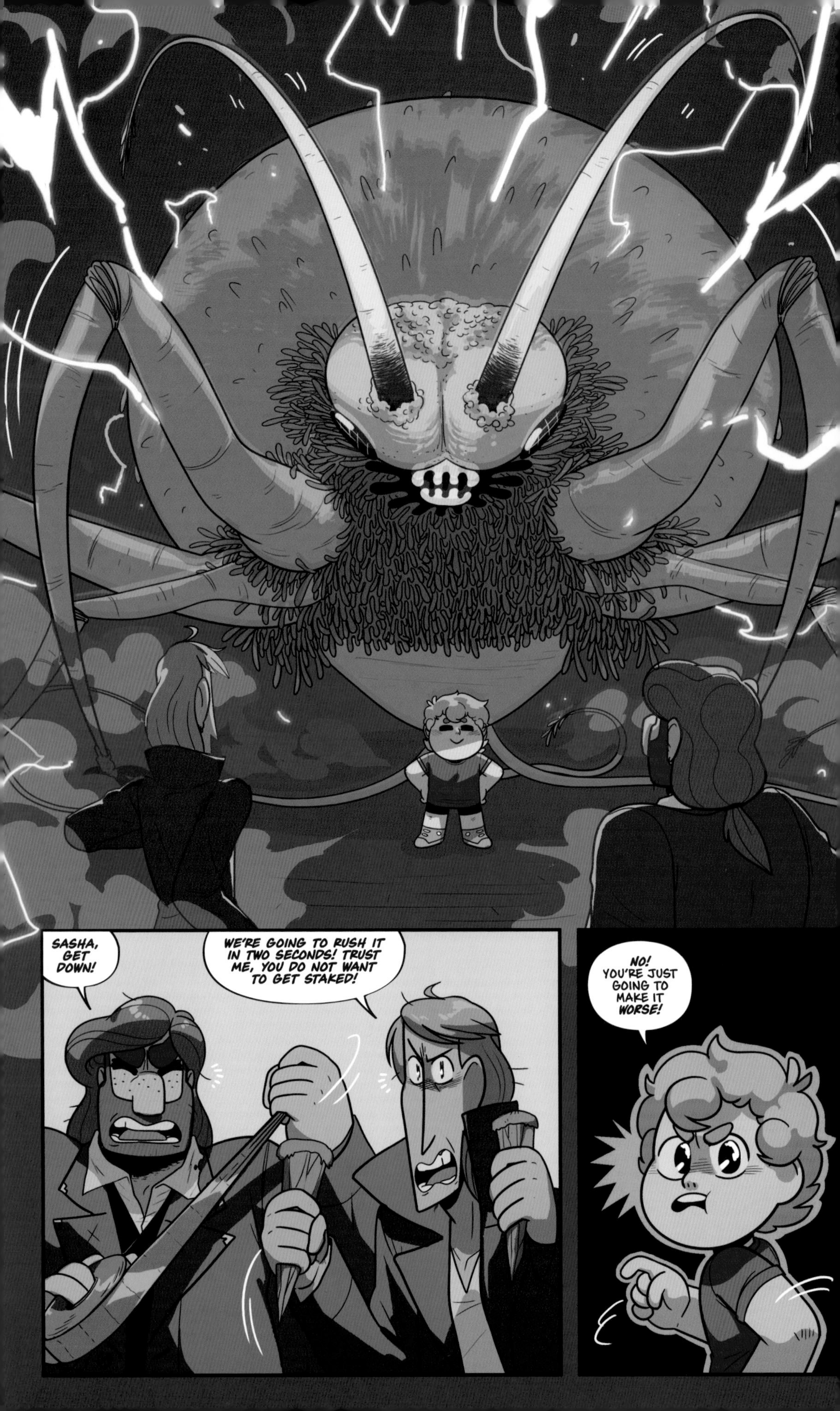
SASHA, GET DOWN!
WE'RE GOING TO RUSH IT IN TWO SECONDS! TRUST ME, YOU DO NOT WANT TO GET STAKED!
NO! YOU'RE JUST GOING TO MAKE IT WORSE!

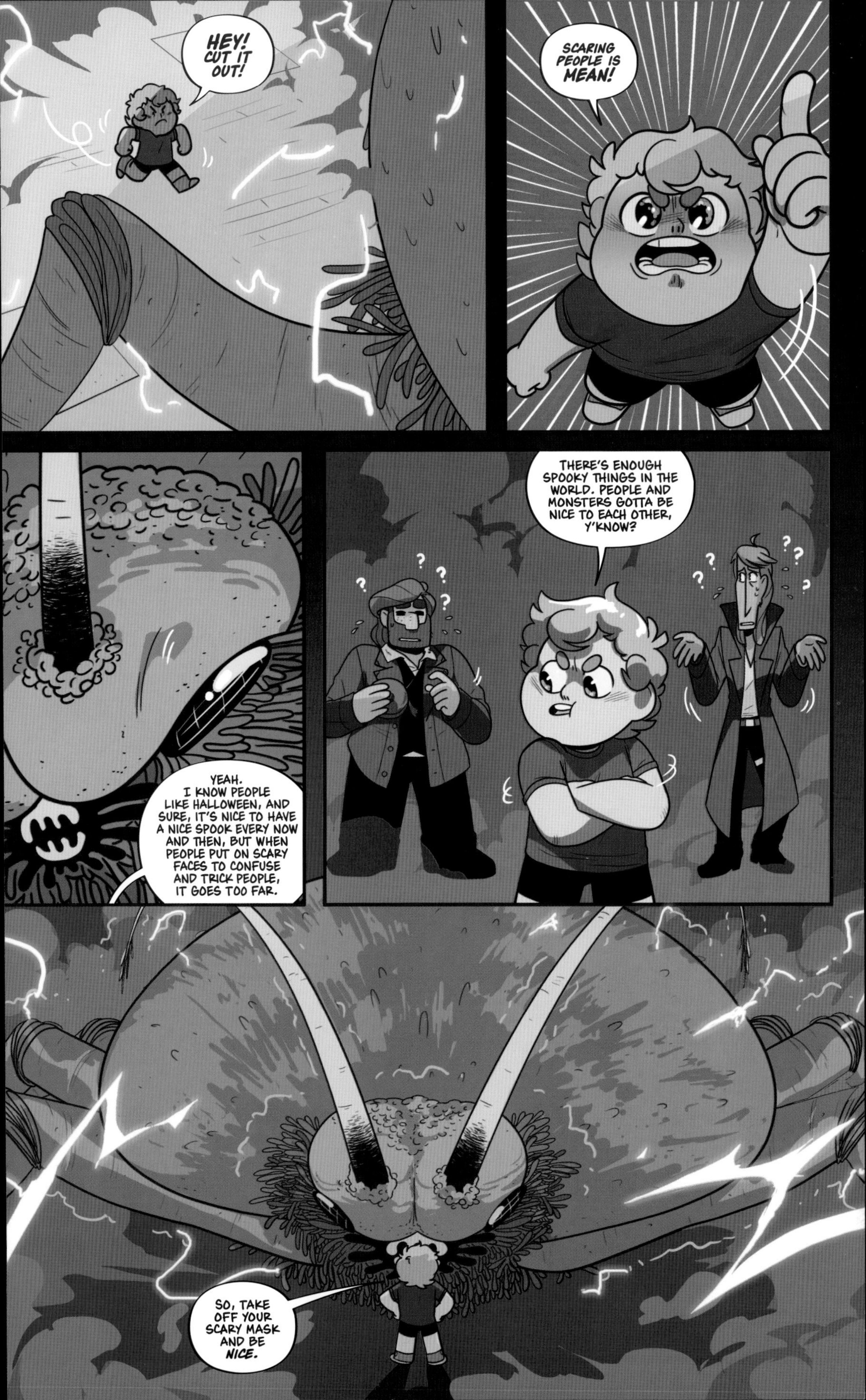
HEY! CUT IT OUT!
SCARING PEOPLE IS MEAN!
THERE'S ENOUGH SPOOKY THINGS IN THE WORLD. PEOPLE AND MONSTERS GOTTA BE NICE TO EACH OTHER, Y'KNOW?
YEAH. I KNOW PEOPLE LIKE HALLOWEEN, AND SURE, IT'S NICE TO HAVE A NICE SPOOK EVERY NOW AND THEN, BUT WHEN PEOPLE PUT ON SCARY FACES TO CONFUSE AND TRICK PEOPLE, IT GOES TOO FAR.
SO, TAKE OFF YOUR SCARY MASK AND BE NICE.

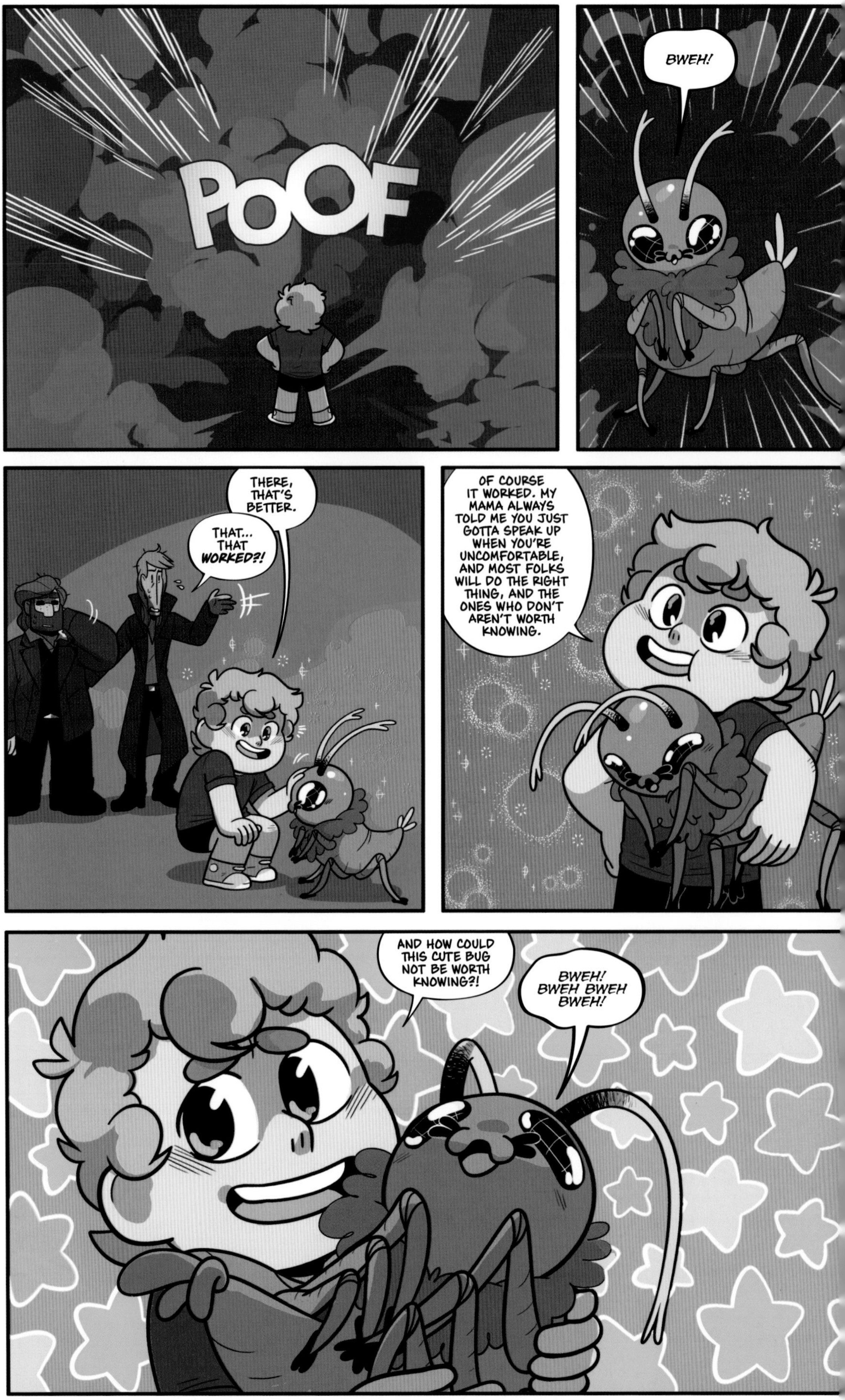
POOF
BWEH!
THERE, THAT'S BETTER.
THAT... THAT WORKED?!
OF COURSE IT WORKED. MY MAMA ALWAYS TOLD ME YOU JUST GOTTA SPEAK UP WHEN YOU'RE UNCOMFORTABLE, AND MOST FOLKS WILL DO THE RIGHT THING, AND THE ONES WHO DON'T AREN'T WORTH KNOWING.
AND HOW COULD THIS CUTE BUG NOT BE WORTH KNOWING?!
BWEH! BWEH BWEH BWEH!

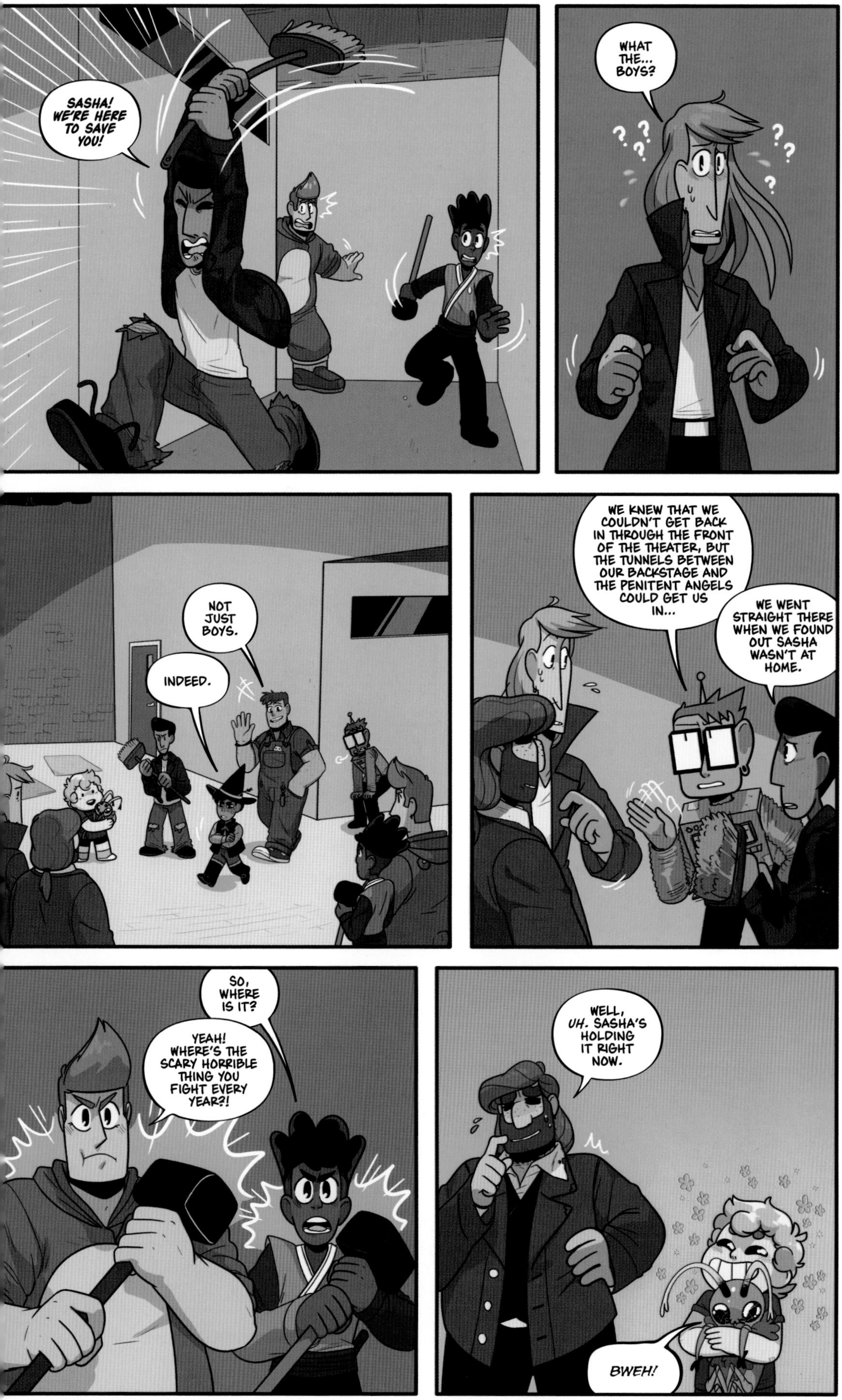
SASHA! WE'RE HERE TO SAVE YOU!
WHAT THE... BOYS?
NOT JUST BOYS.
INDEED.
WE KNEW THAT WE COULDN'T GET BACK IN THROUGH THE FRONT OF THE THEATER, BUT THE TUNNELS BETWEEN OUR BACKSTAGE AND THE PENITENT ANGELS COULD GET US IN...
WE WENT STRAIGHT THERE WHEN WE FOUND OUT SASHA WASN'T AT HOME.
SO, WHERE IS IT?
YEAH! WHERE'S THE SCARY HORRIBLE THING YOU FIGHT EVERY YEAR?!
WELL, *UH*. SASHA'S HOLDING IT RIGHT NOW.
BWEH!

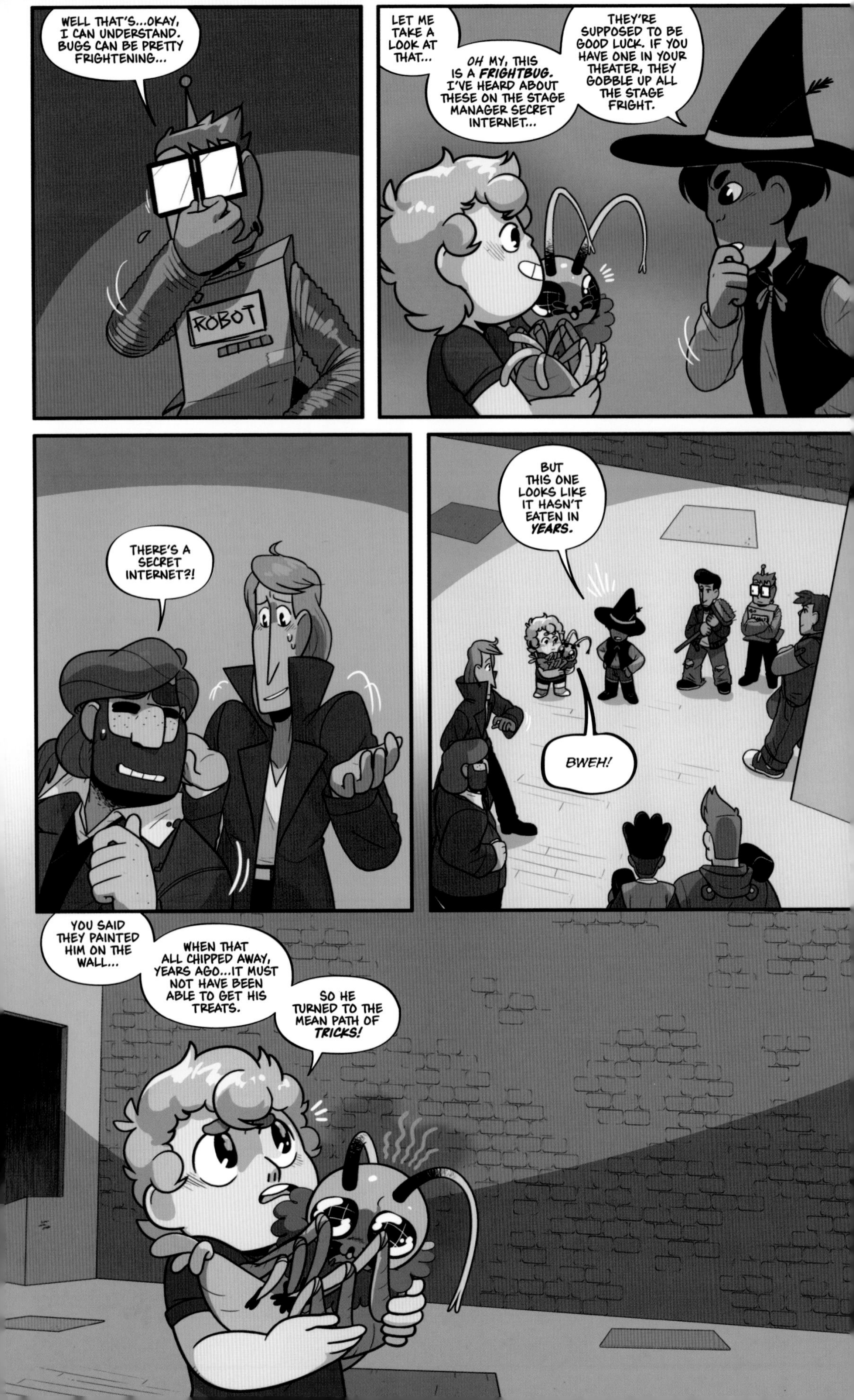
WELL THAT'S...OKAY, I CAN UNDERSTAND. BUGS CAN BE PRETTY FRIGHTENING...
ROBOT
LET ME TAKE A LOOK AT THAT...
OH MY, THIS IS A FRIGHTBUG. I'VE HEARD ABOUT THESE ON THE STAGE MANAGER SECRET INTERNET...
THEY'RE SUPPOSED TO BE GOOD LUCK. IF YOU HAVE ONE IN YOUR THEATER, THEY GOBBLE UP ALL THE STAGE FRIGHT.
THERE'S A SECRET INTERNET?!
BUT THIS ONE LOOKS LIKE IT HASN'T EATEN IN YEARS.
BWEH!
YOU SAID THEY PAINTED HIM ON THE WALL...
WHEN THAT ALL CHIPPED AWAY, YEARS AGO...IT MUST NOT HAVE BEEN ABLE TO GET HIS TREATS.
SO HE TURNED TO THE MEAN PATH OF TRICKS!

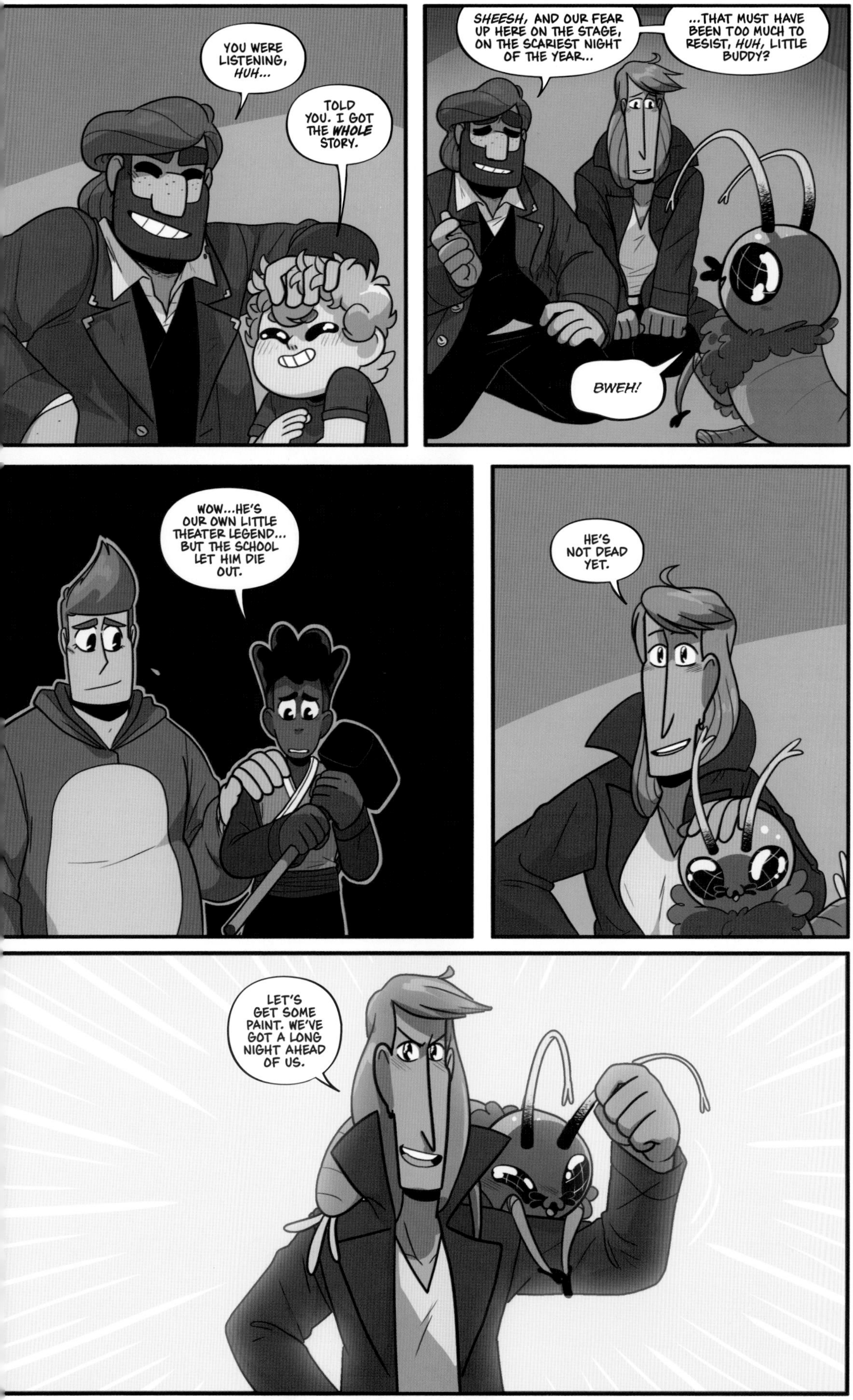
YOU WERE LISTENING, *HUH*...
TOLD YOU. I GOT THE ***WHOLE*** STORY.
SHEESH, AND OUR FEAR UP HERE ON THE STAGE, ON THE SCARIEST NIGHT OF THE YEAR...
...THAT MUST HAVE BEEN TOO MUCH TO RESIST, *HUH*, LITTLE BUDDY?
BWEH!
WOW...HE'S OUR OWN LITTLE THEATER LEGEND... BUT THE SCHOOL LET HIM DIE OUT.
HE'S NOT DEAD YET.
LET'S GET SOME PAINT. WE'VE GOT A LONG NIGHT AHEAD OF US.

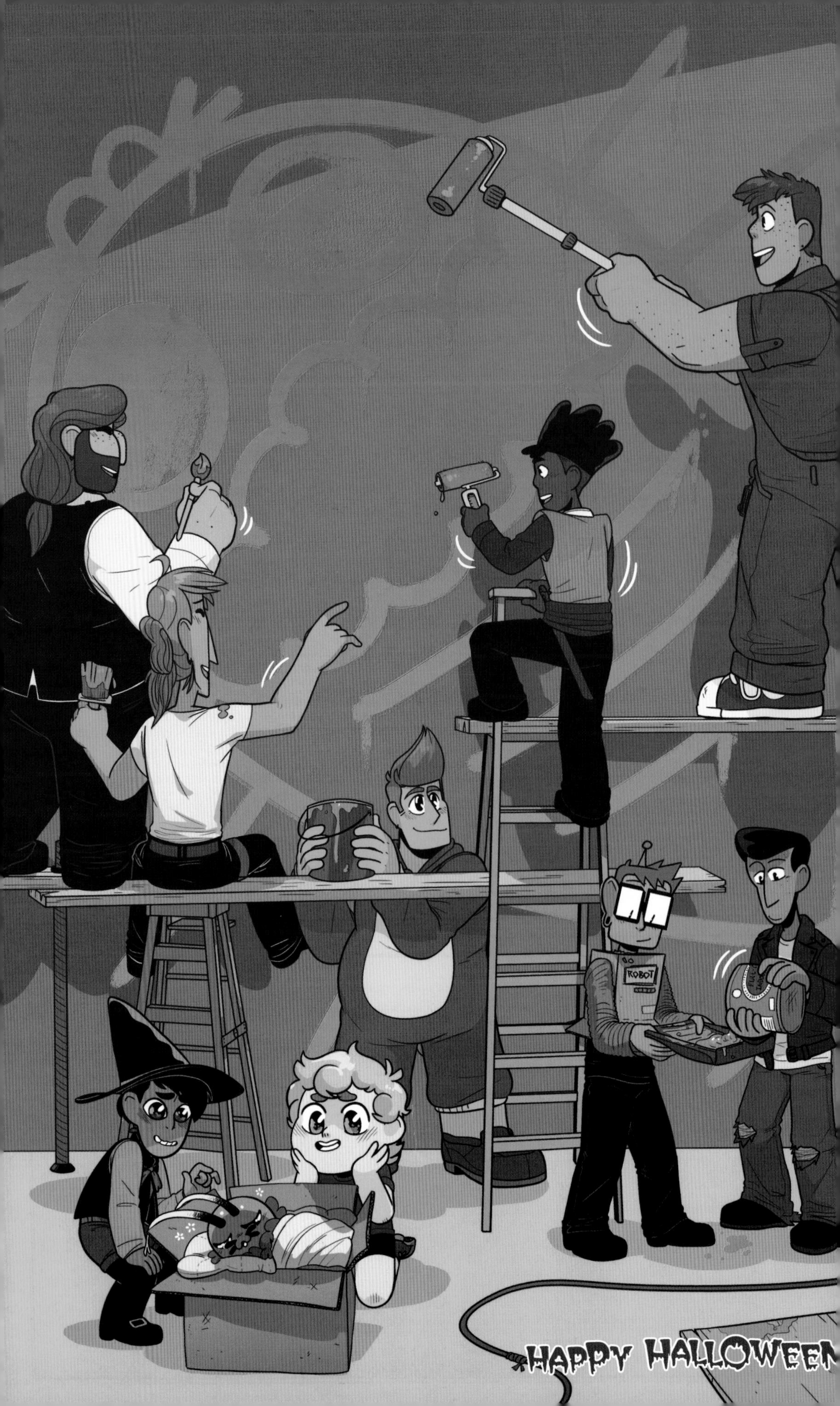
ROBOT
HAPPY HALLOWEEN

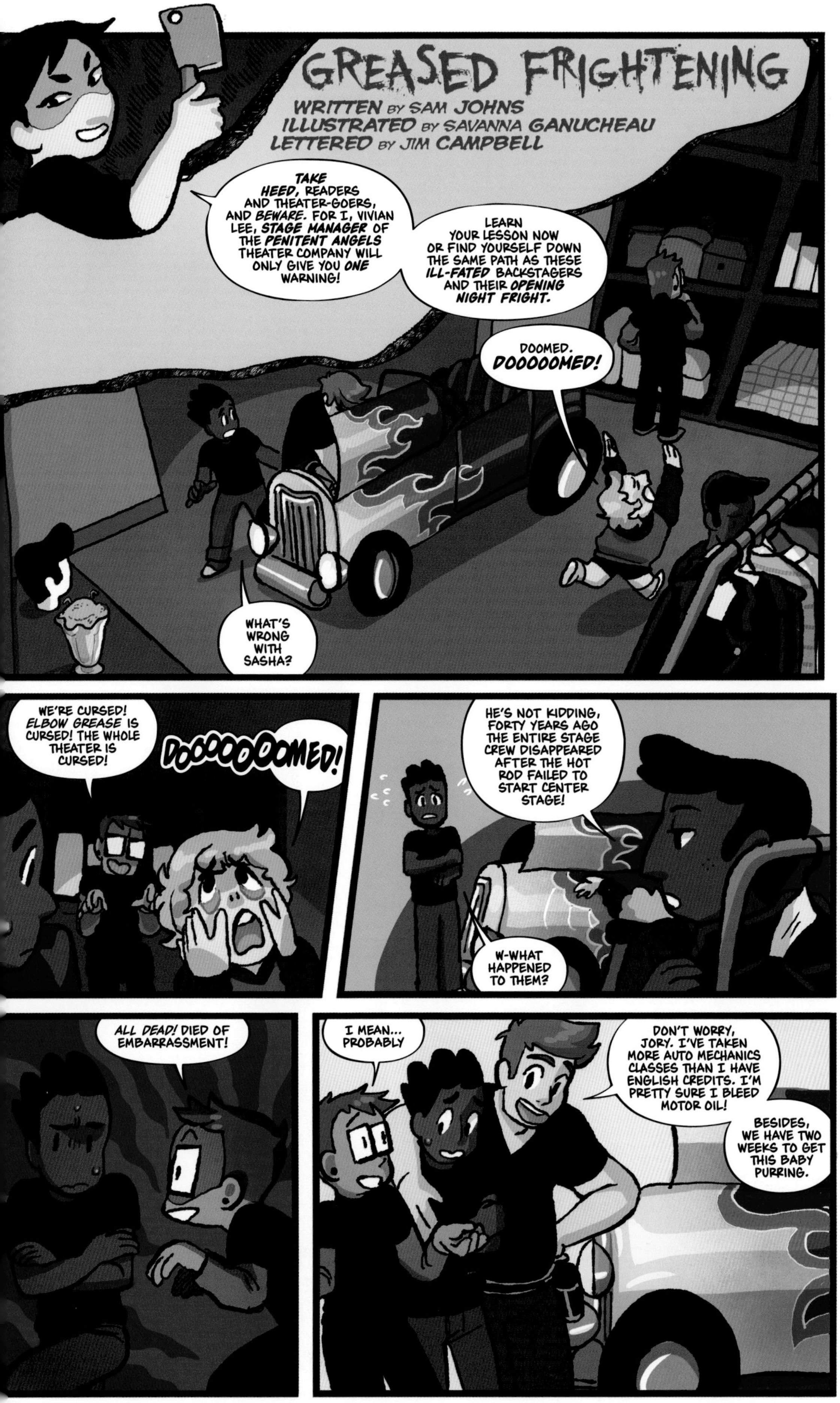
GREASED FRIGHTENING
WRITTEN BY SAM JOHNS
ILLUSTRATED BY SAVANNA GANUCHEAU
LETTERED BY JIM CAMPBELL
TAKE HEED, READERS AND THEATER-GOERS, AND BEWARE. FOR I, VIVIAN LEE, STAGE MANAGER OF THE PENITENT ANGELS THEATER COMPANY WILL ONLY GIVE YOU ONE WARNING!
LEARN YOUR LESSON NOW OR FIND YOURSELF DOWN THE SAME PATH AS THESE ILL-FATED BACKSTAGERS AND THEIR OPENING NIGHT FRIGHT.
DOOMED. DOOOOOMED!
WHAT'S WRONG WITH SASHA?
WE'RE CURSED! ELBOW GREASE IS CURSED! THE WHOLE THEATER IS CURSED!
DOOOOOOOOMED!
HE'S NOT KIDDING, FORTY YEARS AGO THE ENTIRE STAGE CREW DISAPPEARED AFTER THE HOT ROD FAILED TO START CENTER STAGE!
W-WHAT HAPPENED TO THEM?
ALL DEAD! DIED OF EMBARRASSMENT!
I MEAN... PROBABLY
DON'T WORRY, JORY. I'VE TAKEN MORE AUTO MECHANICS CLASSES THAN I HAVE ENGLISH CREDITS. I'M PRETTY SURE I BLEED MOTOR OIL!
BESIDES, WE HAVE TWO WEEKS TO GET THIS BABY PURRING.

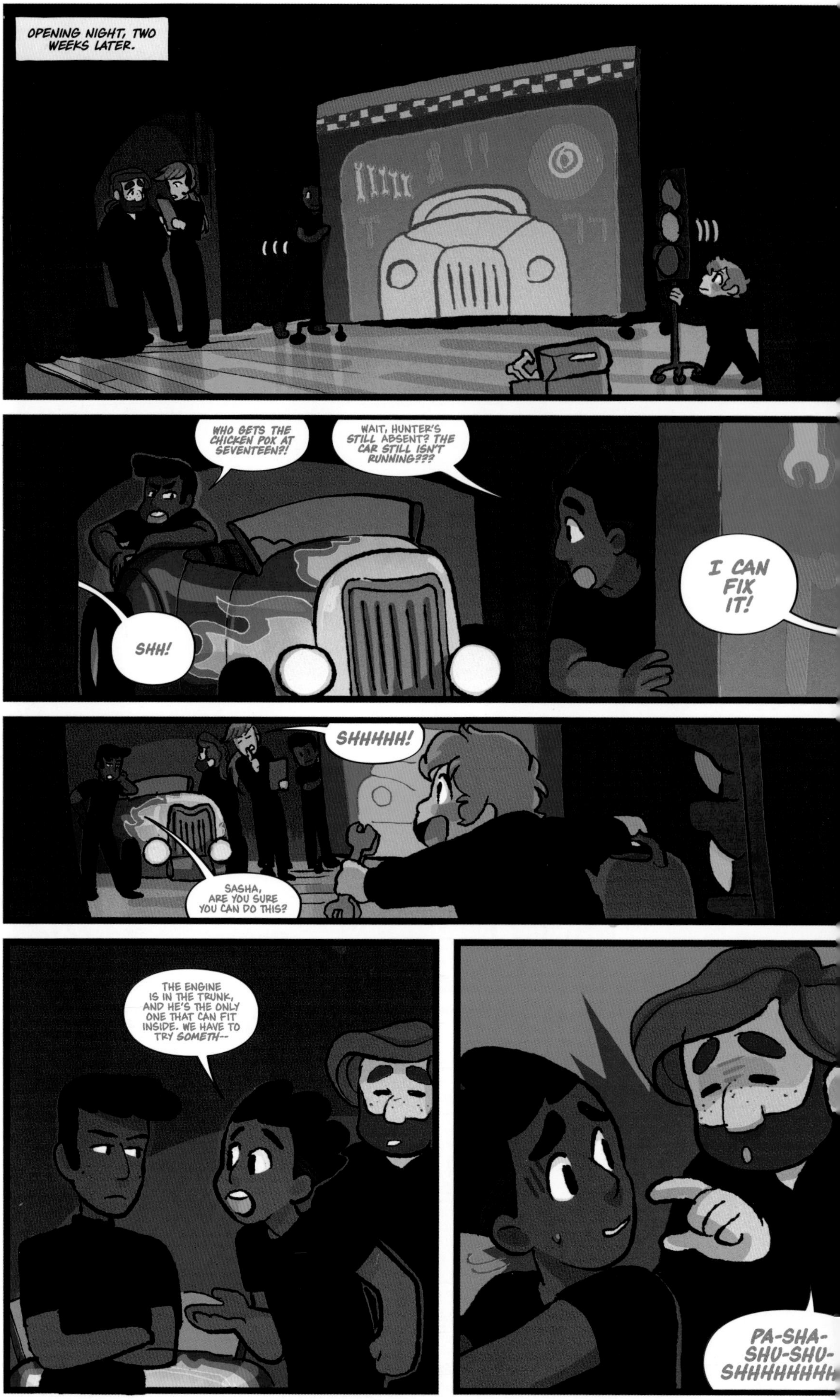
OPENING NIGHT, TWO WEEKS LATER.
WHO GETS THE CHICKEN POX AT SEVENTEEN?!
WAIT, HUNTER'S STILL ABSENT? THE CAR STILL ISN'T RUNNING???
SHH!
I CAN FIX IT!
SHHHHH!
SASHA, ARE YOU SURE YOU CAN DO THIS?
THE ENGINE IS IN THE TRUNK, AND HE'S THE ONLY ONE THAT CAN FIT INSIDE. WE HAVE TO TRY SOMETH--
PA-SHA-SHU-SHU-SHHHHHHHH

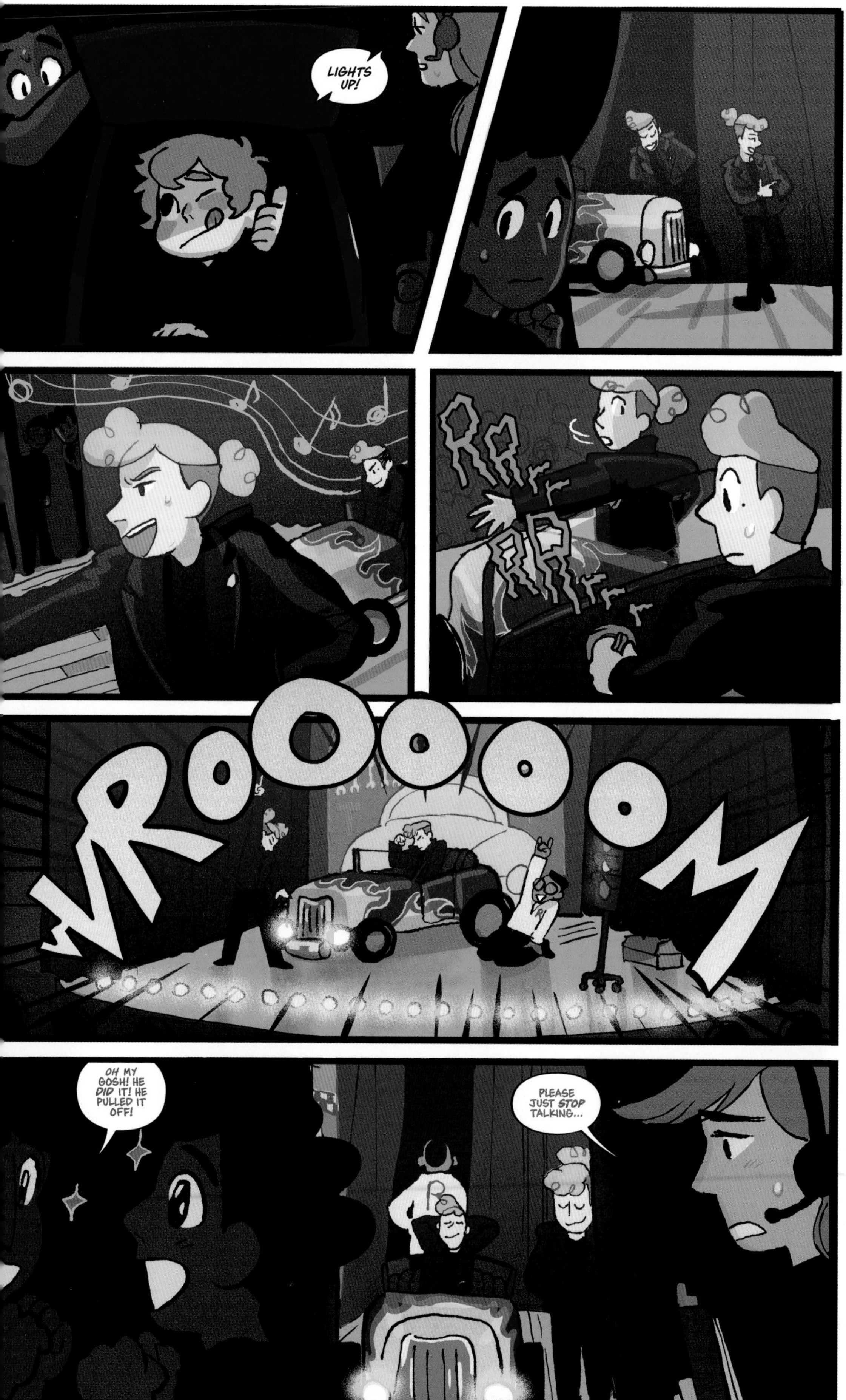
LIGHTS UP!
RRrr
RRRrrr
VROOOOOM
OH MY GOSH! HE DID IT! HE PULLED IT OFF!
PLEASE JUST STOP TALKING...

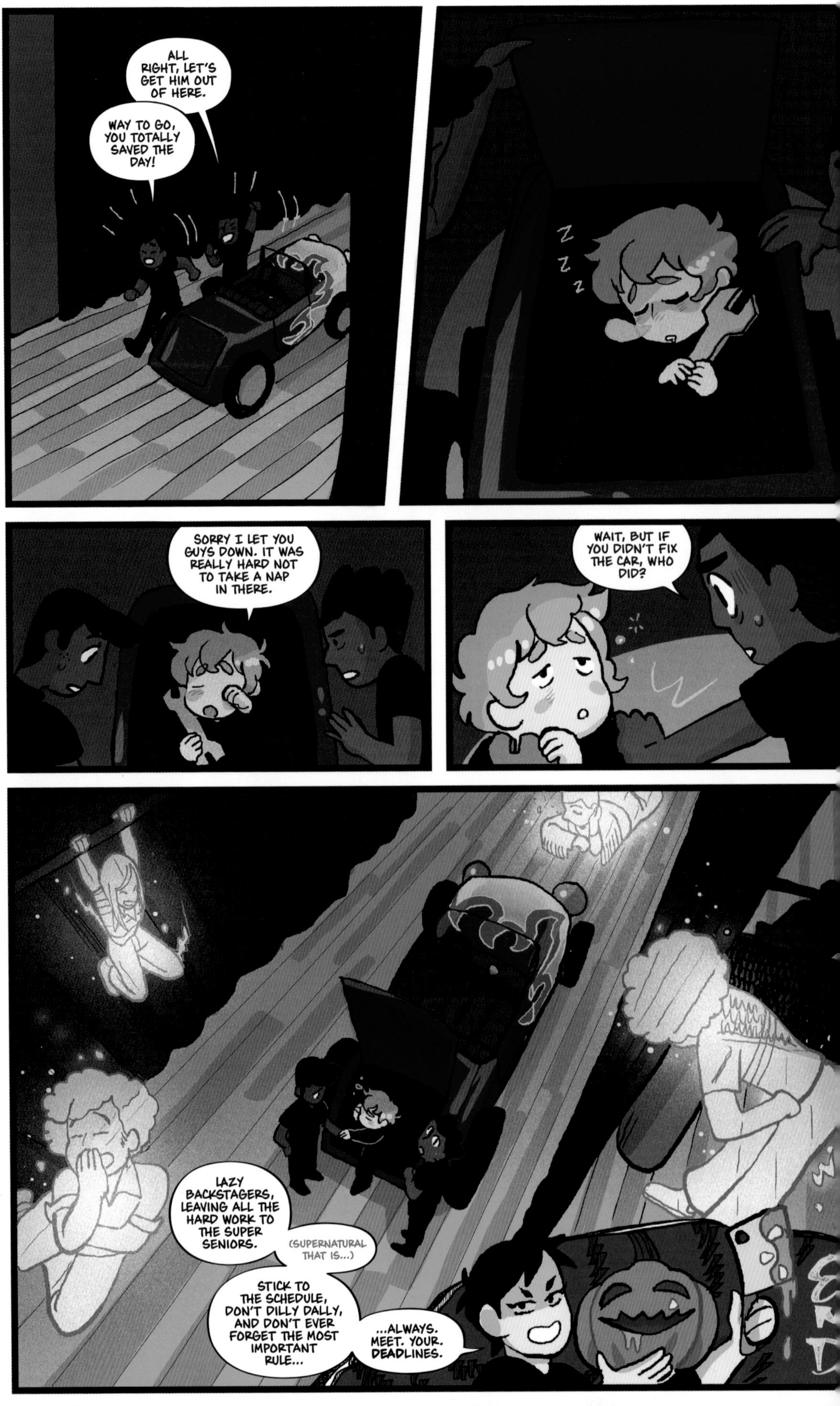
ALL RIGHT, LET'S GET HIM OUT OF HERE.
WAY TO GO, YOU TOTALLY SAVED THE DAY!
Z Z Z
SORRY I LET YOU GUYS DOWN. IT WAS REALLY HARD NOT TO TAKE A NAP IN THERE.
WAIT, BUT IF YOU DIDN'T FIX THE CAR, WHO DID?
LAZY BACKSTAGERS, LEAVING ALL THE HARD WORK TO THE SUPER SENIORS.
(SUPERNATURAL THAT IS...)
STICK TO THE SCHEDULE, DON'T DILLY DALLY, AND DON'T EVER FORGET THE MOST IMPORTANT RULE...
...ALWAYS. MEET. YOUR. DEADLINES.

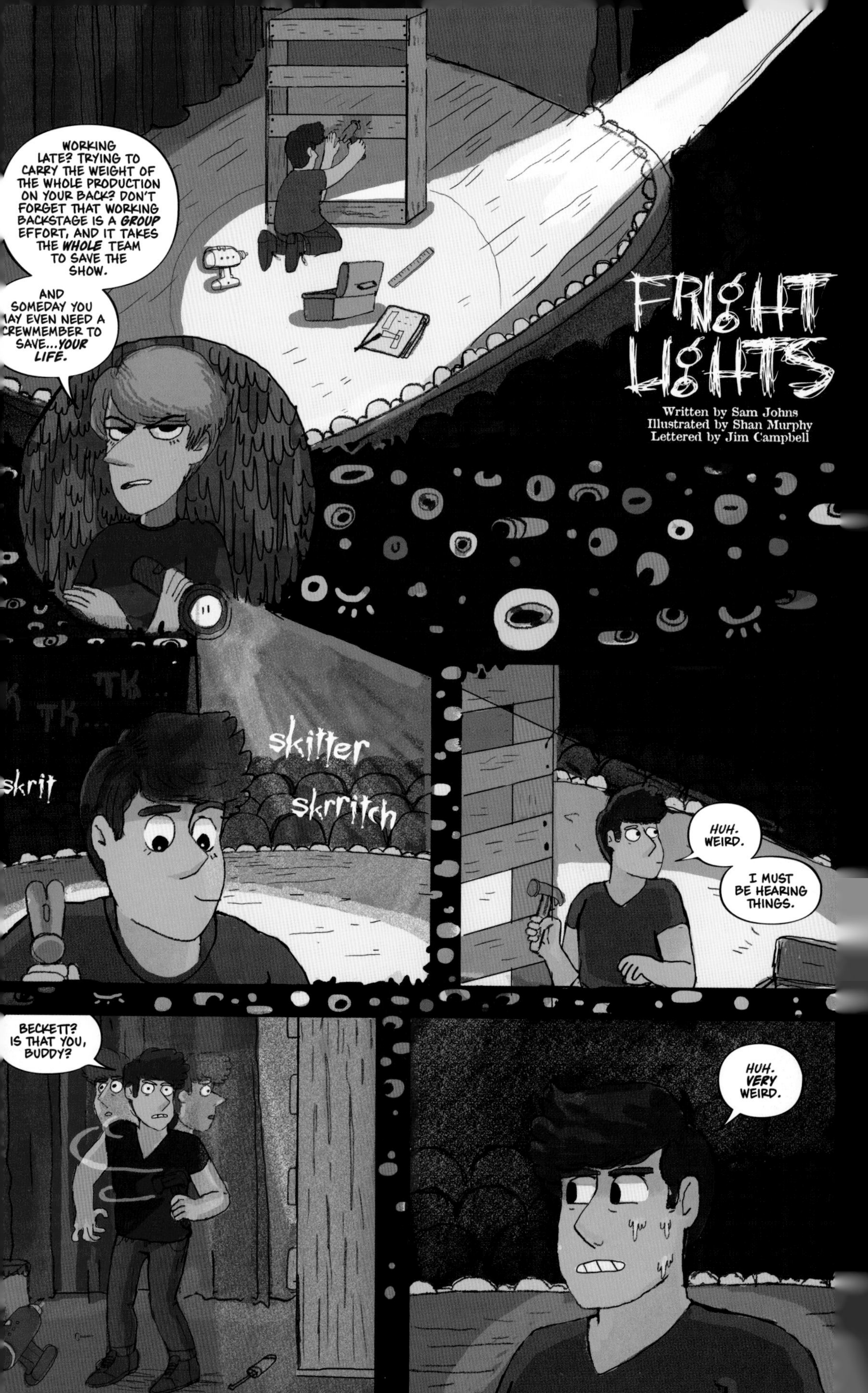

FRIGHT LIGHTS
Written by Sam Johns
Illustrated by Shan Murphy
Lettered by Jim Campbell
WORKING LATE? TRYING TO CARRY THE WEIGHT OF THE WHOLE PRODUCTION ON YOUR BACK? DON'T FORGET THAT WORKING BACKSTAGE IS A GROUP EFFORT, AND IT TAKES THE WHOLE TEAM TO SAVE THE SHOW.
AND SOMEDAY YOU MAY EVEN NEED A CREWMEMBER TO SAVE...YOUR LIFE.
TK... TK...
skitter
skrit
skrritch
HUH. WEIRD.
I MUST BE HEARING THINGS.
BECKETT? IS THAT YOU, BUDDY?
HUH. VERY WEIRD.

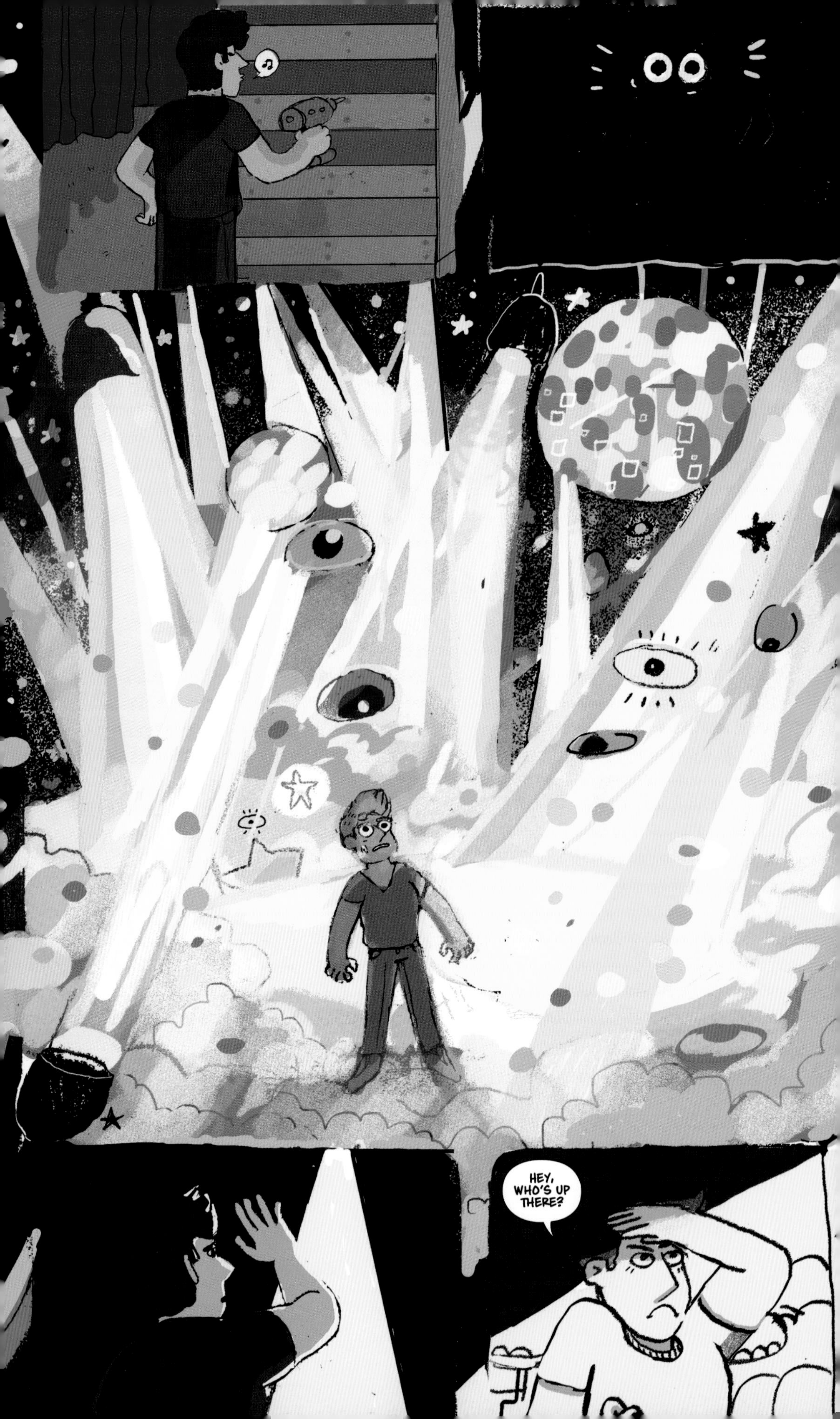
HEY, WHO'S UP THERE?

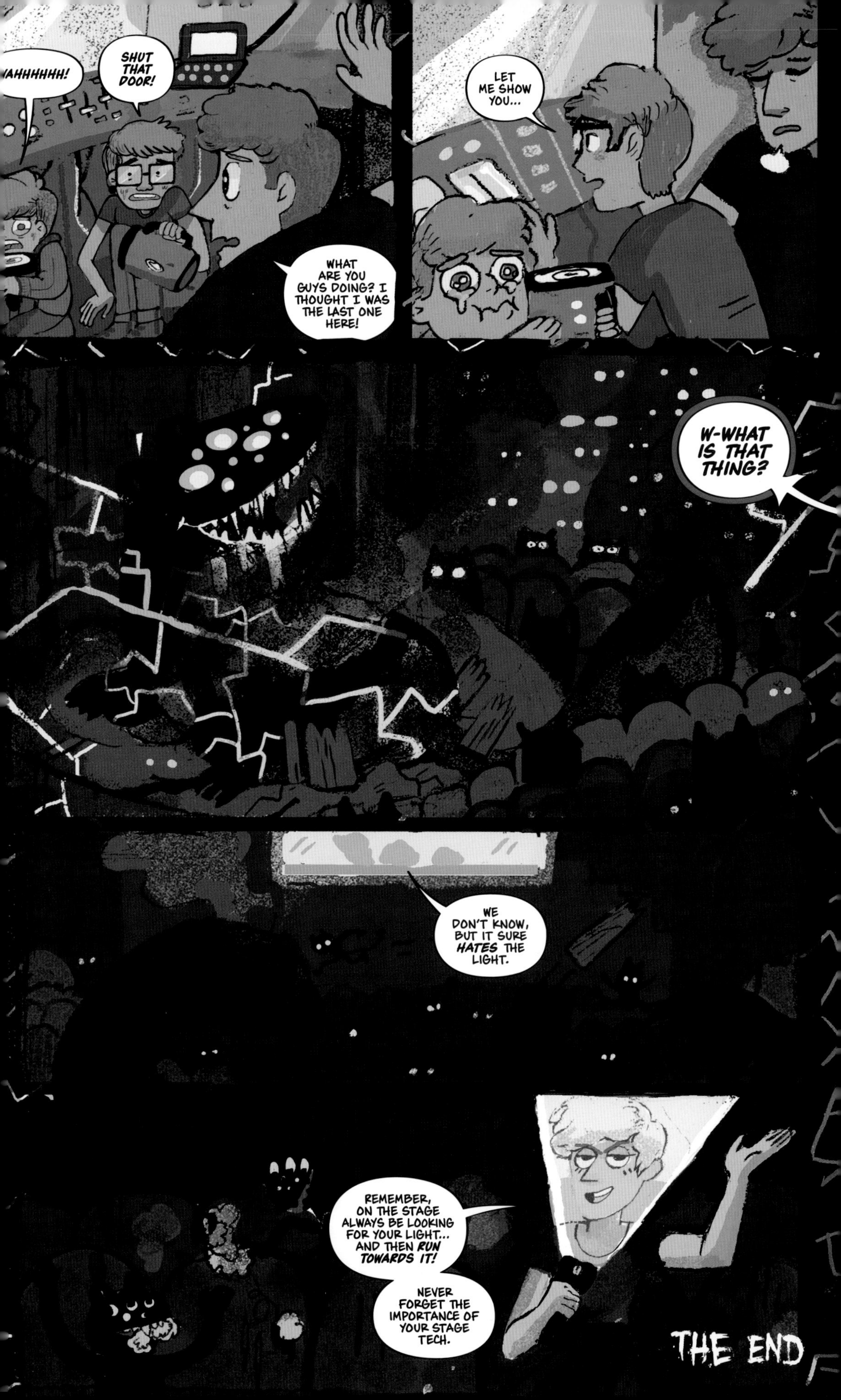

AHHHHHH!
SHUT THAT DOOR!
WHAT ARE YOU GUYS DOING? I THOUGHT I WAS THE LAST ONE HERE!
LET ME SHOW YOU...
W-WHAT IS THAT THING?
WE DON'T KNOW, BUT IT SURE HATES THE LIGHT.
REMEMBER, ON THE STAGE ALWAYS BE LOOKING FOR YOUR LIGHT... AND THEN RUN TOWARDS IT!
NEVER FORGET THE IMPORTANCE OF YOUR STAGE TECH.
THE END

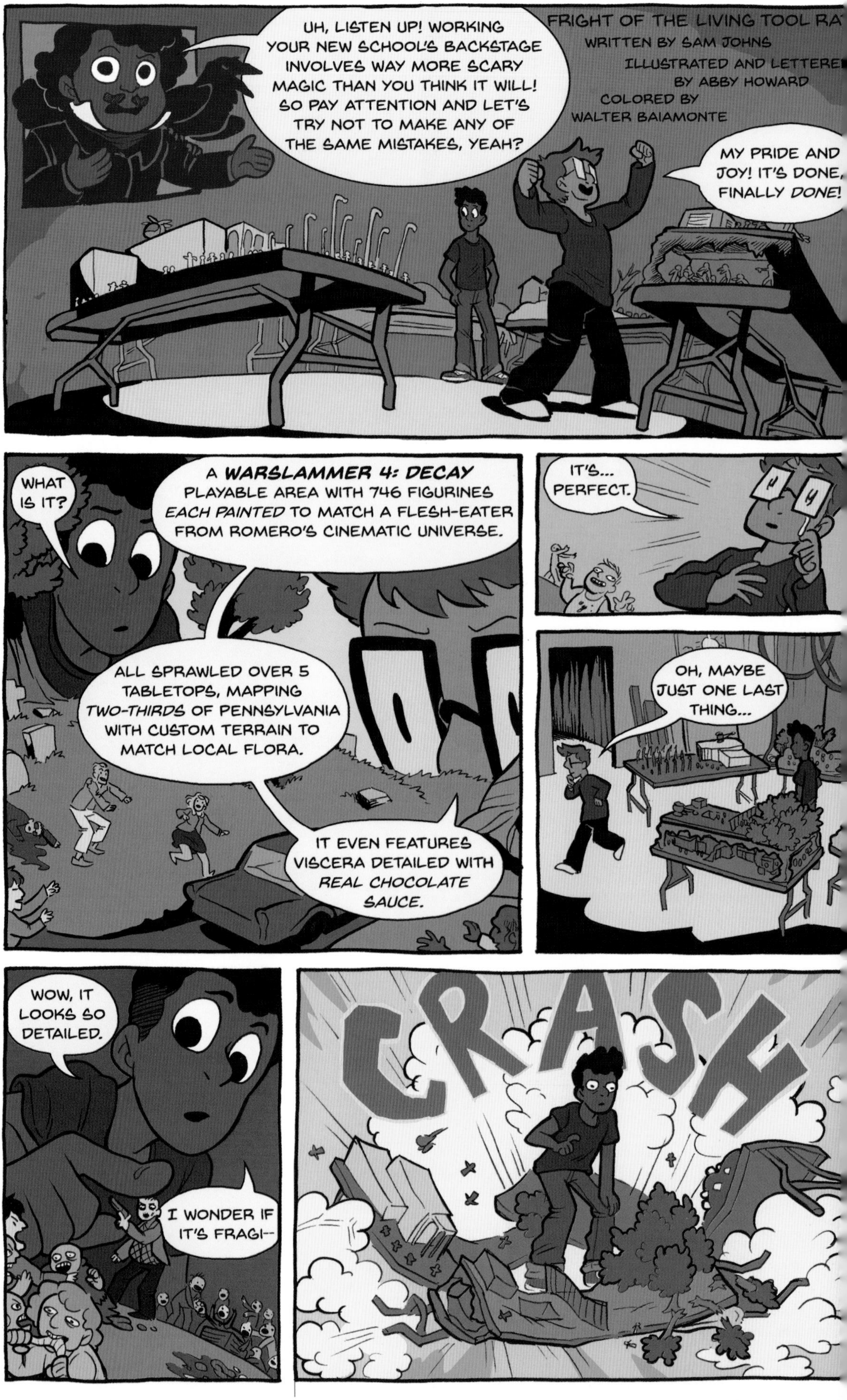
UH, LISTEN UP! WORKING YOUR NEW SCHOOL'S BACKSTAGE INVOLVES WAY MORE SCARY MAGIC THAN YOU THINK IT WILL! SO PAY ATTENTION AND LET'S TRY NOT TO MAKE ANY OF THE SAME MISTAKES, YEAH?
FRIGHT OF THE LIVING TOOL RA
WRITTEN BY SAM JOHNS
ILLUSTRATED AND LETTERE
BY ABBY HOWARD
COLORED BY
WALTER BAIAMONTE
MY PRIDE AND JOY! IT'S DONE, FINALLY DONE!
WHAT IS IT?
A WARSLAMMER 4: DECAY PLAYABLE AREA WITH 746 FIGURINES EACH PAINTED TO MATCH A FLESH-EATER FROM ROMERO'S CINEMATIC UNIVERSE.
ALL SPRAWLED OVER 5 TABLETOPS, MAPPING TWO-THIRDS OF PENNSYLVANIA WITH CUSTOM TERRAIN TO MATCH LOCAL FLORA.
IT EVEN FEATURES VISCERA DETAILED WITH REAL CHOCOLATE SAUCE.
IT'S... PERFECT.
OH, MAYBE JUST ONE LAST THING...
WOW, IT LOOKS SO DETAILED.
I WONDER IF IT'S FRAGI--
CRASH

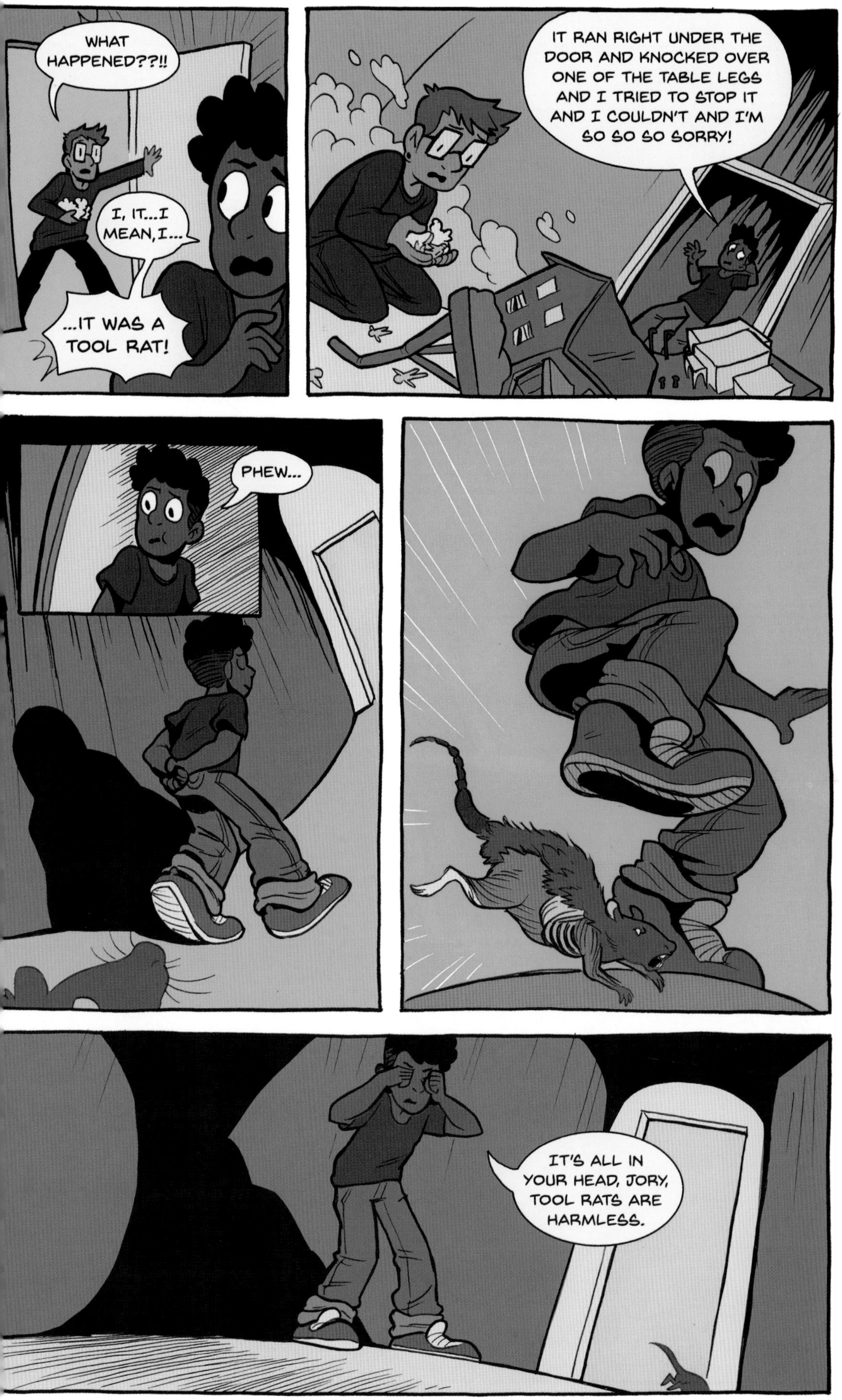
WHAT HAPPENED??!!
I, IT...I MEAN, I...
...IT WAS A TOOL RAT!
IT RAN RIGHT UNDER THE DOOR AND KNOCKED OVER ONE OF THE TABLE LEGS AND I TRIED TO STOP IT AND I COULDN'T AND I'M SO SO SO SORRY!
PHEW...
IT'S ALL IN YOUR HEAD, JORY, TOOL RATS ARE HARMLESS.

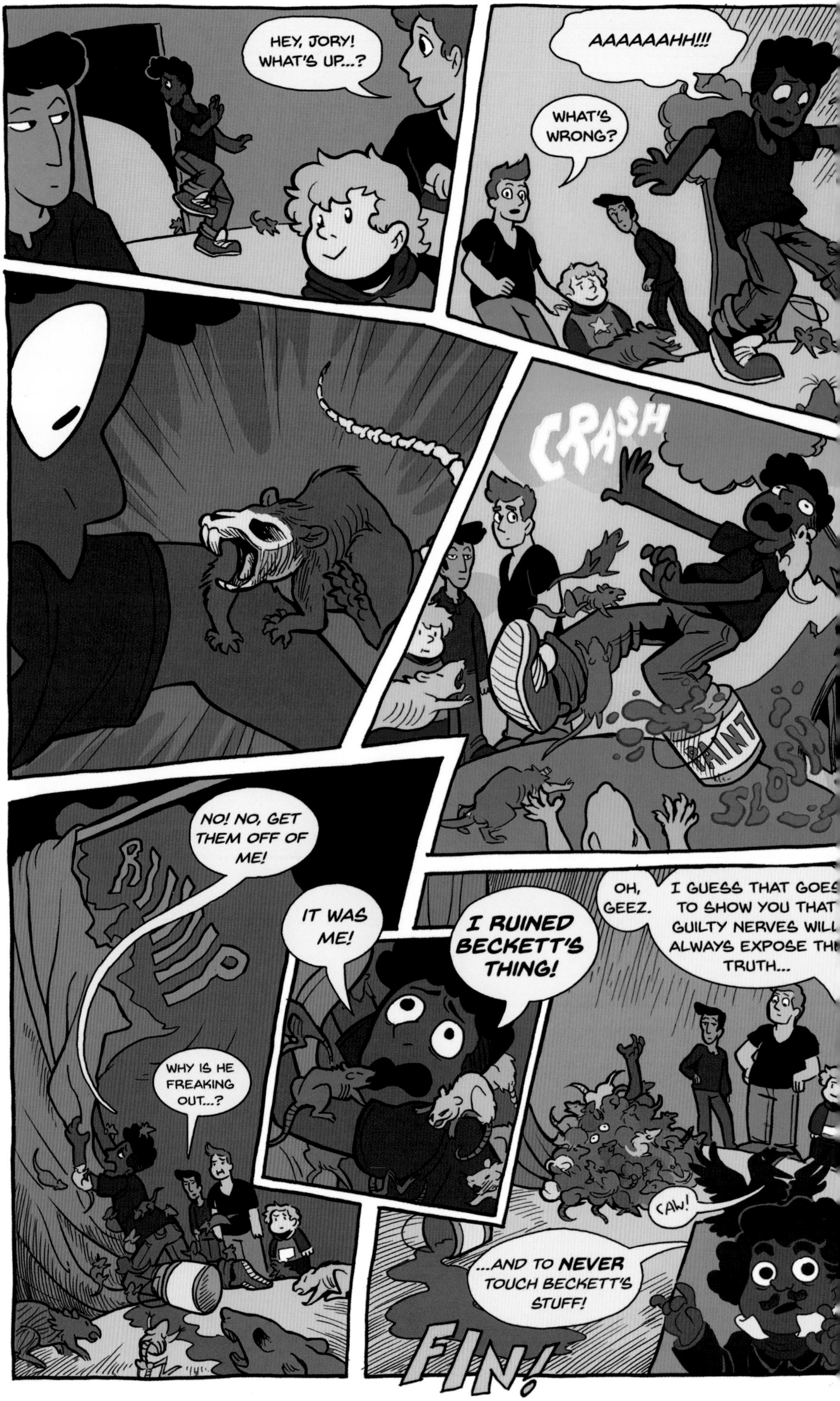
HEY, JORY!
WHAT'S UP...?
AAAAAAHH!!!
WHAT'S
WRONG?
CRASH
PAINT
SLOSH
NO! NO, GET
THEM OFF OF
ME!
RUMP
WHY IS HE
FREAKING
OUT...?
IT WAS
ME!
I RUINED
BECKETT'S
THING!
OH,
GEEZ.
I GUESS THAT GOES
TO SHOW YOU THAT
GUILTY NERVES WILL
ALWAYS EXPOSE THE
TRUTH...
CAW!
...AND TO NEVER
TOUCH BECKETT'S
STUFF!
FIN!

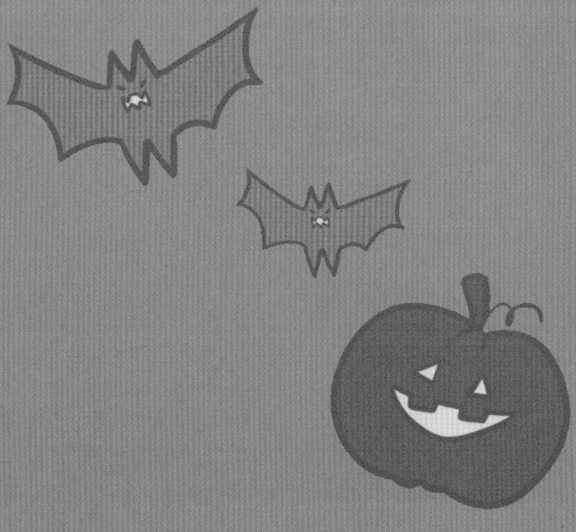

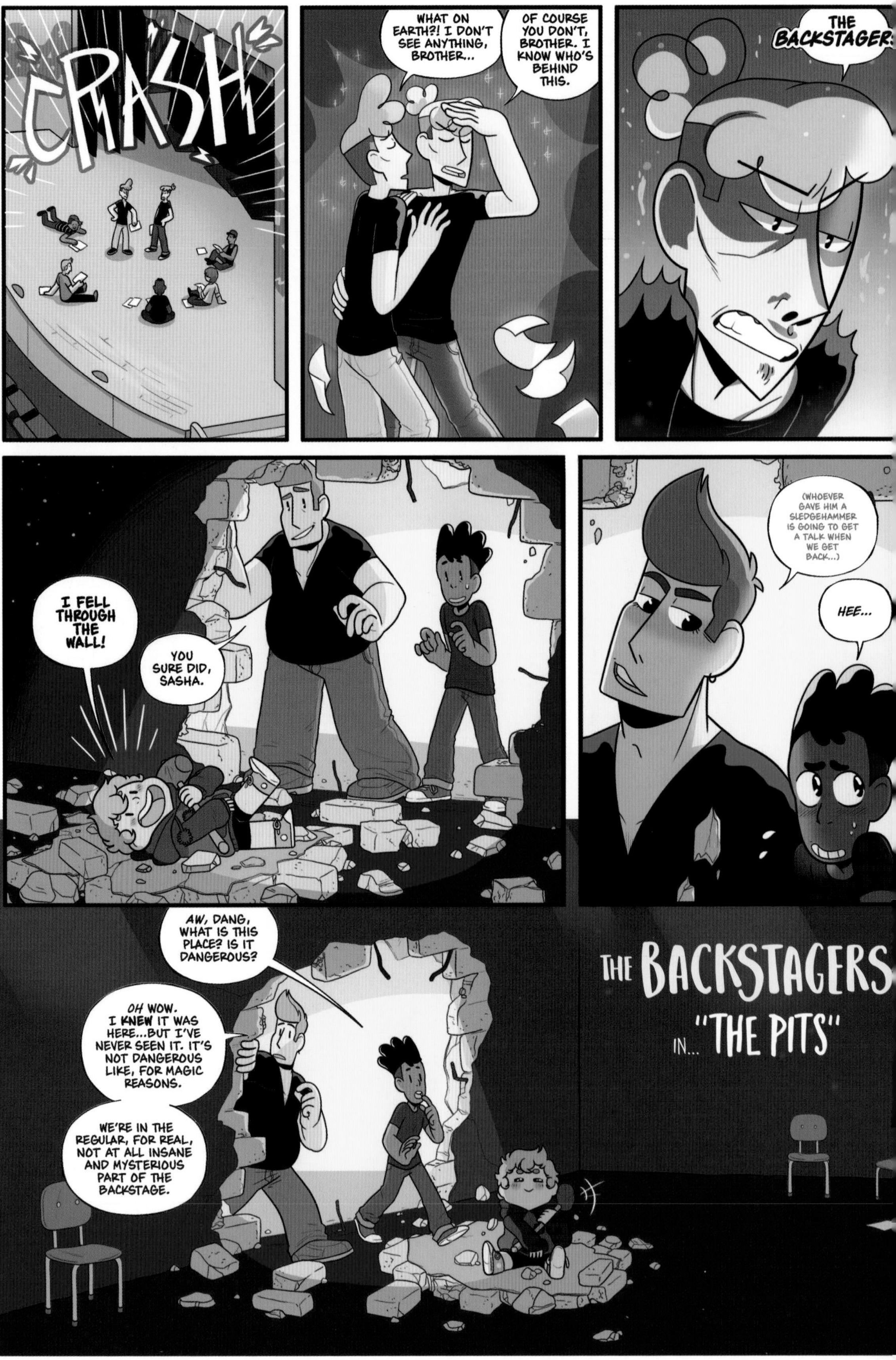

CRASH
WHAT ON EARTH?! I DON'T SEE ANYTHING, BROTHER...
OF COURSE YOU DON'T, BROTHER. I KNOW WHO'S BEHIND THIS.
THE BACKSTAGERS
I FELL THROUGH THE WALL!
YOU SURE DID, SASHA.
(WHOEVER GAVE HIM A SLEDGEHAMMER IS GOING TO GET A TALK WHEN WE GET BACK...)
HEE...
AW, DANG, WHAT IS THIS PLACE? IS IT DANGEROUS?
OH WOW. I KNEW IT WAS HERE...BUT I'VE NEVER SEEN IT. IT'S NOT DANGEROUS LIKE, FOR MAGIC REASONS.
WE'RE IN THE REGULAR, FOR REAL, NOT AT ALL INSANE AND MYSTERIOUS PART OF THE BACKSTAGE.
THE BACKSTAGERS
IN... "THE PITS"

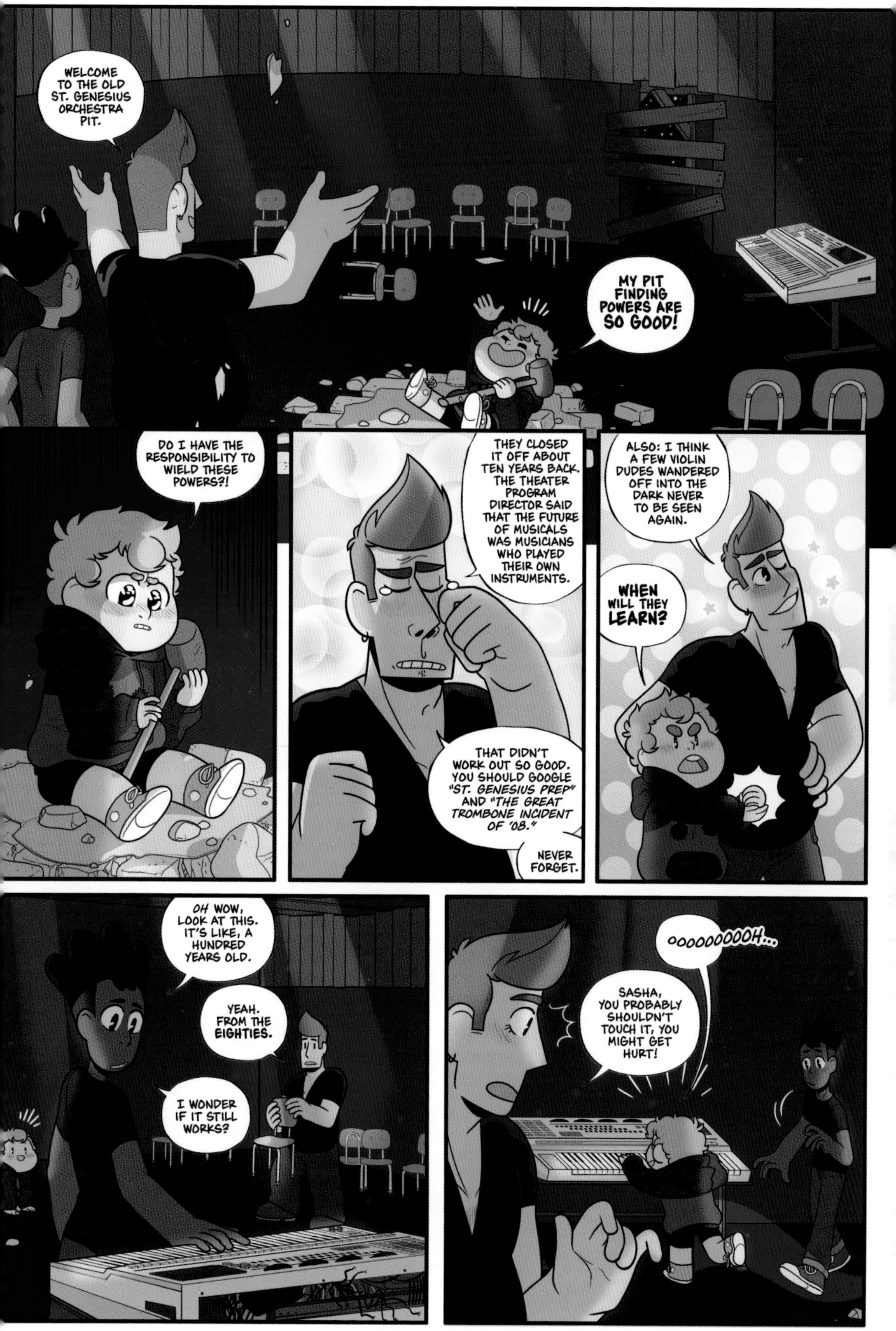
WELCOME TO THE OLD ST. GENESIUS ORCHESTRA PIT.
MY PIT FINDING POWERS ARE SO GOOD!
DO I HAVE THE RESPONSIBILITY TO WIELD THESE POWERS?!
THEY CLOSED IT OFF ABOUT TEN YEARS BACK. THE THEATER PROGRAM DIRECTOR SAID THAT THE FUTURE OF MUSICALS WAS MUSICIANS WHO PLAYED THEIR OWN INSTRUMENTS.
THAT DIDN'T WORK OUT SO GOOD. YOU SHOULD GOOGLE "ST. GENESIUS PREP" AND "THE GREAT TROMBONE INCIDENT OF '08."
NEVER FORGET.
ALSO: I THINK A FEW VIOLIN DUDES WANDERED OFF INTO THE DARK NEVER TO BE SEEN AGAIN.
WHEN WILL THEY LEARN?
OH WOW, LOOK AT THIS. IT'S LIKE, A HUNDRED YEARS OLD.
YEAH. FROM THE EIGHTIES.
I WONDER IF IT STILL WORKS?
OOOOOOOOOH...
SASHA, YOU PROBABLY SHOULDN'T TOUCH IT, YOU MIGHT GET HURT!

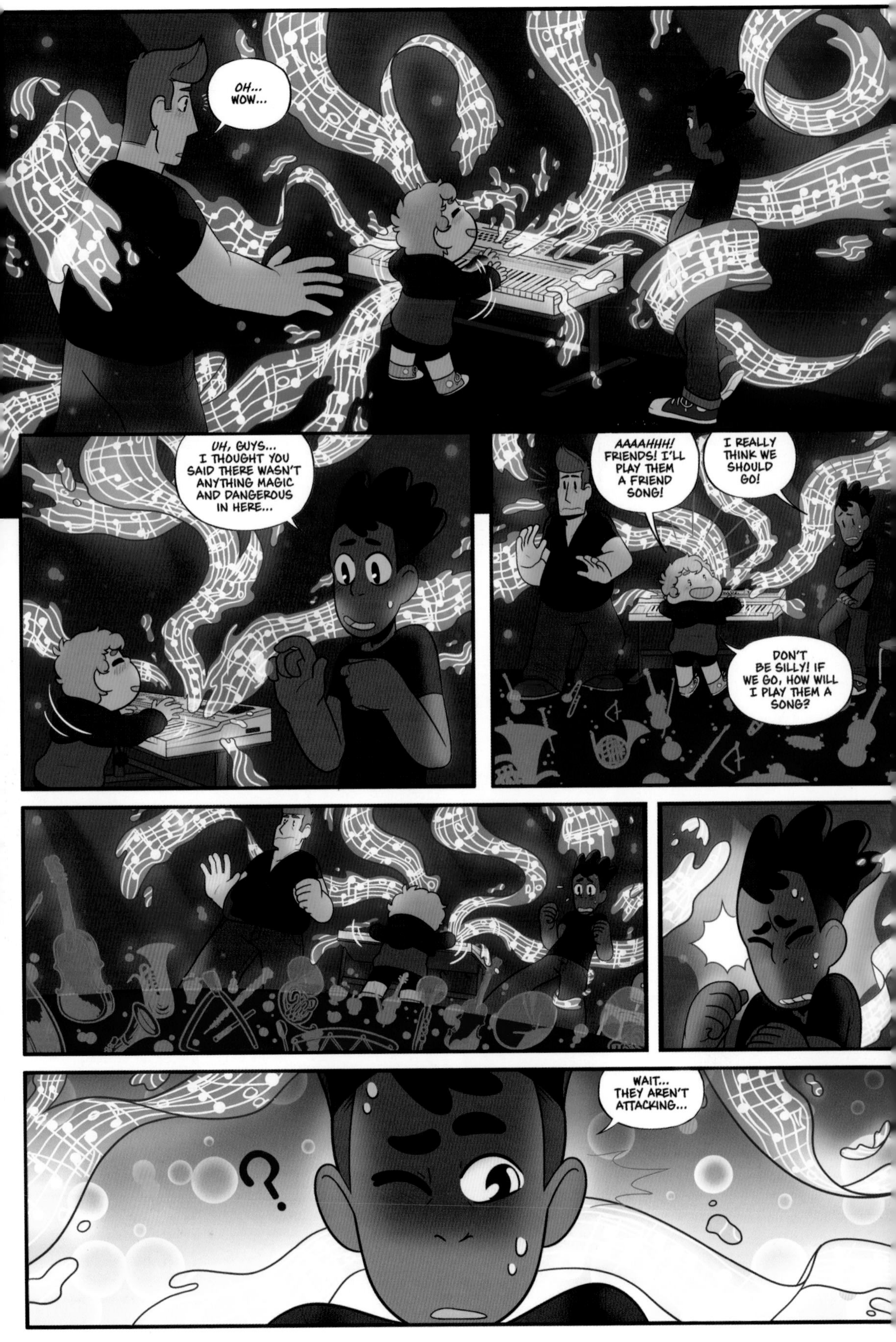
OH... WOW...
UH, GUYS... I THOUGHT YOU SAID THERE WASN'T ANYTHING MAGIC AND DANGEROUS IN HERE...
AAAAHHH! FRIENDS! I'LL PLAY THEM A FRIEND SONG!
I REALLY THINK WE SHOULD GO!
DON'T BE SILLY! IF WE GO, HOW WILL I PLAY THEM A SONG?
WAIT... THEY AREN'T ATTACKING...
?

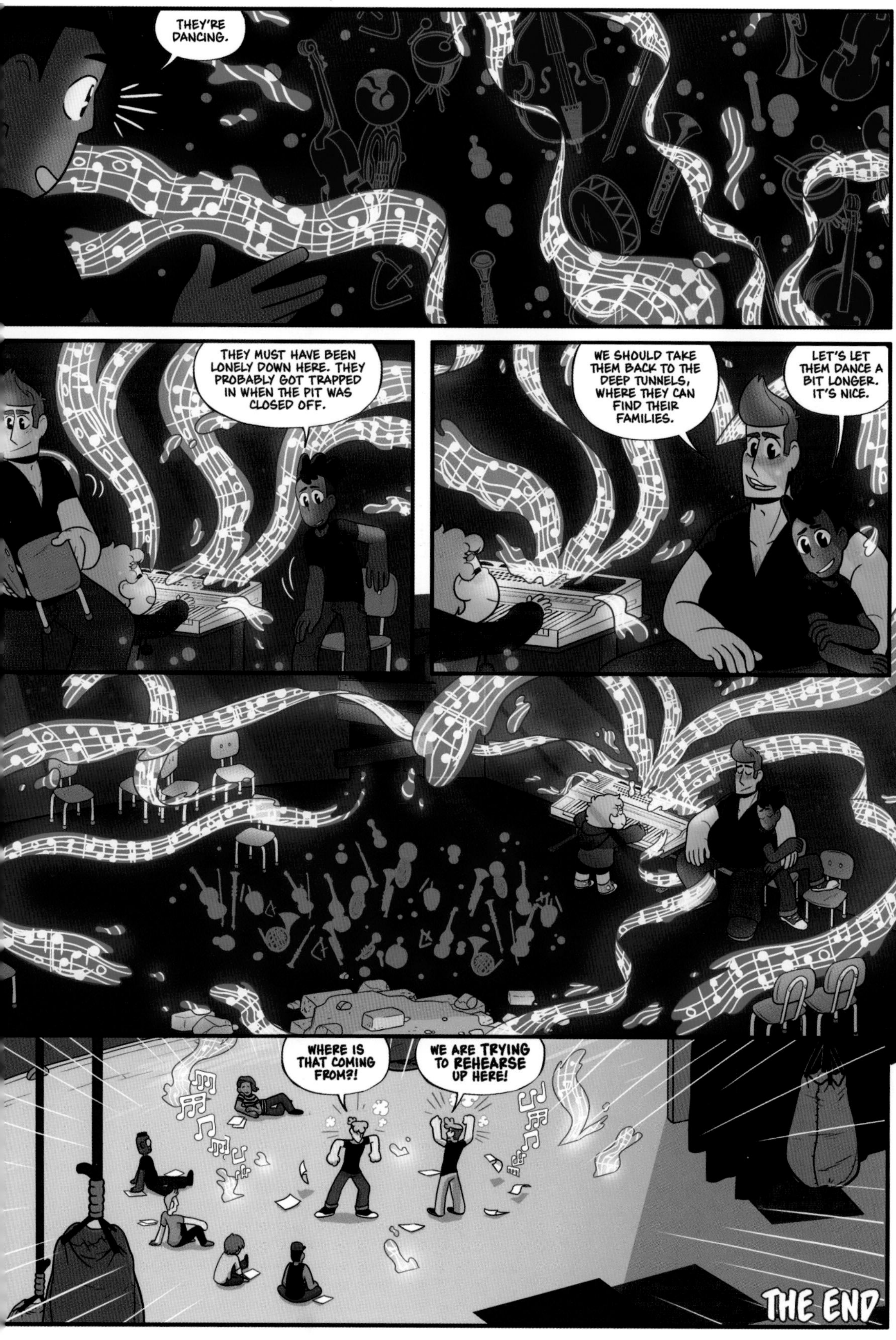
THEY'RE DANCING.
THEY MUST HAVE BEEN LONELY DOWN HERE. THEY PROBABLY GOT TRAPPED IN WHEN THE PIT WAS CLOSED OFF.
WE SHOULD TAKE THEM BACK TO THE DEEP TUNNELS, WHERE THEY CAN FIND THEIR FAMILIES.
LET'S LET THEM DANCE A BIT LONGER. IT'S NICE.
WHERE IS THAT COMING FROM?!
WE ARE TRYING TO REHEARSE UP HERE!
THE END

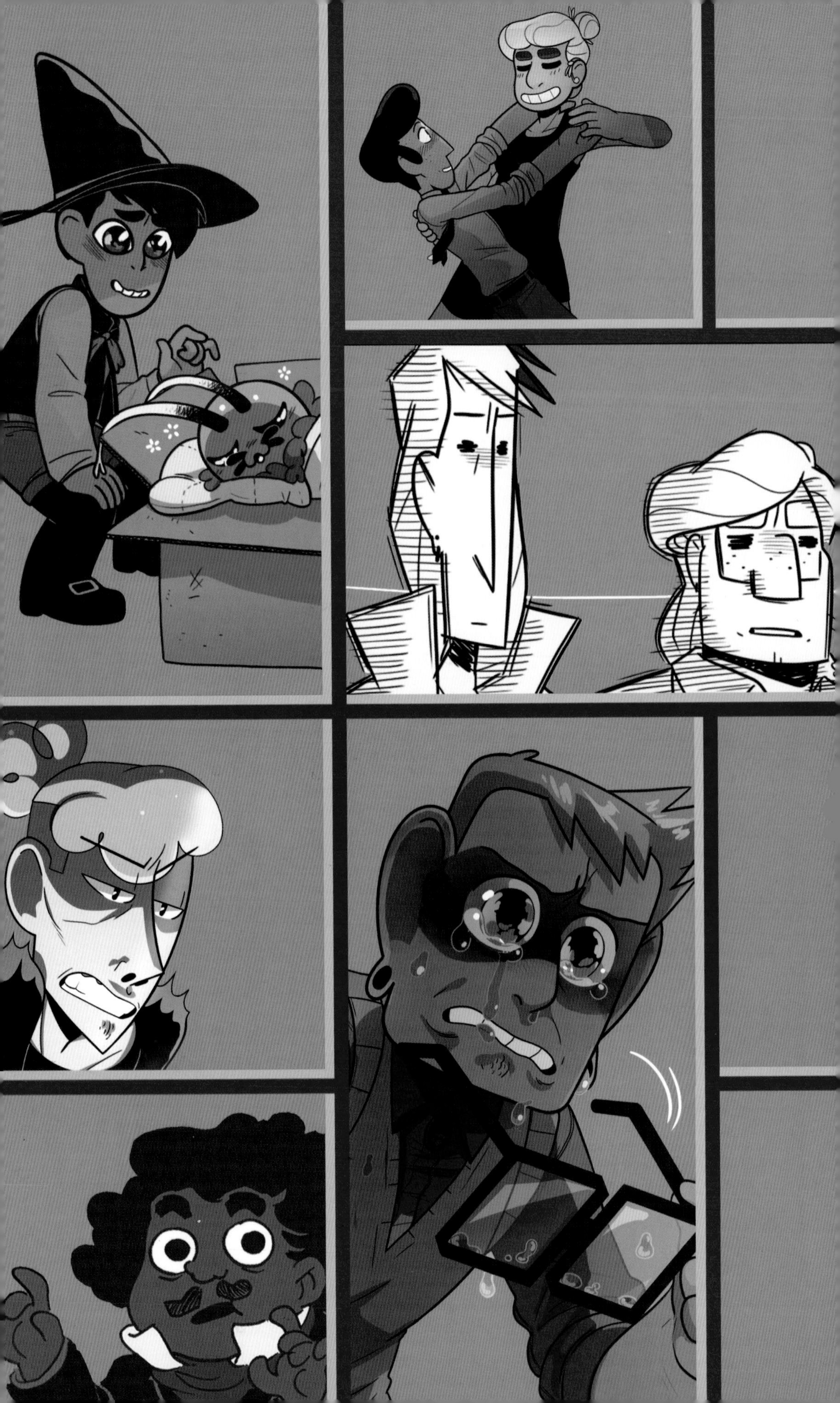

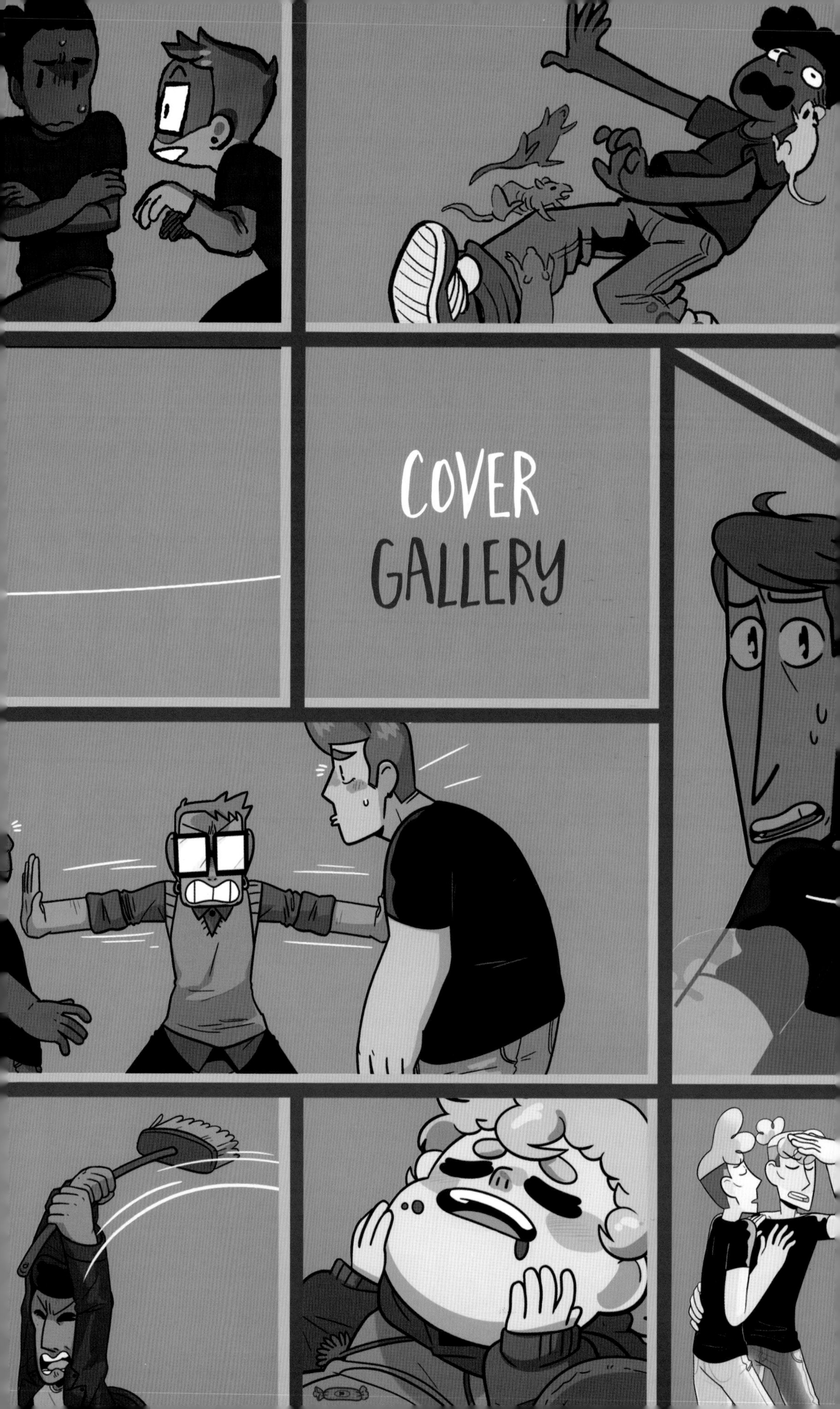
COVER
GALLERY

THE BACKSTAGERS: VALENTINE'S INTERMISSION MAIN COVER BY

RIAN SYGH

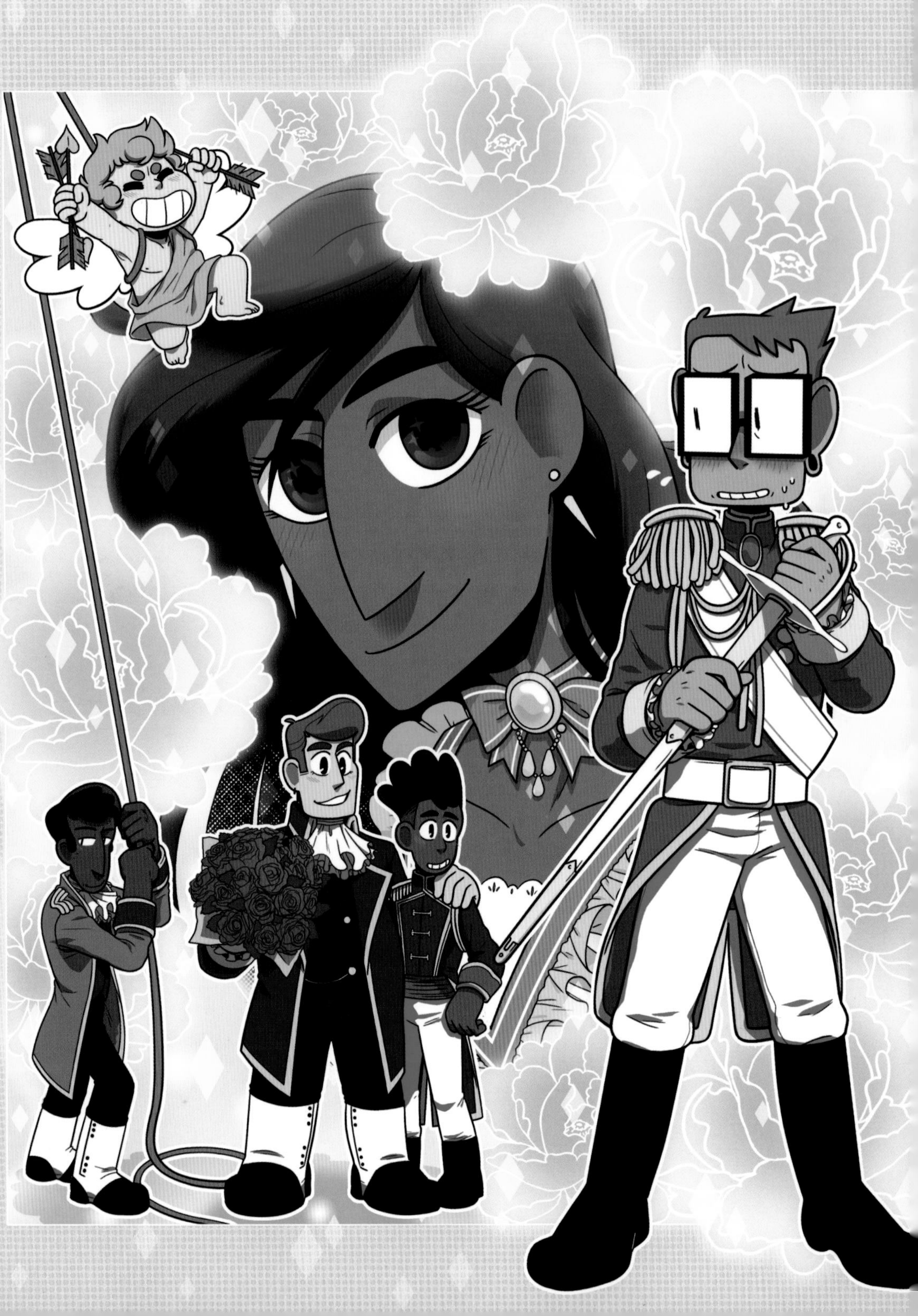

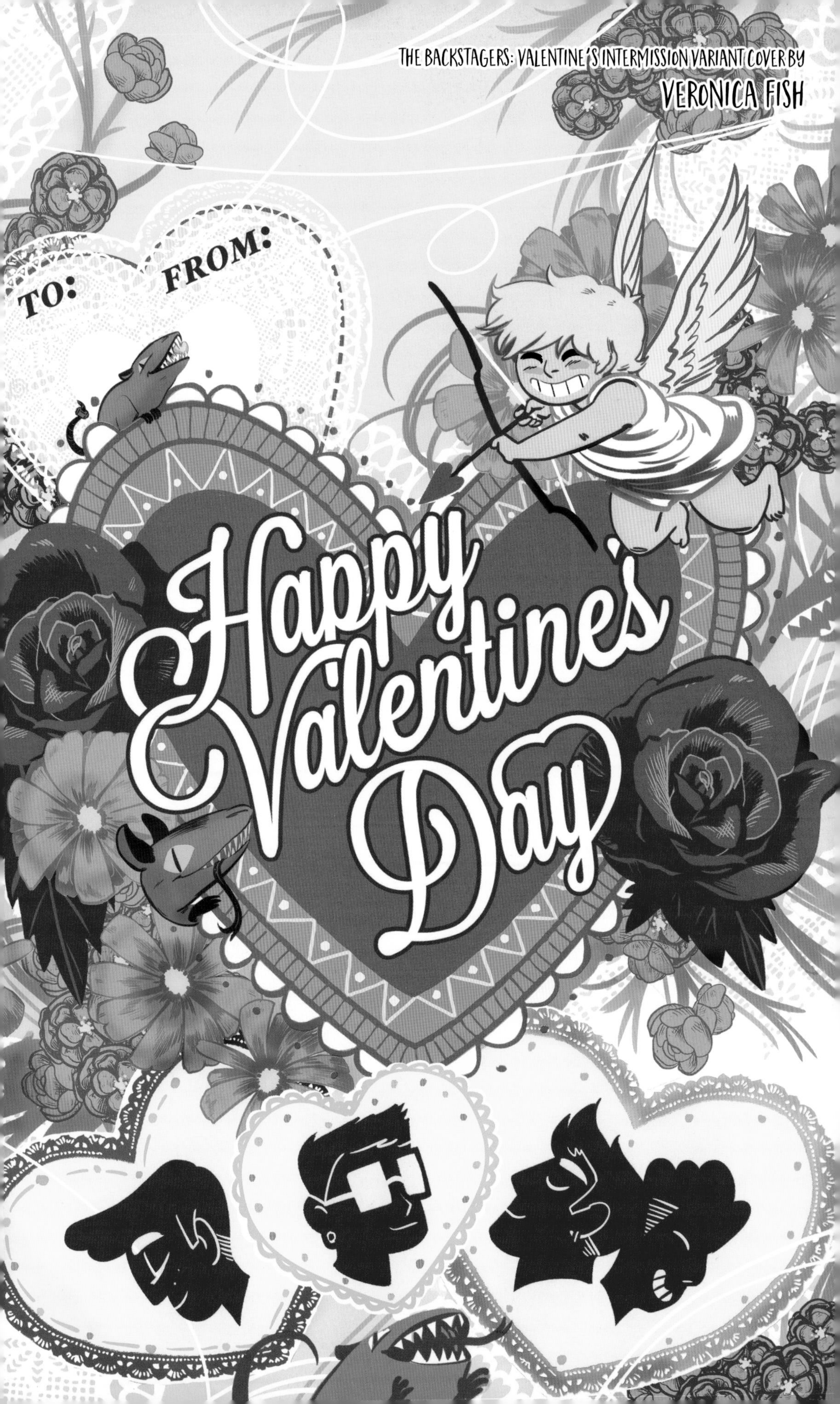
TO:
FROM:
Happy Valentine's Day

THE BACKSTAGERS: VALENTINE'S INTERMISSION VARIANT COVER BY
VERONICA FISH

THE BACKSTAGERS: HALLOWEEN INTERMISSION MAIN COVER BY

RIAN SYGH

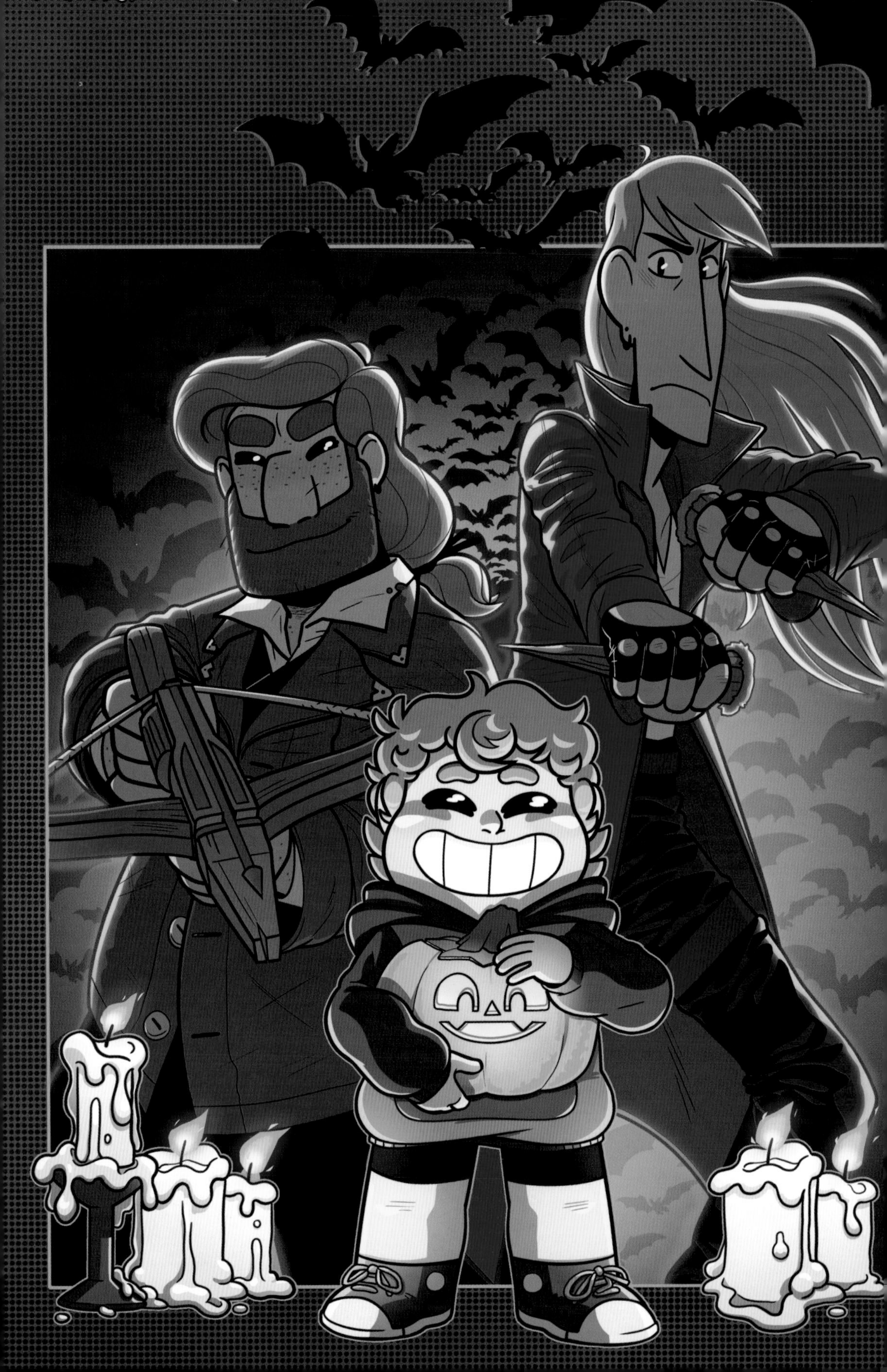

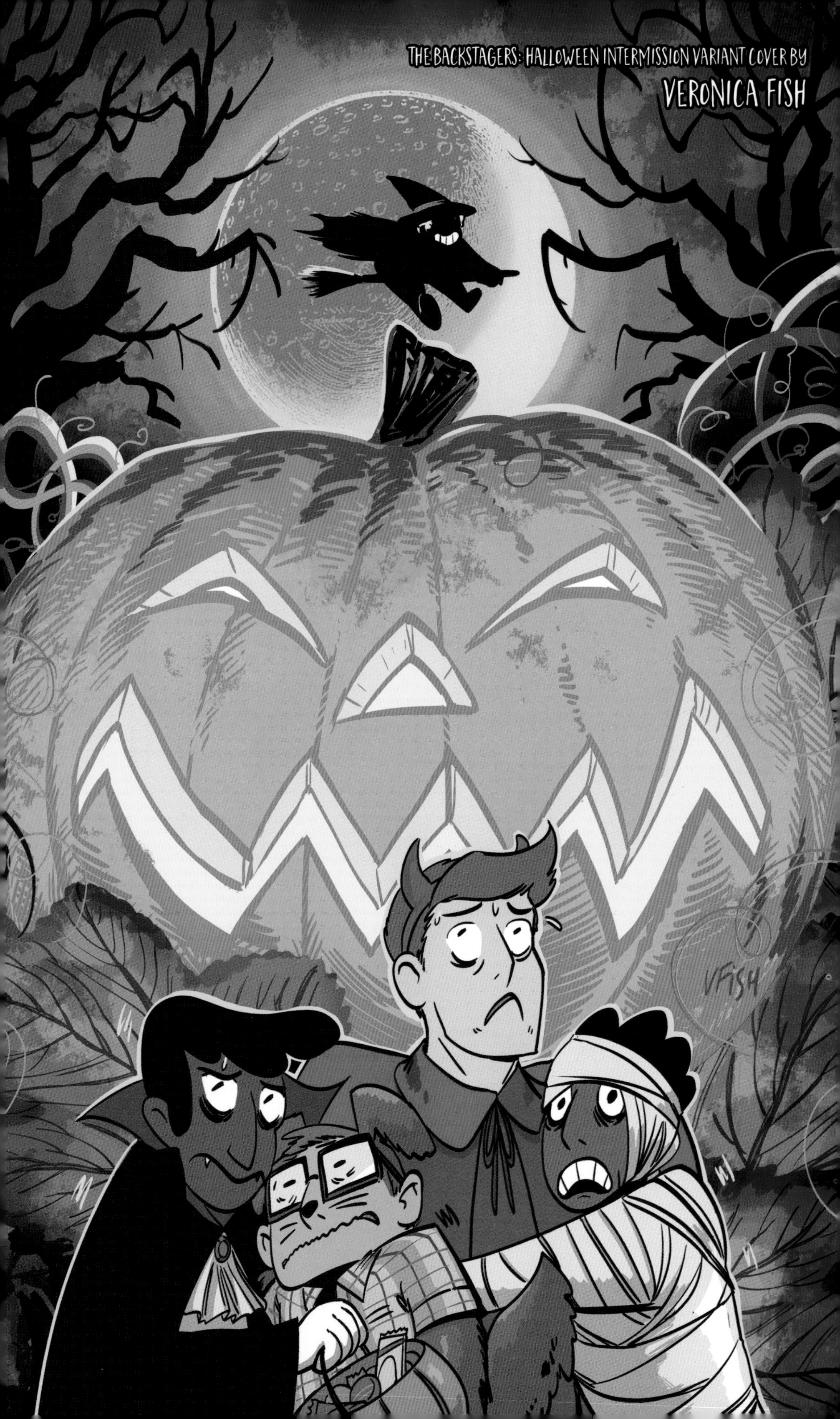
VFISH

THE BACKSTAGERS: HALLOWEEN INTERMISSION VARIANT COVER BY
VERONICA FISH

HALLOWEEN INTERMISSION: PAGE ONE

PANEL ONE: ESTABLISHING SHOT – ST. GENESIUS HIGH SCHOOL, THREE YEARS AGO (It looks mostly the same, but if you wanted one of the buildings to be under construction as a cool detail, we can go for it)

    PRINGLES: Aw, geez. School's been out for like 20 minutes.

PANEL TWO: PRINGLES and ROMAN are standing on the stage with MEAT, all in costume, all impatient

    PRINGLES: Where the heck are they??

    ROMAN: The Cinemonsterthon XI starts at six on the dot, gents, and I'm not missing a single freakin' trailer.

PANEL THREE: ROMAN holds up a passionate fist and we see a dramatic tear drop emerge from the corner of his eye.

    ROMAN: I freakin' LOVE trailers.

PANEL FOUR: MEAT looks at them with FRANKENSTEINIAN confusion, and a deep longing for POPCORN. PRINGLES pats his back, encouraging

    MEAT: Popcoooorn…

    PRINGLES: Yeah, buddy, we'll get you that popcorn, I promise.

PANEL FIVE: ROMAN, a little intense

    ROMAN: They must've booked it off campus when the final bell rang. Probably didn't want to admit to their fellow Backstagers that they were too scared for twelve straight hours of the SCARIEST MOVIES KNOWN TO MAN OR BEAST!

PANEL FIVE: PRINGLES, clearly very nervous about going to this movie marathon

    PRINGLES: Wait, not going was an OPTION?

    PRINGLES (SMALLER FONT): Not an option I was going to take, obviously.

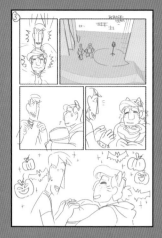

▌LLOWEEN INTERMISSION: PAGE THREE

▌EL ONE: We see TIM and JAMIE, in their Witchboy and Cat costumes, peak out from behind ▌ curtains…

▌EL TWO: They walk out onto the stage, and we see that they are carrying SLEEPING BAGS.

JAMIE: Are you sure this was a good idea, Tim?

▌EL THREE: TIM looks at JAMIE, EXCITED.

TIM: Jamie, this was the best idea in the entire history of people having ideas. My ▌ Dads think I'm sleeping over at your place. Your mom thinks you're at my place.

TIM: All those guys, they don't think we've got the guts to stick it out in the ▌ theater on Halloween night.

▌EL FOUR: JAMIE looks at him, nervous…

JAMIE: And I mean…Do we got the guts?

TIM: Together? We got the guts. We've got more guts than all of the cinemonsterthon ▌ movies times ten.

JAMIE: Y-yeah?

▌EL FIVE: TIM takes his hands, almost trying to let his enthusiasm CATCH

TIM: Trust me…

TIM: THIS IS GOING TO BE THE BEST HALLOWEEN EVER

Stage Manage
African American. 1
Big beaming smile an
a bit too muc
confidence fo
his own goo

Stage Manager. Latino. 17. He's the anxious one in between the two stage managers.

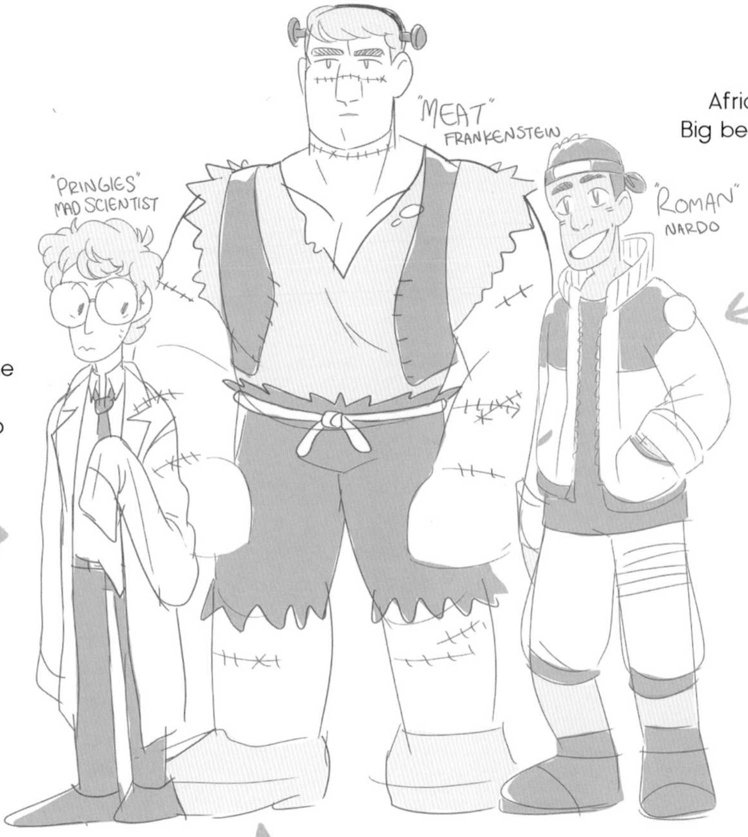
"MEAT"
FRANKENSTEIN
"PRINGLES"
MAD SCIENTIST
"ROMAN"
NARDO

16. He is basically just high school Frankenstein – A kind of surprised vacant expression on his face, and he is like three feet taller than the people around him.

Tim's hair is either way shorter or WAY LONGER. Either way, he hasn't figured it out yet, and he has braces. I think he started figuring out how to dress kinda cool in Junior year, but he's a ways off yet.

He is a nice chubby bo
with floppy hair, but N
BEARD. He still has a nice bi
smile, but looks a little mor
nervous.

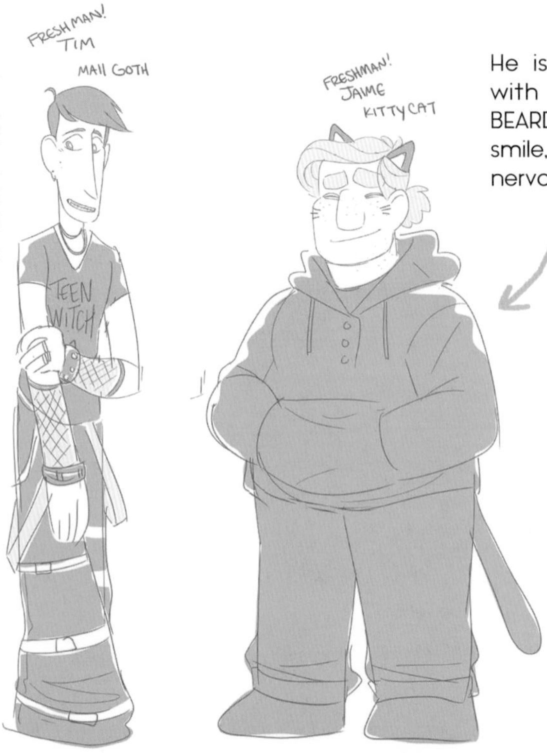
FRESHMAN!
TIM
MALL GOTH
FRESHMAN!
JAIME
KITTY CAT
TEEN
WITCH